"It would be better if people thought we were man and wife."

"I see," Will said. "And just how do we make them think that?"

"Well, we simply pretend we are. In public, I mean," she added quickly.

He sat gazing at her, and even in the darkness of the train car she could see a positively evil glint appear in his eyes. "Well, Emma," he finally said, "I'll be delighted to pretend you're my wife." Without another word, he wrapped an arm around her and pulled her to him.

For an instant, she was too shocked even to struggle. Then she tried to jerk away. But he was holding her so tightly she couldn't move.

"Relax," he whispered. "There's nothing wrong with a tired wife resting against her husband."

"Will! Just stop this. Stop it right now. It isn't seemly." But the funny thing was, there was something about it that didn't feel wrong at all. That felt, in fact, positively right....

ABOUT THE AUTHOR

First, dozens of readers wrote to say how much they loved Dawn Stewardson's first time-travel story, *Blue Moon*. Then, *Romantic Times* magazine gave the book a Special Achievement award. Finally, Dawn decided to write a spin-off.

Readers of *Blue Moon* will recall that the hero had a young son, Will, who traveled through time with him to the twentieth century. Now, in *Moon Shadow*, Will returns to the Old West.

Dawn Stewardson makes her home in Toronto with her husband, John, in an old house on the shores of Lake Ontario.

Books by Dawn Stewardson

HARLEQUIN SUPERROMANCE

329–VANISHING ACT
355–DEEP SECRETS
383–BLUE MOON
405–PRIZE PASSAGE
409–HEARTBEAT
432–THREE'S COMPANY

HARLEQUIN INTRIGUE

80–PERIL IN PARADISE
90–NO RHYME OR REASON

Moon Shadow

DAWN STEWARDSON

Harlequin Books

TORONTO • NEW YORK • LONDON
AMSTERDAM • PARIS • SYDNEY • HAMBURG
STOCKHOLM • ATHENS • TOKYO • MILAN

Published November 1991

ISBN 0-373-70477-1

MOON SHADOW

To the readers of *Blue Moon*
who asked for a sequel.
And to John, always

CHAPTER ONE

THE KNOCK didn't startle Emma. She'd been expecting something. Her sensibilities, as her mother had dubbed those feelings when they'd surfaced in childhood, had been quiet for quite a spell. But the past few days she'd been having dreadful worries about John. And this morning she'd woken with a premonition that something unusual was going to happen today. Something so unusual that Saturday, the sixteenth of July, 1887, would be a day she would never forget.

She quickly slipped the pie she'd just assembled into the oven, wiped the flour off her hands onto her apron, and headed to the front of the house.

At the door, she paused to glance in the mirror. Her face was flushed from the kitchen's heat. She brushed up a loose tendril of her long hair, catching it in a hairpin, then opened the door. And when she looked out, the most peculiar sensation seized her. She felt as if time was suddenly standing still.

On her porch stood a man with the warmest black eyes she'd ever seen. She simply gazed up into them, mesmerized for a second... or was it a minute... or longer?

She knew, with absolute certainty, that this man's arrival was the unusual event she'd been expecting.

Finally she managed to draw her gaze from his eyes and consider the rest of him. He was a perfect example of what the writers in *Ladies' Home Journal* referred to as "a fine figure of a man." Tall, lean, clean-shaven and dark-haired, with a face that was all strong lines and angles. Far too attractive a face for her to feel comfortable looking at it for too long. She focused, instead, on his elegant attire.

She'd never before seen wool as smoothly woven as that of his suit. And the bowler he held politely in one hand appeared to be real silk.

He made her think of a San Francisco Nob. She could easily imagine him walking out of one of the millionaires' mansions on Nob Hill and strolling down California Street to the financial district. But what was he doing in a small Nevada town like Mountainview?

He stood watching her with an uncertain expression that tempted her to ask what was wrong. She resisted, though. She sensed a strangeness about him. She couldn't define precisely what the strangeness was, but it was sending her sensibilities into chaos.

"I'm sorry, I seem to have the wrong house," he finally said.

His voice was deep but soft. And just his one sentence confirmed her assumption that he was well-educated.

She nodded her understanding and began to close the door. The unusual event had been brief. That was strange... not at all the major occurrence her premonition had led her to expect. But that was probably for the good.

"Perhaps you could direct me," the man added quickly. "A fellow at the old McCully house sent me

here, but he obviously gave me a false lead. I'm looking for John McCully's place.''

She paused behind the half-shut door, then slowly
opened it again. "This is John's house.''

The man's uncertain expression deepened. "But you
can't be Abigail. Or Hildy. You're not old enough.''

"You know my family?'' she asked curiously.

"Yes. I mean, I did. Years ago. I'm Will Lockhart,
an old friend of John's.''

Emma shook her head slowly. "I'm afraid your
name doesn't mean anything to me. But I'm Emma,
John's other sister.''

"Emma? I don't recall your parents having a third
girl. You must be even younger than you look.''

"I'm twenty-seven.''

The man stared at her for another moment, then his
face broke into a grin.

The sight of his even white teeth, and the intriguing
way his mouth dipped a touch to the left when he
smiled, started a funny little fluttering in her chest.

"You're the baby," he said. "I'm sorry, but I forgot that you were a girl.''

She swallowed uneasily. Men didn't make her in-
sides flutter. Nor cause any other internal reactions.
She'd taught herself not to allow them to—had been
aware, since childhood, that keeping company with a
man could only lead her to disaster. So the persistent
sensation this man's presence was causing was most
disconcerting.

"I really do apologize," he added. "The fellow I
spoke to said John lived with one of his sisters. The
local schoolmarm. And I just assumed it was Abigail
or Hildy.''

"No. Abigail and her husband are in the Dakotas. And Hildy and her family live in Missouri. I'm the one who teaches school here."

"Well, I didn't mean to be insulting. Not remembering you, I mean. But John and I were only boys. And we never referred to you as anything except the baby. But, Emma . . . yes, I recall now. Of course you were a girl . . . are a girl . . . a woman, I mean, Emma."

She nodded, hoping he'd stop repeating her name. The way his voice seemed to caress it, as if it wasn't at all common, made her nervous.

"I'm Billy," he continued. "I go by Will, now, but has John ever mentioned the name Billy Lockhart?"

"Why . . . why, yes, of course he has. Many times. You and your father moved to Boston, didn't you?"

Will nodded.

So, Emma amended her thoughts, this man, Will Lockhart, didn't live on San Francisco's Nob Hill. But in Boston he likely lived on prestigious Beacon Hill. "It's been so many years since John's seen you," she offered.

"Yes. Twenty-five. He and I were both nine when I left."

Emma nodded again, trying to imagine what on earth had brought him to their door after all that time. "And you still live in Boston, Will?"

"Yes. I'm an astronomer there."

"An astronomer," she repeated, trying not to smile. But she would be hard put to think of a more esoteric occupation. It certainly wasn't one there was any call for in the West.

"You know," he elaborated, "I study stars and planets and their movements."

"Yes, I know what astronomers do. John's often wondered what became of you. My mother has, too. She was very fond of you."

Will gave a relieved-looking smile. "I'm glad I haven't been forgotten, because I've got to talk to John about something extremely important. Do you know where I can find him? Right now, I mean?"

"Not exactly," she said slowly, watching his reaction.

His smile faded to a worried expression. "But he won't be difficult to locate, will he? It's essential that I see him today."

Emma took a step back. She needed a little time to puzzle this situation through. "Please come inside, Will. I should have invited you in before this. And perhaps you'd like a cold glass of lemonade?"

He nodded, stepping through the doorway. "If it's not too much trouble."

"No, no trouble. It's already squeezed. I'll just fetch you some."

She headed into the kitchen, thinking rapidly. How very odd that Will Lockhart had come looking for her brother after twenty-five years. How strange he seemed so anxious to see John just when she'd begun having sensibilities about some terrible thing happening to him.

She took the lemonade from the icebox, reached for a glass and absently started to pour. And then a thought made her hands begin to shake so badly she almost dropped the pitcher.

What if Will Lockhart was somehow a part of the terrible thing she sensed was going to happen to her brother?

WILL TOSSED HIS HAT onto one of the parlor chairs and considered the idea of kicking himself. He hadn't acted like such a total, complete fool in front of a woman since...Lord, when had he *ever* been such a donkey?

By the time he'd finished apologizing for not remembering Emma existed—not as a female, at least—he'd been practically babbling.

Hell, he'd been an idiot, while she'd been calm and collected and perfectly at ease. His arrival hadn't seemed to disturb her in the slightest. It was almost as if she'd been expecting him. But she'd taken him so by surprise that he still wasn't thinking quite straight.

Some schoolmarm. *Spinster* schoolmarm, to quote that fellow precisely. When she was absolutely gorgeous. Enormous blue eyes and smooth, pale skin with a natural blush. And long chestnut hair that had golden sun streaks meandering through it. Even the way she had it all pinned up, even wearing a floor-length, shapeless cotton dress and a flour-smudged apron, she was beautiful.

A spinster. How could any woman so lovely, with full lips that were simply made for kissing, be thought of as a spinster? Instead, Emma ought to be considered the woman of men's dreams.

But the last thing he was here to do was think about a woman. He was here to see John. Apparently, doing so wasn't going to be quite as easy to manage as he'd hoped, though.

Emma, he realized, hadn't answered his question about exactly how difficult it might be to locate her brother. But he'd gotten the sense it could take the major part of the day.

He glanced around the small parlor, trying to ignore the smell that was wafting from the kitchen. There was an apple pie baking in there—his absolute favorite dessert. And the aroma was making his mouth water.

He eyed the wooden-backed settee, the uncomfortable-looking chairs, and decided not to sit down. Instead, he wandered over to the glass-fronted oak bookcase that stood against one wall.

The bottom shelf contained neatly stacked issues of *Harper's Weekly,* the *Atlantic Monthly* and *Ladies' Home Journal,* the top shelf volumes of...he paused, gazing at the collection of Mark Twain novels.

Way back when, his father and Mark Twain had been the closest of friends. Of course, when he'd lived near Mountainview, in 1862, the writer had been a young man in his twenties, a down-and-out prospector who wrote occasional newspaper articles to support himself. But that was back when he was still known as Sam Clemens, long before he'd adopted his famous pen name. By 1887, Mark Twain had become an inordinately successful author.

Will's gaze drifted to the center shelf. It held children's books that Emma must use in teaching. One of them caught his eye, and he lifted the glass door to take it out. A worn *McGuffey Reader.* The same title he'd used in school so many, many years ago.

"Bring back memories of your school days?" Emma asked softly.

He turned, the little book still in his hand. "Yes, memories," he repeated, noticing she'd removed her apron and tidied her hair. "But I was surprised to see all the current magazines. I wouldn't have thought..."

Emma laughed quietly. "Did you assume we were all ignorant country bumpkins in Mountainview? I *have* been out into the big wide world, Will."

He forced a smile, feeling like an idiot all over again.

"I went to San Francisco when my parents moved there," she explained, "and stayed until after I'd completed teacher's training. And I visit them now. As often as I can. We're very close—because I'm the baby, I guess."

He nodded, putting down the book and taking the glass of lemonade she was holding out to him, trying to make up his mind whether asking if he could remove his jacket would be terribly rude. He decided he'd better not risk it, even though the house had to be ninety degrees.

"So," Emma said slowly, "I don't imagine you've come all the way from Boston simply to see John, have you?"

"Not exactly. I'm on my way to California, have business to attend to there. But I wanted to stop off here. As I said, I have something very important to talk to him about."

"Perhaps you could tell me what it is. Then I could tell him when I see him."

"No, no, that wouldn't quite work."

She gave a teasing little smile that started him thinking, once more, about how kissable her lips looked.

"I'm really very reliable," she told him.

"Oh, I didn't mean to imply you weren't. It's just that...well, what I've got to tell John is going to sound peculiar, so I have to speak to him in person. I *will* be able to see him today, won't I? As I mentioned, it's awfully important."

Emma paused before speaking. "Will," she finally said, "I'm afraid John isn't in Mountainview just now."

He stared at her, his spirits sinking. "Where is he?"

"Well, he used to work for a man named Buck Dursely, as his business manager."

"Yes, I remember Buck. He had the claim on Broken Hill."

"That's right. A few months ago, though, he decided to close the mine and move to California. He wanted John to go along—to work for him there. But John took it into his head that he'd like to try his hand at cattle ranching."

"John, a cowboy? What does a guy from a mining town in Nevada know about being a cowboy?"

Emma shrugged. "John says any man with a horse can be a cowboy. But he doesn't plan on just rushing into ranching. Not without getting experience, I mean. He decided to spend some time learning, as a ranch hand on a good spread, before he invests his money in land and cattle. So he's gone off to work for a few months."

"Gone off?" Will repeated uneasily. He didn't imagine there was a single good spread very close to Mountainview and—

"Yes, John's someplace in Arizona right now."

Will visualized a map of the United States, and his spirits continued sinking until they were as low as he imagined they could get. The southeast tip of Nevada bordered on Arizona. But between them, they covered an awful lot of territory.

So that was it. He'd come all this way and failed. Of course... of course, he *could* spend more time looking for John. In fact, if he had to, he could spend until August 1. And he did have the gold dust.

Absently he patted his breast pocket, reassured by the feel of the little pouch his father had pressed on him. It had been at the last moment, so he hadn't had a chance to check on what it would be worth. It was probably a small fortune, though.

"It's left over from the old days," Hank had said. "I didn't need all the gold I brought with me from Mountainview. And just on the off chance you run into any problems..."

Not that there were going to be any problems. But the gold *would* give him the means to search for John a little longer than he'd intended.

Only, Emma had said "someplace in Arizona." What guarantee was there that even if he traveled to Arizona he'd be able to find John? He had to try, though. Yes, he definitely had to try.

Emma eyed Will closely, wishing he'd tell her about whatever he thought was so important. Because the sensibility she'd been having about her brother was frightening her half to death. It was telling her that toward the end of July something utterly dreadful was going to happen to him.

Her feeling had grown so strong over the past few days that she'd been tempted to wire John a warning. But he didn't hold with her sensibilities. Didn't hold with anything that wasn't cold, hard fact. He'd completely outgrown his childhood belief in superstitions before the family had even realized she suffered from this affliction, from these premonitions. And he dismissed them as nonsense. He would certainly pay no heed to a caution from her.

She gazed up at Will's face. He seemed lost in thought, and she wished she could read minds instead of merely having sensibilities.

Finally he focused on her once more. "Emma, how long does it take to get to Arizona from here?"

"Well, by train you can get to Utah, then down to the Arizona border, in a day or so."

"A day or so," he repeated.

"And a night, of course. It would take about twenty-five or twenty-six hours, I think."

"I see . . . Emma, if I went to Arizona, what do you figure the odds would be of my locating John . . . say within a week or so?"

She shook her head slowly, recalling the strangeness she'd sensed about Will when she'd opened the door to him. Had it meant he was a threat to her brother? Until she could determine that, she wasn't about to admit she knew precisely where John was.

"What do you think, Emma? What would my odds be?"

She considered for a moment longer. Will's turning up after a twenty-five-year absence, claiming to have something important to tell John, something that would sound peculiar, was too extraordinary to be coincidental. But Will had once been John's best friend, which made her think that whatever he had to talk to her brother about was more likely to help than harm. Just in case, though . . .

"Well, Will," she said, hoping she sounded nonchalant, "your odds on finding John would be good as long as you had someone with you who knew the

West. And I'm free until school begins again in the fall."

"NO," WILL SAID FOR the twelfth time, smacking the kitchen table for emphasis. "No, no, no, absolutely not." Emma wasn't going with him. He didn't care what she said or did, she wasn't going.

He'd come expecting to be here and gone within a single day. Now it looked as if he'd be away far longer. But he certainly didn't want a woman with him, slowing him down.

Emma cut him a second piece of the still-hot apple pie and passed it across the table.

He had half a mind to refuse it. If he wasn't so hungry and it wasn't his absolute favorite dessert and it wasn't so incredibly good, he would have. He nodded his thanks, wondering if she knew the saying, "the way to a man's heart is through his stomach."

"Will," she said as he started eating again, "I keep reading articles that say Eastern men are far more reasonable than those out West. But I can't see that your saying, 'no, no, no, absolutely not' is being the least bit reasonable."

"Emma, it isn't a question of my being reasonable. It's a question of the idea's being ridiculous. You're an unmarried woman—a schoolteacher. What would people here think about your traveling with me?"

"They'd think that you're an old friend of John's and we're going to see him."

"That isn't what I mean and you know it. They'd think..." He paused, searching for the word his father used to use. "They wouldn't think it seemly. They'd think you...you know what I'm saying."

A blush crept up her face, but she shook her head. "They wouldn't think anything of the sort, Will. I'll admit that it would be a problem for most women. But not for me. I've never in my entire life kept company with a man. Every citizen of Mountainview knows that I have no interest in men—not in *that* way. So they'd think nothing more than that we're going to see John."

Will almost choked on his pie. Emma, this woman who'd practically set him drooling when she first opened the door, had no interest in men? Not in *that* way?

She couldn't be saying what she seemed to be saying. Could she? He'd never before known his instincts to be wrong about... well, wrong in *that* department.

But women married young out here in the wilderness. So if Emma had reached the ripe old age of twenty-seven without even having kept company with a man...

"Just think about the positive side," she pressed. "I know a lot about the West and you don't."

"I do so!" Maybe not a *whole* lot, he amended silently. But that wasn't the point. The point was that he neither wanted nor needed Emma with him. After all the reading up he'd done, he'd hardly be a fish out of water. He'd get on a train, go to Arizona and find John McCully. How difficult could it be? Hell, there simply weren't that many people in Arizona.

"I suppose you know everything about avoiding the Apaches, do you?" Emma said. "The Arizona Territory's crawling with them, you realize."

"The Apaches?" Oh, Lord, his voice hadn't cracked, had it? He cleared his throat.

"Yes, the Apaches. I imagine you're aware they're the most treacherous of all the tribes? That warfare is their principal vocation? That they've devised some of the most sadistic tortures ever?"

Will cleared his throat a second time—just for good measure. "The Indian problems are pretty well over," he said firmly. His books had told him that.

Emma rolled her eyes, making him wonder uneasily about those books' reliability.

"And precisely how," she went on, "do you imagine a tenderfoot astronomer from Boston is going to track down a man in the middle of Arizona?"

"I'm not a tenderfoot!"

"You aren't?" Her gaze traveled slowly over his expensive suit, not leaving the slightest doubt what she was thinking.

He tucked his feet under the chair rail, trying to hide his patent leather boots.

"The Arizona Territory is estimated to be 113,000 square miles in area," she offered in a superior tone.

"Never mind trying to impress me with school-marm geography, Emma. I'll find John. On my own."

"Oh? How? Are the stars going to guide you?"

"I'll... well, I'll just ask after him."

She merely wrinkled her nose.

He glared at her in reply.

"Will... Will, I just have to check on something." She rose from the table. "I'll be back in a minute. Have another piece of pie if you'd like."

He glanced at it, considering, as she hurried from the kitchen, but her talk about Apaches hadn't done much for his appetite. Maybe he'd been a bit hasty, deciding to go to Arizona after John. Maybe Emma was right about how difficult it would be to find him. But if he didn't go... well, he *had* to, didn't he? After all, he owed Johnnie McCully his life.

Memories of that long-ago day were as clear as those of yesterday. And thinking back, he didn't feel like thirty-four-year-old Will Lockhart. He felt like nine-year-old Billy once more.

He and Johnnie had gone into the hills for a picnic. The summer sun was beating down, its heat making Cheyenne pant noisily as he ambled along beside them. The dog trotted ahead to the stream, eager for a drink.

"I should of brought him a bowl," Billy said. "My pa says I should always..." Suddenly pain struck, the worst he'd ever had, searing through his chest as if it were burning holes inside him. He couldn't breathe, couldn't walk another step. His legs gave way, and he crumpled to the grass, gasping for air.

"Billy! Billy!" Johnnie cried. "Don't have a spell here! Billy, I'll run and fetch someone."

He couldn't answer. The pain was scorching his throat, was stabbing him everywhere. He tried not to cry, but tears began streaming down his face, turning Johnnie into a blur as he ran.

The seizure grew worse, so bad he couldn't stand it. And then the world turned black... until he felt Erica's arms cradling him, heard her softly murmuring.

He tried to tell her he was fine but, instead, began gagging with choking coughs that shook his body. The pain started racing through him again, setting him on fire.

Then Johnnie was there, pressing a cold, wet rag to his forehead...running off to the stream and returning with the cloth wetter and colder...again and again...until the scorching pain subsided and breathing was possible once more. Until, finally, Billy thought he might not die, after all.

Will shuddered, back in Emma's kitchen, his heart pounding. "Just a recollection," he whispered to himself. "Just a recollection from long, long ago." A recollection of Johnnie McCully saving his life. How could he even consider not doing the same in return?

He couldn't. No matter how big Arizona was or how many Apaches were still roaming it, John McCully wasn't going to be killed on July 25. Not when Will knew it was going to happen and could prevent it.

CHAPTER TWO

EMMA STOOD IN HER bedroom, telling herself to calm down and think. She was losing this argument. Will didn't want her to go along, and she could hardly force him to take her. Yet John's safety was at stake. She simply knew it was. And if there was any way she could help, she had to.

Of all her brothers and sisters, she loved John the most. He'd always watched out for her when she was growing up, had never let the younger boys pick on her just because she was the baby. And when she'd come back from San Francisco to teach, he'd bought this house for them.

She'd do anything for John. And right now, what she had to do was convince Will to let her go with him to Arizona.

She took a deep breath, walked back to the kitchen and sat down across from him once more. He'd taken her up on her suggestion about a third piece of pie. She prayed that was a good omen and managed a smile.

"Will, let's discuss my going with you more logically. I can help you. I know how the world works beyond the pale of Eastern civilization. And aside from that, you haven't seen John in twenty-five years. You two could pass on a trail and not know it. Besides, I have to go with you because . . . well, I've simply got a feeling I have to."

"What do you mean, a *feeling?*" he asked, eyeing her with apparent curiosity.

She shrugged uneasily. She shouldn't have said that, knew better than to mention her sensibilities.

"Do you mean," Will asked, "that you have a feeling something is going to happen to John?"

She merely stared at him. What would make him think that? Could he read her mind?

"You know, Emma, I had the sense, earlier, that my arrival didn't really surprise you. You don't have ESP, do you?"

"I . . . I don't have what?"

He smiled at her—a smile that sent a new variation of sensations through her. These ones made her feel warm and tingly. And he was looking at her almost as if he had some understanding of sensibilities.

"Sorry, Emma. I guess word of ESP hasn't reached Mountainview yet. But some people have a heightened sensitivity. You know, they have premonitions."

She nodded slowly, not at all clear what this ESP was, but certainly clear about premonitions, only too aware of how frequently she had them. Yet she'd always been told never even to mention the subject. So why was Will discussing it with such nonchalance? And why, if this ESP was commonly known back East, hadn't she read about it in one of her magazines?

Will was still smiling at her. She wished he'd stop because something had apparently gone awry with the immunity to men she'd so consciously developed over the years. And that meant she was going to have to be on her guard every minute she was with him on the trip. But she *was* going with him. Even if it meant arguing the point all day.

"Listen...Emma," he said quietly, "I'd decided that if I had to do any explaining about this, I might try telling a little white lie—might say that while I was studying the planets, their alignment had given me a message about John. But now that I realize you'll understand, well, the fact is that I kind of have premonitions, too."

"What do you mean...kind of?"

"Well, I mean, I know about some things that are going to happen in the future. And that's why I have to see John. I've got the same sort of feeling you do. That he'll be coming into trouble soon. On July 25, to be exact."

July 25. And her feeling had told her toward the end of July.

She gazed uncertainly across the table at Will. She'd never before met anyone else who suffered from sensibilities. But...but maybe the fact that he did explained these strange responses she was having toward him. Maybe her immunity wasn't working because her sensibilities were attuned to his.

And maybe that was why he felt free to talk openly about having them. Because surely he didn't do that with just anyone...did he?

"Will?"

"Yes?"

"The feelings you get?"

"Yes?"

"You don't usually discuss them with people, do you?"

"Ahh . . ." He sat gazing at her as if he couldn't decide how to answer the question.

"Well, sometimes I talk about them," he finally admitted.

Oh, mercy, he told people he had premonitions. Or else, from what he'd just said, he lied and claimed that planets gave him messages. But that was just as dangerous a way of explaining how he foresaw things. Either way, people would think he was crazy. And John would laugh off a warning from Will just as he would from her.

"Will?"

"Uh-huh?"

"You wouldn't tell John about your premonition, would you? Or tell him the planets talked to you? He doesn't hold with that sort of thing."

"Oh. I thought he might. When we were boys, he was very superstitious."

"He isn't any longer. He outgrew it."

"Oh. Well, then, I guess neither of those stories would fly. I'll have to think of something else."

Emma nodded slowly. Flying stories? Will certainly used strange turns of phrase. But there was no point in worrying about that. And with luck, he'd concoct a believable explanation and John wouldn't even suspect his old friend suffered from sensibilities. After all, it had taken her awhile to recognize the symptoms in Will, and she was familiar with them.

He finished his last chunk of pie, drained the glass of lemonade and rose. "Well, I'll be on my way now, Emma. But don't worry any more about John. I'll find him. And everything will be all right."

Emma thought more rapidly than she'd ever thought before. If Will went off into the wilds of the Arizona Territory alone, he might start talking to strangers about his sensibilities or messages from the stars. And if he did that, he'd never live to find John, let alone warn him. Some skunk would decide Will was a sissy. Or feebleminded. Or a lunatic. Maybe even a feebleminded, sissy lunatic. At any rate, he'd be considered fair game for target practice.

What kind of help would he be to John if he were dead?

Blast it. If Will Lockhart was going to reach her brother, he needed a keeper. And she seemed to be the only candidate for the job, so she just *had* to go.

"Oh, one more thing," Will said, reaching into his suit pocket, pulling out a small leather pouch and handing it to her. "That's gold dust. We don't use it as exchange in Boston, but I was told it would be good to carry. Could you give me an idea what that amount's worth?"

She glanced up at him, certain he must be joshing. He seemed deadly serious. But how could he be carrying gold and not know its value? Even setting aside the matter of his sensibilities, Will Lockhart was a most peculiar man.

She made a small weighing motion with her hand. "Gold's going for about sixteen dollars an ounce. So maybe a hundred dollars?"

He looked taken aback. "I...I'm afraid I don't know much about Western prices, either. How long do you figure a hundred dollars would last me out here?"

"Well," she said slowly, still half suspecting he couldn't be serious, "how long it would last would depend on what you were buying and where you were buying it. In some places, sugar, coffee and tobacco sell for their weight in gold.''

"Ahh ... then you're saying this wouldn't last me long. I mean, by the time I purchase a train ticket and all.''

"Will, your train tickets will cost about six dollars for every couple of hundred miles. And there's a fair piece of rail line from Nevada over to Utah and down into Arizona.''

"I see.'' He paused, clearing his throat.

"Will, you don't have only this gold with you, do you? I mean, you have currency, don't you?''

"Ahh ... well, Emma ... you see, there's a bit of a problem with that. I...I'm afraid I have a funny hang-up about carrying a lot of money.''

"You have a funny what?'' *Hang-up,* he'd said. But what in gracious' name did that peculiar word mean? On top of his strange turns of phrase, she didn't understand half the words he used.

"I mean ... by hang-up, I mean that carrying a lot of money makes me uncomfortable. So I never do it. You know what a phobia is?''

She nodded.

"Well, carrying money's a kind of phobia with me.''

Emma tried to look understanding but knew she was looking as if she thought Will was plumb loco. Never mind feebleminded or a sissy. With every word he uttered, *lunatic* was seeming the more appropriate description for him.

Between using expressions he'd undoubtedly created all on his own and not knowing about so many everyday things, it would be easy to believe he'd been living in a foreign country.

It was exactly as her mother had warned her from childhood. And that fancy physician in San Francisco had echoed the warning. People who were afflicted with sensibilities had a high likelihood of developing insanity.

Her marrying, that doctor had said, would be a dreadful mistake. Because if she bore children, she'd run the risk of passing on her affliction to them. And even if she never developed a disorder of the mind, her children might.

She smiled nervously at Will. Proof that the affliction could lead to insanity was standing right here in front of her. Will Lockhart was undoubtedly mad as a hatter. She'd never even heard of anyone being afraid to carry money. And if doing so made him uncomfortable, why didn't carrying gold bother him? His mind simply didn't work in a rational fashion.

"Will..." she began, "if you don't like to carry much money, what do you do when you need more? Wire a bank in Boston for it?"

"Yes," he said quickly. "Yes, that's precisely what I do." He pressed his lips together and frowned, as if his mind was racing.

Maybe, Emma thought, panic rushing through her, he was going to change his mind about heading after John. She simply couldn't let that happen. She had to get them on their way before it did.

"Today's Saturday," she said.

"Pardon?"

"I said that today's Saturday. The banks closed at noon. And tomorrow's Sunday. You won't likely be able to get any money for a couple of days, will you?"

"No... no, not for a couple of days."

"Well, I really don't think you should wait until you can get money from Boston. I mean, wasting the next few days isn't a good idea. Locating John might take some time, and we don't want to cut this too close."

"No. No, cutting this too close is that last thing I want to do." Will thought furiously. He had to get to John, hated the thought of not being able to warn him. But how was he going to make it to Arizona and back without money?

He shook his head slowly, looking down at Emma. He simply wasn't going to be able to help John, after all. But how could he tell her that? And how could he just turn his back on what he'd come here to do? How could he let Johnnie die?

"I can get money today," she said.

"You can what?"

"I can get money today. As much as we need."

"But you just said the banks closed at noon."

"Not from the bank. Mr. Dursely is holding money for John. A lot of money. Some of it's wages, but it's mostly a bonus. That's what John's going to use to buy his ranch. I can go over to Mr. Dursely's right now. He's still in town. He has an office in his house, and I know he keeps cash in his safe there. And if I tell him we have to take some of that money to John, he'll give me whatever amount I ask for."

"But Emma, I—"

"It's the simplest solution, Will."

He nodded reluctantly. It might be the *only* solution. Just offhand, he couldn't think of another one. But Emma had said *we. We have to take some money to John.* Well, there was still no way he was going along with that part of her plan.

He didn't want company. And she would slow him down. And hell, if there actually *was* the odd Apache or two in Arizona, that gorgeous hair of hers would be a magnet for one who wanted a prize scalp. The last thing he needed was a traveling companion who'd attract Indians.

"Just give me time to change my clothes and pack a few things," she said. "Then we can go straight from Mr. Dursely's to the rail station and catch the afternoon train. Where's your luggage, by the way? Did you leave it at the depot?"

"Ahh . . . my luggage. Well, I guess that's another problem. I let it go on ahead to San Francisco . . . thought I'd be following it along later today."

Emma shrugged. "That really isn't a problem. John left most of his clothes here, and the two of you are about the same size. I think even his boots should fit," she added, glancing at Will's feet.

She was, he decided with annoyance, barely managing not to smirk at his patent leather boots.

"I'll pack a bag for you, too," she said, turning away.

"Wait a second," he said sharply. "Wait just a damned second. Forget about changing and packing things for yourself. I said I'll find John on my own, and that's exactly what I'm going to do. I'll come along to Buck Dursely's with you. I'd like to see him

again, anyway. And you ask him for the money. Then
I'll take it and head after John.''

"Don't be silly," Emma said, smiling angelically.
"You're already putting yourself out enough, taking
all this time to go looking for him. The least I can do
is make sure you don't feel uncomfortable while
you're doing it.''

"What's that supposed to mean?''

"Why, Will, you just finished telling me that carrying a lot of money makes you feel uncomfortable.
That you never do it. That you have a phobia about it.
So I'll carry the money. Mr. Dursely will give it to me,
and I'll carry it.''

"Emma, I don't—''

"No,'' she said quickly, holding up a hand to stop
him. "No, no, no, absolutely not. I won't hear another word of objection. With you doing all this for
John, I'd feel awfully guilty if I didn't go along to
Arizona and keep you from being uncomfortable.''

Will shook his head, wishing it would stop spinning. He wasn't accustomed to lying. And right now,
his lies were piling up so fast and furiously that he
could barely keep on top of them.

Hell, maybe he should just tell Emma the truth, that
when he was nine years old he hadn't simply moved to
Boston but had traveled through time to 1989 and had
been living in the future for the past twenty-five years.
Maybe he should explain that's why he had no nine-
teenth-century currency. All he had, aside from his bit
of gold dust, was modern money and a slew of credit
cards.

But he knew what she'd think if he started in about
time travel, if he told her his clothes were a period

outfit he'd rented from a costume place, if he said he wasn't actually an astronomer but an astrophysicist who worked in a space station. Right. He knew exactly what she'd think. So instead of saying anything, he closed his eyes, visualizing the tombstone he'd seen during a visit to Mountainview in the year 2014:

In Memory of John R. McCully
Born February 12, 1853
Killed July 25, 1887
Rest in Peace

Killed. When he'd seen that word, Will had known he had to travel back in time to save his best childhood friend. As boys, John and he had been inseparable—until Will's father and Erica had taken him to the future.

It had been 1862 when Erica accidentally stumbled through that time hole in the Broken Hill Mine and mysteriously appeared in Mountainview. Of course, in her world the year had been 1989, and she was as incredulous at finding herself in the previous century as Hank Lockhart was at learning she'd come from the future.

But by the time the two of them had figured out how to get her back through the time hole, they'd fallen in love. So Hank and Will had gone to the future with Erica, where Will's consumption was cured by modern medicine.

No wonder he'd grown up with a fascination for the mysteries of time and space, particularly for the enigma of time holes—those tiny chinks in the time continuum that were occasionally opened by the gravitational pull of blue moons.

They were difficult to find since they seldom opened. And when they did, it was only for the time they lay under the blue moon shadow. But there was nothing like a Ph.D. in astrophysics, plus the thousands of hours Will had spent playing on Space Station Freedom's supercomputer, to help him pinpoint the hole he needed. He knew its general location, in Broken Hill, from their trip with Erica. And the computer had calculated when it would open.

So early this morning he'd entered Broken Hill and gone directly to the tunnel that led to the time hole. As he'd turned a corner, he'd glimpsed an eerie blue light glowing in the distance—just as he recalled from that childhood trip. And sure enough, he'd emerged from that mine on July 16, the same day he'd entered. Only he'd entered in the year 2014 and emerged in 1887.

The time hole would be under the moon shadow for seventeen days, until August 1. With any luck, that would be enough time to save John from being killed.

"Will?" Emma said, capturing his attention again. She was looking at him curiously so he forced a smile. He didn't try to explain, though. He could hardly tell her the truth, tell her he knew her brother would be in danger on July 25 because he'd seen John's tombstone. She'd figure Billy Lockhart had grown up to be crazy as a loon. Anyone would. That's why he'd concocted his cover story about passing through on his way to San Francisco in the first place.

BUCK SAT BEHIND his desk, staring blankly at the papers on it. If he hadn't been a danged fool, hadn't given John such a big bonus, the man would still be here, where he was needed, instead of off watching a herd of stupid cattle. Tarnation! He'd give anything to have John back working for him again.

He liked to be certain he could trust the men who managed his affairs, but those fellows he'd hired in San Francisco...well, he supposed they would turn out to be fine. It was only that they hadn't been with him for ten years, the way John had.

"Buck," he muttered to himself, "you'd best get your business here all tidied up just as soon as you can." Yup, he'd best get himself to San Francisco so he could keep a close eye on what was happening out there.

Absently he let his thoughts linger on how John D. Rockefeller would react to real competition from Dursely Oil. Then he pictured his mansion on Nob Hill. Mary Beth was spending a fortune on new furniture, but that was all right. She was a good woman. And he was a lucky man.

He looked down at his desk again and forced his eyes to focus on the bank document. He'd better try, one more time, to get all the way through this. He'd signed the original over a week ago and sent it back to San Francisco. But ever since, he'd been worrying.

The First Coastal Bank of California, he slowly read, underlining each word with his finger, *agrees to lend Mr. Buckingham Dursely...*

Lend. He hated the idea of borrowing money. He was a millionaire. Why did he have to borrow?

John had explained why, of course. For the same reason they'd raised all that money by selling company shares on the New York Stock Exchange.

The oil business required vast amounts of capital. It wasn't merely a matter of sticking derricks into the ground. Not that just doing that wasn't danged expensive.

But in addition, Dursely Oil had to lease land for drilling, needed storage facilities and refining equipment, and had to establish transportation systems to get the oil to market.

And all that was going to take far more money than he had. Borrowing was the way to expand, John had assured him. But all those shares of Dursely Oil the bank was holding as collateral...that made Buck very, very nervous.

He knew he was concerned for nothing, though. He didn't understand all the details of this loan agreement, but John certainly did. After all, he'd helped draft the original terms. And he'd said there wasn't the slightest risk that Buck could ever lose control of the company.

He just wished John had been here to check things over. John would know if this official copy the bank had printed up contained any errors. But, of course, banks didn't make errors. So worrying was foolish.

Besides, John D. Rockefeller had borrowed every cent he possibly could when he'd started up Standard Oil. And if borrowing was good enough for Mr. Rockefeller, it was good enough for Buck Dursely.

The knock on the front door lifted his spirits a mite. It started him thinking about how Mary Beth was right now interviewing servants in San Francisco. Pretty soon, he'd have him a butler to open doors. But today there was no one here 'cept himself. He shoved back his chair and headed to the front of the house.

Through the window, he could see it was Joe, from the Wells Fargo office, standing on the porch with a telegram in his hand.

"It's from San Francisco," Joe said when Buck opened the door. "From one of your men at Dursely Oil."

He handed Joe a quarter, thinking that if he waited another minute, the man would probably quote the message, word for word. Telegrams might be faster than letters, but they sure weren't as private.

He started to open the message as Joe headed off, then saw Emma McCully coming up the walk with a young man and stuffed the paper into his pocket.

"Emma!" he said when the two reached the porch. "Good to see you, gal. I'm mighty lonesome with the family gone ahead to California."

She smiled up at him. "I've brought an old friend of yours, Mr. Dursely."

He gazed at the fellow, searching his memory. There was definitely something about those black eyes that reminded him of someone...he plumb couldn't think who, though.

The man extended his hand. "Emma's not being fair, Buck. The last time you saw me I was nine years old. I'm Billy Lockhart."

"Why...why, I'll be hanged!"

"I hope not," Emma said, laughing.

Buck grabbed Billy's hand and shook it heartily. The young man looked familiar 'cuz he was the spitting image of his pa. "It's really you, Billy. After all these years."

"It's really me. I go by Will, now, though."

"Tarnation! This sure enough is a surprise." He couldn't take his eyes off Billy—all growed up to be a man. Little Billy who'd had that crazy wolf-dog. The danged dog had once warned Buck off a rattler that would have bit him for sure.

"Just recollecting on that big gray dog of yours," he told Will. "What'd you call him again?"

"Cheyenne."

"Cheyenne...yup, I remember now. Only dog I ever knowed with yellow eyes. Took him to Boston with you, didn't you?"

Will nodded. "And he lived to a ripe old age. Finally died in his sleep, in front of our fireplace."

"Always liked that dog," Buck said. "Course, I always liked your pa, too. He was the one who convinced me not to give up on Broken Hill, you know."

"Yes, Dad's told me the story."

"Yup. Your pa and the purty woman who came to visit him from Boston. I was danged discouraged, back then. But they told me I'd strike it rich if I just stuck with it. And I did. It was almost like they knew what was going to happen in the future. Whatever become of that purty woman?"

"Dad married her. And they're still in Boston."

Buck realized Emma was looking at him expectantly and remembered his manners. "Emma. Billy. Will, I mean. You two just come right on in, now. We got ourselves a passel of catching up to do."

"NOW, ARE YOU SURE THAT'S enough money, Emma?" Buck asked, easing the door of his safe closed.

"I'm positive, Mr. Dursely. And thank you again."

"No thanks necessary. It's John's money, not mine."

"And we'll take it straight to him, won't we, Will?" she said, smiling at him so sweetly that he gritted his teeth.

He did *not* want this woman going with him. She was too darned appealing for her own good. Or more important, under the circumstances, for *his* good.

Hell, even Buck, a married, paunchy man of about fifty, had smoothed his graying hair and sucked in his gut the moment he'd seen her. What if they ran into some rough-and-ready dude who hadn't seen a good-looking woman in months? How he'd react to Emma wasn't exactly difficult to imagine.

She might never have kept company with a man, but every minute longer Will spent with her made him more convinced that she simply hadn't met the *right* man. He'd clearly misinterpreted her meaning about not being interested in men, because she simply exuded a smoldering sensuality.

And hell, never mind some rough-and-ready Old West dude. He wasn't keen on coping with Emma's sensuality himself. Living two months at a stretch on the space station for the past few years hadn't done much for his social life. The only women he generally had a lot to do with were rocket scientists. And he'd never met a rocket scientist who looked anything like Emma McCully.

He couldn't see any way around her going with him, though. Not when she already had that money tucked securely in her handbag. And when she was so damned determined to go.

He wiped his brow, wondering how in hell Emma was managing to look cool in that long-sleeved, high-collared dress. It was some kind of silky brown fabric—fitted to the hips, accentuating the most delightfully curvaceous breasts and tiny waist he'd ever seen, then all draped in front and jutting out into a bustle at the back.

The skirt reached below her ankles, barely exposing any of her tiny black kid shoes. They looked so delicate, with their little raised heels, that he wondered how she'd manage the walk to the train station, let alone cope with whatever walking might be required in Arizona.

And that hat she was wearing was nothing but feathers and whimsy. It might be attractive on her...well, it might be terrific-looking. But it wasn't going to be a darned bit of good for keeping the sun off her pale skin.

"I still can't get over it, Will," Buck said.

Will forced his eyes away from Emma as Buck gave the safe's dial a final spin and continued speaking.

"Can't get over seeing you again. You sure don't look the same. And all dressed up in those city slicker duds."

"You sure don't look the same, either, Buck. And your duds aren't too bad themselves." And he looked, Will reflected, one heck of a lot more content with life than he had as a young man. He seemed happy and prosperous as the devil—a far cry from the old days.

"You know, Buck, the last time I saw you, you were covered in mine dirt and didn't have two quarters to rub together."

"Didn't have many teeth, either, did I?" Buck grinned broadly, revealing a full set of gleaming white teeth that were far too perfect to be real. "That was one of the first things I did after I struck it rich—got me a good dentist in San Francisco to make me these choppers."

"They look great," Will offered, recalling that the young Buck Dursely had been down to about three teeth.

"You know, Will, I've just been so damned lucky. Got me more money that I can spend, a good wife and five young 'uns. Wish you could of met Mary Beth, that the family wasn't in San Francisco already.

"But you know women. Mary Beth couldn't wait to get settled into the new house. It's a danged mansion, Will. On Nob Hill. Can you beat that?"

"You're really living the life of Rilcy, huh?"

"Of who?" Buck asked.

Damn. Both Buck and Emma were eyeing him strangely.

"Just a back East saying," he told them. "It means a life of ease." He'd have to be more careful with his expressions. There were only so many times he could get away with explaining things that sounded peculiar as "back East" sayings.

"Well, I owe some of my good life to you," Buck said. "You and your pa. Between your dog saving me from that snake and your pa encouraging me to stick with Broken Hill... Well, you ever need anything, Will, anything at all, you just let me know. I'd be danged happy at a chance to help you out. I never forget them that's done me a good turn."

"Hell, it was Dad and Cheyenne who did you good turns, not me," Will said, laughing. "What are you going to do in San Francisco, though? You won't miss the mine?"

"Nope. Got something new planned. In fact, I've got it operating already. I've gone into oil. Formed a company called Dursely Oil. Couple of years back, California's crude output reached 500,000 barrels a year. And I decided that's where my future lies. I'm going to be an oil baron. There's some fella back East owns too much of the industry. I'm going to take him on."

"Oh? Who's that?"

"Fella in New York. By the name of John D. Rockefeller. First billionaire in history, they say."

"John D. Rockefeller?" Will repeated. "Hell, Buck, he was one... *is* one of the shrewdest business-men ever."

"Well, I don't rightly know just how shrewd he is," Buck said. "But I do know that he owns ninety per-cent of the American refineries and all the pipeline and oil cars of the Pennsylvania Railroad. I figure that's too much for one man. Mean to take a good share of it away from him."

Will slowly shook his head. He'd always been in-terested in the business world—had done a lot of business courses in his undergraduate years. And the thought of having a chance to take on John D. Rock-efeller's monopoly was incredible. If Buck was any kind of businessman himself, he'd probably have a ball as an oil baron.

"We'd better be leaving now, Mr. Dursely," Emma said. "We don't want to miss the train."

"I still think the two of you are loco, Emma, heading out into the Cattle Kingdom like this. You know what they say about King Colt rodding the range."

"King Colt?" Will said.

"Your pistols, of course. Those range riders shoot first and ask questions later."

"Well, Will and I don't intend to ride any ranges," Emma said. "Once we get off the train, we'll take a nice, safe stage."

Will glanced at her curiously, wondering why she sounded as if she knew exactly where they'd be going. Probably, he decided, because Buck would think they were twice as loco if he knew the truth—that they'd likely end up scouring half of Arizona on horseback before they located John. And that was certainly going to be a treat, after not having been on a horse for twenty-five years.

"A *safe* stage?" Buck said with a snort. "Safe? I suppose you ain't heard of highwaymen? Or the Apache Kid?"

"The Apache Kid?" Will repeated. He certainly hadn't heard of the Apache Kid. And he certainly didn't like the way Buck had spit out the name.

"The meanest Indian you could ever meet," Buck elaborated. "And he just happens to be terrorizing Arizona these days. How are you at shooting, Will?"

"Ahh . . . well, there's not much call for guns back in Boston."

"You ain't saying you're not packing hardware, are you?"

Will cleared his throat uncomfortably. This trek to Arizona was sounding worse by the minute.

"Tarnation," Buck muttered, crossing the room and opening a cupboard. "How could Hank Lockhart take his boy back East and turn him into a danged tenderfoot?"

Will glanced at Emma. She was clearly trying not to laugh, and her amusement annoyed him. This was the second time today he'd been called a tenderfoot, and he didn't like it. Where did these two get off, thinking they were so damned superior?

"Here," Buck said, drawing Will's attention back to him. He was holding out a gun and holster. "Here, take this Colt Peacemaker. It's nice artillery. I keep five beans in the wheel, and here's a box of extra lead plumbs."

Will took the gun and tucked the cartridges into his jacket pocket.

"And you, Emma," Buck was saying, "you take this little Remington .22. Mary Beth doesn't carry it all that often. But it tucks in real nice between your... well, you can conceal it in a lot of places."

Will resisted the urge to look over and see if Emma was actually tucking the gun into her bodice. Instead, he concentrated on strapping the Colt around his hips, feeling like a complete imposter. He certainly hoped that "five beans in the wheel" meant the hammer was resting on a sixth, empty chamber, that he wasn't likely to shoot himself in the foot, right here in Buck's office.

Once he finally got the belt adjusted, he and Emma started for the front door.

"You remember what I said, now," Buck offered as Will slipped one case under his arm and picked the other up by its handle. "Remember that if there's anything I can ever do for you, just ask."

"I'll keep that in mind. And thanks." Will gestured Emma through the doorway, ahead of him.

"And hell," Buck went on, "if you ever happen to get to San Francisco, I can always use good men. That's why I was so danged upset when John insisted on lighting out for Pleasant Valley, instead of coming West to work for Dursely Oil."

Will paused, half out of the house, and glanced back in. "Pleasant Valley?"

"Where John is. Where you're going," Buck elaborated, as if Will wasn't too bright.

Where John was... where they were going... Apparently John's whereabouts was common knowledge. Which meant that Emma's help wasn't needed to track him down in those 113,000 square miles of the Arizona Territory.

Will looked at her. She was staring intently at the porch floorboards, so he turned back to Buck.

"Pleasant Valley. Of course. The name simply slipped my mind. Well," he muttered, taking hold of Emma's arm with his free hand and propelling her down the porch stairs. "Let's get started for Pleasant Valley, Emma. You've told me so much about it that I can hardly wait to see it."

At the bottom of the steps he turned and gave Buck a quick farewell salute, then marched off down the dusty street ahead of Emma, hoping she'd trip over those stupid little shoes she was wearing.

Buck had the door half shut when he remembered the wire that had been delivered. He pulled it out and slowly read it, feeling his stomach start to churn.

After a minute, he began at the first word again, praying he'd misread. He hadn't.

Carefully he folded the telegram and put it back into his pocket. Then he wandered unseeingly into the parlor and poured a large glass of whiskey.

He sank into his chair and sat trying to think what he should do, but unable to think about anything except how proud Mary Beth was to have an oil baron as a husband...about what she'd think if she knew he was in danger of losing his company.

CHAPTER THREE

EMMA HURRIED after Will, wondering if he was ever going to stop stomping along at breakneck speed. They'd been walking for almost fifteen minutes, had practically reached the train depot, but he wasn't showing any sign of slowing . . . or any awareness that she was behind him.

What if he'd decided never to speak to her again? What if he'd decided to get on the train for San Francisco, instead of the one heading for the main line east?

Oh, maybe she should have admitted that she knew where John was. But then Will would have set out alone for sure. And he shouldn't be allowed loose on Arizona by himself.

Not that the fact he tended to insanity was instantly obvious to people. Mr. Dursely hadn't seemed to see anything amiss. And from the way Will took to glaring whenever anyone called him a tenderfoot, he clearly believed he could manage the trip on his own.

But he didn't fool her. Not for a second. If she was going to ensure that he warn John, she first had to ensure that he made it to Pleasant Valley without getting himself shot so full of holes he wouldn't float in brine.

Ahead of her, Will reached the station platform and stepped up onto it, not even breaking his stride. In the distance, she could hear the faint, rhythmic chugging of the train. It would be arriving in just a couple of minutes.

She almost ran the last few feet to the platform, hiked her dress up a little, and managed the high step. Will was already nearing the far end. Finally he stopped, set down the bags, then turned and watched her approach.

She swallowed hard. Those black eyes of his, she realized uneasily, didn't always look soft and warm. She stopped in front of him and tried a smile. It had no apparent effect.

"Pleasant Valley," he snapped. "I assume Pleasant Valley is in Arizona."

"Yes . . . in the Tonto Basin . . . that's in the shelter of the Mogollons."

"You knew exactly where John was all along."

"I . . . yes, I did. He had a job lined up before he left. He's working on the Tewksbury spread, by Cherry Creek. It's not far from Flagstaff."

The long, mournful sound of a whistle reached them, announcing the train's imminent arrival.

"Why didn't you tell me?" Will demanded angrily.

"I . . . Will, when you first arrived, I simply wasn't sure I could trust you."

"What? What the devil did you think I'd come here for?"

"I didn't know. I wasn't even certain you were who you said you were. For all I knew, you could have been Black Bart."

"Who?" Will demanded.

"A highwayman. A *famous* highwayman." Mercy, didn't eastern newspapers print any news about the West?

"All I knew for sure," she pressed on, "was that I'd been having a feeling about something awful happening to John. And then you appeared out of nowhere. I just couldn't tell you where he was until I knew why you wanted to see him."

"Well, now you know why I want to see him. And you know I'm not Black Bart. And I know where John is. So there's absolutely no need for you to come one step farther with me. Here." Will picked up her case and held it out to her. "Just give me enough of that money to get me to Pleasant Valley and back, then take this and go home."

"But carrying money makes you uncomfortable," she said.

"I'll cope."

"But...but, Will, I'm still worried about John. I really do want to come along."

"Well, I'm afraid I really don't want to go off into the unknown with someone who lies. So just hand over some of that money and I'll go buy my ticket."

Emma screwed up her nerve and shook her head. "No."

"No?" Will practically shouted. "What the hell do you mean, no?"

"I mean that John is my brother and this is his money and I'm going to Pleasant Valley."

"Why? Give me one good reason why you should."

He gave her the most infuriatingly smug look she'd ever seen, as if he was certain she couldn't possibly come up with a *poor* reason, let alone a good one.

Well, blast him. If he was so worried about the truth, she'd darned well give it to him. She took a deep breath and plunged ahead before she lost her courage.

"Look, Will, I don't mean to be the least bit insulting, but you have some rather strange ways about you. I'm sure they're nothing more than Eastern peculiarities, but...well, they could run you into a mite of trouble before you catch up to John. So I think I'd best come along and...and watch out for you."

"What?" This time he did shout. "You? You watch out for me?"

"Yes. And carry the money, of course," she added, clutching her handbag more securely. "So you don't feel uncomfortable."

Will's face turned purple as she spoke. "That's it. That is more than I can take. The only reason I came here was to keep your brother from being...was to warn your brother he might be in for some trouble. And when I get here, what do I run up against? A woman who doesn't trust me, who lies to me, and who has the unmitigated gall to tell me I need baby-sitting. Well, I'm not one of your schoolboys, Emma. I'm a grown man. And I'm going back to Buck's. I'm going to borrow some money from him so I won't have to listen to you insult me."

She stared down at the platform, calling herself sixteen different versions of stupid. *Baby-sitting* was undoubtedly another of his personally concocted words, but it didn't take a genius to figure out its meaning.

So much for telling the truth. Now he wasn't only riled about her deception, he was furious at being insulted.

Blast those articles about *progressive* Eastern men. Blast Susan B. Anthony and the National Women's Suffrage Association and all the rest of them.

Their propaganda had actually started her believing that men were becoming more receptive to women's opinions, when, obviously, she'd been an idiot to believe anything of the sort. Mr. Will Lockhart of modern-day Boston, Massachusetts, was no different than any other 1887 man. As far as he was concerned, women weren't supposed to open their mouths. But, blast it all, she still needed him to go to Arizona and warn John. She still needed someone her brother would listen to.

She looked up. "Will?"

"What?" he snapped.

"The train's almost here." She pointed down the track. The locomotive had appeared around the curve, and the clickity-clack of wheels was fast growing deafening. Smoke billowed from the smokestack, forming a long, trailing gray cloud above the coaches.

The engineer blasted an earsplitting whistle, and the chugging began to slow.

"Will, it only stops for fifteen minutes. You don't have time to get to Buck's and back here again."

"Then I guess I'll have to take a train tomorrow, instead of this one."

Emma bit her lip, desperately trying to think of a response. Whether Will wanted to believe it or not, he shouldn't go alone. Aside from the bizarre things he might say to people, she'd watched him strapping on that gun. He'd looked as if he'd expected it to bite him. She *had* to go with him. And they had to go now. By tomorrow, he might change his mind about going altogether.

"Will, I'm sorry I said what I did. I...I didn't really mean that you needed watching out for." She took a deep breath. She wasn't good at lying.

"Will...Will, the plain truth is that I'm terribly afraid to go to Arizona alone. Yet I've got this feeling I really *have* to go."

The words practically choked her, but she managed to get them out, then stood eyeing Will closely, waiting for his reaction. Susan B. Anthony and the rest of them certainly wouldn't approve of this approach, but...but Will's angry expression was softening.

She began breathing a tad easier and pressed on. "Will, I just didn't want to admit to being afraid. But whether I'm frightened or not, my feeling is also telling me that it's important I leave today. So I'm going inside to buy my ticket. And...and I'd feel ever so much safer if you didn't wait to take a train tomorrow. Please come with me now."

CHARLES K. MATTHEWS ushered the man out the rear of the First Coastal Bank of California, then closed the door behind him and rebolted it, absently registering the fact that dusk was falling. His wife always complained about his staying so late on Saturdays.

"When the bank closes at noon," she'd say, "I don't understand why you're barely home in time for dinner." This was inevitably accompanied by a suspicious gaze that said she didn't entirely believe he'd spent his afternoon at the bank.

He could hardly tell her that things might go wrong if he wasn't accessible when messages arrived. What was the point in setting up an elaborate system of contacts, in paying handsomely for the information produced, if he didn't get it in time to take full advantage?

If he hadn't learned, the precise moment he had, about McCully leaving Mountainview, he'd have missed this opportunity entirely.

He strolled across the bank's elegant marble floor, trying to decide if this latest news presented a problem. Did it matter that one of Dursely's men had wired Dursely about the declining share prices and warned him he was in danger of losing his company? Would Dursely suspect foul play or not? Would it even occur to him there might be a relationship between the loan agreement and the price drop?

Charles shook his head thoughtfully, deciding no. He'd realized the moment they'd met that Dursely wasn't a brilliant man—that McCully was the brains behind his boss. And with McCully not there to do the thinking...

Of course, it would be only prudent to check on how Mr. Buckingham Dursely had reacted to the news.

Charles paused at his office door and polished the brass plaque with the sleeve of his suit jacket. Then he pulled out his handkerchief and burnished each letter in turn: Charles K. Matthews, Vice President.

When he'd finished, he cast a covetous eye to the other side of the corridor, to the president's office door. "Soon," he murmured to himself. "Very, very soon."

He patted his flat stomach with satisfaction. He'd look the part of bank president far better than the incumbent—he was as fit at forty-five as he'd been at twenty-five. His head of dark hair was still full. And the thick mustache he'd grown, emulating Mr. Rockefeller's, was most distinguished-looking.

Yes, he'd look the part. And he *would* be getting the position very, very soon. Because Mr. John D. Rockefeller would be very, very pleased with Mr. Charles K. Matthews.

SINCE THEY'D BEGUN waiting for the Utah Central, which would take them on to Salt Lake City, the twilight had given way to complete darkness. One lone light shone on the platform outside, and the interior of the dreary little Ogden depot was so dimly lit that Emma was feeling edgy.

Aside from herself, Will and the stationmaster, the characters in here were as unsavory-looking as all get out. And even the stationmaster was shifty-eyed.

She glanced at Will, sitting on the bench across from her, grateful he'd so quickly gotten over his fit of temper. And grateful, she silently admitted, that he was with her.

When she'd told him she was afraid to make this trip alone, she'd been out-and-out lying. But not being afraid in the daylight of Mountainview or in the plush dining car of the Central Pacific train they'd initially boarded, were very different things to not being afraid in the middle of a pitch-black night in Utah.

Right here and now, she was very glad she wasn't on her own. No, it was more than that. She was glad it was Will who was with her. Which was crazy, of course, since she was perfectly aware that he was somewhat touched in the head. And, considering he barely knew how to strap on a gun, she couldn't imagine he'd be much help if they ran into trouble. But there was something about him that she found strangely reassuring.

Maybe it was that he was so tall ... or the lean way he was muscled ... or the strength of his even features ... or how large his hands were. The few times he'd taken her arm, she'd been extremely aware of those hands. Each time he touched her, she felt the most peculiar little stream of warmth curling within her body.

She sharply reined in her thoughts. Emma McCully did *not* think about men in physical terms. Emma McCully did not think about men, period. And she certainly had no intention of starting to do so when it came to a tenderfoot astronomer whose sensibilities had him verging on a serious disorder of the mind.

Mercy! Even if that fancy physician hadn't explained the laws of heredity to her, years ago, by now she'd read enough about modern genetics to know that bearing the children of *any* man would be foolhardy of her—let alone those of a man who had the same affliction she had.

But ... but why was she even thinking about such absurd things? She'd always known she could never marry and have children. Her students were her children. She loved them as if they were really her own. And when it came to men ... well, taking a husband meant bearing children. So even the idea of a man in her life was ridiculous.

Yet, since Will had appeared on her porch, her eyes had been straying to him. And whenever they'd strayed, her body had started reacting in ways it never had before . . . in most disquieting ways.

Will glanced over, caught her watching him, and she felt herself blush.

"I . . . I was just thinking," she mumbled, fumbling in her handbag to avoid his gaze, "that you should be carrying at least a little of this money. Twenty dollars or so wouldn't make you feel too uncomfortable, would it?"

"I imagine I could handle that," he said, taking the bills she extended. He stuffed them into his pocket and pulled out his ticket, examining it once more, then looking over at her again. "We're sure not going to get much sleep tonight, are we? I mean, even aside from those damned hard seats in the coaches, we're going to be up and down all night like a jack-in-the-box, changing trains."

"We only have to take a few different lines."

He gave her a wry glance. "A few? I'm not even going to ask how you'd define a lot. Hell," he muttered, returning his attention to the ticket. "After this, there's still the Utah Southern to catch in Salt Lake, then the Wasatch and Jordan Valley, then the Atlantic and Pacific line at the Utah-Arizona boundary, right?"

She merely nodded, reminding herself he was used to a gentler life in Boston, but wondering how he'd ever made it all the way from there to Mountainview.

Of course, he'd probably spent his nights in a Pullman Palace Car, so he'd have been more comfortable. She'd admit the unpadded wooden seats in the unreserved coaches weren't luxurious. But there hadn't been any point in paying for sleeping car tickets when they had all these changes to make.

It was strange that he'd seemed so surprised to learn about them. Surely he hadn't expected the Central Pacific was going to take them down into Arizona. Everyone knew that each state and territory had several different railways, and that a lot of them had no more than ten or twenty miles of track.

She breathed a sigh of relief at the sound of a distant whistle. She'd be glad to be out of this depot.

Only a few minutes later the train was grinding to a halt outside. "Boooaard," a conductor called from the platform. "All aboooaard that's going to Salt Lake City."

"That's us," Will said, picking up their cases from the floor and rising. "And once we're on this one," he added with a resigned-looking grin, "we'll only have three more trains to wait for before we pull into Flagstaff."

Emma followed him silently to the station door. Now probably wasn't a good time to correct that assumption. Apparently he hadn't realized the Atlantic and Pacific line ran to Prescott, not Flagstaff. They'd be getting off in the middle of the desert and taking a stagecoach on to Flagstaff.

But she'd save mentioning that for tomorrow. If he hadn't been on a stage before, he'd ask her what they were like. And she wasn't up to telling him that he'd enjoy the thorough jolting a Concord would give them about as much as calves enjoyed the branding iron.

Outside, beyond the single lamp above the platform, the sky hung black as mourning crepe. There wasn't a star to be seen, and the moon was nothing but a pale gray haze behind dark clouds.

They walked past the baggage car, through the soft glow emanating from the windows of the dining coach, then on past the Palace Cars. They were in darkness, most of the curtains drawn.

Inside, she knew, porters had transformed the day coaches into private sleeping cubicles. She tried not to think about the beds as she followed Will toward the unreserved coaches at the end of the train.

When they reached the first of them, he slipped his hand beneath her elbow and helped her up onto the one high step. She smiled to herself. In Mountainview, she wasn't often made to feel she was an elegant lady. And it was a feeling she liked. Or...or was it the secure feel of Will's touch that she liked?

No, she told herself firmly. That definitely wasn't it. She wanted nothing to do with Will. Not in *that* way, at least. And not with *him* of all men.

She stepped up into the train, out of the fresh night air and into the smoky coach. It was almost as dark as the night. The two gas lamps, suspended from the ceiling above the aisle, provided barely enough light to see by. And rather than their faint gleams being reassuring, they cast eerie, menacing shadows.

Her eyes quickly adjusted to the dimness, and she saw that the majority of passengers, those who'd been on board when the train had pulled in, were asleep. Or trying to sleep.

The odd person was sitting upright; the occasional cigarette glowed. But for the most part, dark shapes of motionless bodies were curled into the straight-backed wooden benches, seeking comfort they couldn't possibly find.

In the aisle seat beside her sat a large, heavily bearded man wearing a filthy buckskin jacket. It smelled, or he smelled, of rancid bear grease...in combination with the stench of whiskey. The drunken leer he was giving her made her shiver.

From behind, Will rested his hand lightly on her arm. "There are a couple of empty benches farther along," he murmured, stepping forward to stand between her and the leerer.

Once again, his presence made her feel more secure. Once again, his touch ignited that funny little curl of warmth inside her. She started along the aisle, stepping around the occasional bag or basket.

A different smell seemed to be rising from each bench she passed. None was pleasant. Some almost made her gag. She stopped at the benches Will had spotted—two empty ones, facing each other.

She slipped into one of them and slid over to the window. Will put a bag on each bench and sat down across from her, his knee brushing hers for a moment.

Quickly he moved it away. But not so quickly that she wasn't aware of her reaction, of the way her heart leapt, the jump in her pulse rate.

What was she doing here, alone with this man? What had possessed her to insist on coming with him? His nearness made her feel as threatened as the interior of the coach did. In an entirely different way, of course, but every bit as threatened.

A shrill whistle split the air, and the train jerked forward an inch or two. A couple more uneven jolts,

and the chugging became more regular. The wheels'
clickity-clacks grew rhythmical, and the train rum-
bled into the night, gradually picking up speed, beginning to sway with its own motion.

Will leaned across to her, so near that she could feel
the warmth of his body and smell his scent...a woodsy
aroma that seemed heavenly fresh...that almost made
her forget he was a threat...almost made her wish he
would stay this close.

"Emma," he whispered, "everyone seems settled
in. And I'm dying of thirst. Do you think it would be
safe to save these seats with our bags and go to the
dining car?"

She shook her head. "From the looks of a few of
these folks, we'd come back to find our bags gone and
our seats taken. Why don't you go and I'll wait here?"

"No."

He leaned back, and she felt the strangest combination of relief and regret.

"I'll just stay here, too," he added. "I wouldn't
want to come back and find both the bags and you
gone."

She swallowed hard at his words. Would he actually care if something happened to her? She swallowed a second time—hadn't realized how dry her
throat was until he'd mentioned the dining car.

"Will, maybe you could just make a fast trip and
bring back something to drink. I'm awfully thirsty,
too."

He gazed at her uncertainly for a moment, then
looked around. "Everyone *is* pretty quiet."

"I'll be fine. Really. I'll just close my eyes, count to
a hundred, and you'll be back."

Hesitantly he rose. "I'll be quick, Emma."

She nodded, managing a smile. "I know. Just to the count of a hundred."

Will started along the aisle. She watched, for a moment, as he quietly strode down the dark coach, past the sleeping passengers, then squeezed her eyes tightly shut and began to count—slowly and silently, in rhythm with every second chug-chug of the train.

It was silly, of course. Something she might have her children do. But it would pass the few minutes until—

She felt the man's presence an instant before he spoke. Felt it and smelled it ... the stench of whiskey combined with rancid bear grease.

"Yer fancy man leave you all alone, honey?" a gruff voice growled as her eyes flashed open.

She stared into a grimy beard—hot, sour breath on her face, making her nauseous.

"Thought you'd like some company while he's gone," the man muttered, grabbing the bag from beside her and tossing it onto the other bench.

CHAPTER FOUR

EMMA GAZED UP at the drunk, terrified. He stood swaying in front of her, threatening to topple down onto her any instant. Her mind scrambled unsuccessfully for the right words to send him away.

But suddenly they weren't necessary. As if from nowhere, Will materialized and clamped a hand on the fellow's shoulder. "The lady's with me," he said firmly.

The other man shrugged Will's hand off and turned quickly, making Emma suspect he wasn't quite as drunk as he was pretending to be. She held her breath.

Will's right hand was resting on the handle of his Colt, but she had no illusions about his having a fast draw. And drunk or not, the other man wore his own gun with careless ease.

He stared at Will for a long moment, then edged a step backward. "Just thought *the lady* might be lonely," he snarled, turning away and lumbering down the dark aisle.

Emma began breathing again and silently told her heart it could slow to normal speed. Maybe that strangely reassuring feeling that Will's presence gave her wasn't so strange, after all.

He stood watching until the other man had settled back into his own seat, then sank down beside her. "You okay?"

"Fine." At least she was certain she'd be fine after a few more deep breaths.

"That creep didn't hurt you, did he?"

She shook her head, not bothering to ask for a definition of *creep*. Will's meaning was obvious. "He just startled me. But what made you come back so quickly?"

"I don't know, exactly. I got halfway to the dining car, then had a feeling I should turn around."

A feeling. Strange, how having sensibilities was usually such an awful affliction, but, every now and then, it was very convenient. "Well, I'm thankful for your feeling, Will. And thankful you acted on it. I... you were wonderful."

A slow grin spread across his face. "You mean, I didn't do too badly for a tenderfoot, huh?"

She laughed quietly, telling herself she'd better stop calling him that.

"Emma, is that sort of thing likely to happen again?" he said seriously.

She shrugged, not liking the expression that had replaced his grin. It clearly told her he wished she was back in Mountainview.

"I think," she replied, "that fellow just had the wrong impression."

"What do you mean?"

"Well...I think he assumed..." She paused, waiting in vain for a look of understanding from Will.

"You know... the way he called me *the lady*," she finally explained, trying to ignore the way her face was growing warm.

Will simply continued staring blankly at her.

"And... and before you arrived he called you a *fancy man*."

"A what?"

"A fancy man," she managed again. She certainly couldn't use any words more explicit than that without turning absolutely crimson. "I think it's your Eastern clothes, Will. I guess you should have changed into something of John's before we started out. Because he thought you were a fancy man and... and since I was with you..."

She just couldn't say it aloud. But Will would have to be an idiot not to realize the man had thought she was nothing better than a hurdy-gurdy dance hall girl.

"Oh," he finally said, breaking into another grin.

"Will! It isn't funny. Not the least bit funny."

"It's not? But I thought you were the woman who assured me people wouldn't think a thing about you traveling with me."

She glared at him. She hadn't realized he had such a disagreeable sense of humor. "What I assured you," she enunciated precisely, "was that no one in *Mountainview* would think anything of it because they know me. But out here in the middle of Utah...well, it isn't funny, Will."

He shook his head, clearly torn between thinking this was hilarious and being annoyed with her. But, blast it. She wasn't to blame for a drunk's actions. And there was nothing the least bit hilarious about being mistaken for something she wasn't.

"Will, stop smiling. I don't like being taken for...for...well, I don't like it at all."

"No? Well there's something I don't like at all, either, Emma. I don't like the sense that I'm going to have to watch out for you every minute. I knew you shouldn't have come along. I told you a million times there was no need. But you tricked me into letting you."

"I tricked you?" she said, trying to sound innocent.

"Of course you did. First you pretended locating John was going to be difficult—that I needed your help. And then you squirreled the money away so I couldn't go without you. And then...and then, that story about being afraid to travel on your own was a lie, wasn't it? I'll bet, when we were still back in Mountainview, you weren't the least bit frightened, were you?"

"But, Will, I was." She smiled weakly, feeling a dreadful suspicion her guilt was written all over her face.

"You weren't! I can see that you weren't."

Blast it. Dreadful suspicion confirmed.

"You can be a darned aggravating woman, Emma. You tricked me into agreeing to let you come along. And your being where women are few and far between is going to cause all kinds of problems, isn't it?"

"No! It isn't."

"Oh? Then what do you call what just happened? You know, I should probably let you in on a little secret. I'm no expert with a gun."

She tried to look surprised.

"So," he went on, "I can do nicely without trying to bluff any more guys into thinking I might be Billy the Kid. But I can't see you getting on a train for home and making the trip back by yourself. Not if that creep is any example of the sort of companions you'd have. So what are we going to do? I don't suppose you have any ugly pills in your bag, do you?"

"Will, it's not me that's the problem," she said. "It's the way *you* look. It's those *fancy man* clothes."

He eyed her skeptically, as if considering whether that could be a possibility. "I'll change then," he finally said. "When we stop at Salt Lake, I'll put on something of John's. And after that we'll have no more problems with men coming on to you. Is that right?"

"Coming on to me?"

"A back East expression," Will snapped. "But after I change, will men leave you alone?"

She shrugged uneasily.

"What's the shrug mean?"

"Well, your changing will help, but . . ."

"But what?"

"Well, since we're traveling together, it would be better if people thought we were man and wife."

"I see," Will said, turning the two words into twelve syllables. "I see. And just how do we make them think that?"

"Well, we simply pretend we are. I mean, instead of telling that drunk *the lady* was with you, you could have told him I was your wife."

"I see," he said again, his tone even more annoyed. "First you trick me, and now you expect me to be an actor."

He sat gazing at her, and, even in the darkness of the coach, she could see a positively evil glint appear in his eyes. It made her wonder if maybe she shouldn't risk taking a train back to Mountainview on her own.

"Well, Emma," he finally said. "I'll be delighted to pretend you're my wife. But I'd never have guessed you were that kind of woman."

She stared at him for a moment as his meaning sank in. *"Pretend!"* she hissed, the moment it did. "I said, pretend. And I only meant in public."

"In public, the way we are now, you mean?"

"Yes."

"Fine. We'll pretend." Without another word, he wrapped an arm around her shoulder and pulled her to him.

For an instant, she was too shocked to even struggle. Then the instant passed and she jerked away. Rather, she tried to jerk away. He was holding her so tightly she couldn't move.

"Relax," he whispered. "There's nothing wrong with a tired wife resting against her husband."

"Will! Just stop this. Stop it right now. It isn't seemly."

He didn't even look at her—simply stretched his legs out, crossed one foot over the other on the bench across from them, and closed his eyes. "'Night, wife," he murmured, giving her an infuriating little squeeze. "Sleep well."

She made a final, unsuccessful attempt to free herself, then sat fuming. How dare Will manhandle her like this? Maybe she *had* tricked him a little. Maybe he had *some* right to be upset with her. But no gentleman would ever grab her and hold her against her wishes. Will Lockhart was definitely no gentleman.

She sat stiffly against him, waiting for him to tire of his game and release her.

He didn't. Instead, his breathing gradually slowed and deepened.

He'd fallen asleep! If she could move her arm, she'd give him a sharp dig with her elbow. But she couldn't move at all. Not away from him, at least.

If she remained the way she was, though, stiff as a board, her neck was going to develop a terrible crick.

She sat the way she was until she could feel that darned crick forming. Then, tentatively, she let her body sag a little. Uneasily she rested her cheek against Will's chest.

He made a quiet, murmuring sound and shifted his position a bit.

His arm relaxed around her, and she sighed quietly with relief. She could move away.

She didn't, though. Unseemly as sitting this way was, unsettling as it felt to be resting against a man, wrong as she knew that was for an unmarried woman to be doing, there was something about it that didn't feel unseemly at all. Or unsettling. Or wrong. That felt, in fact, positively right.

Back in Mountainview, she hadn't given much thought to what this train trip would be like—that she would be sitting in the dark, surrounded by strangers while hurtling through the blackness of Utah at what must be at least fifteen miles an hour. The reality of it was frightening.

But being close to Will was making her feel safer than she should rationally feel. So it might not be the proper thing for her to do, but...

She remained cuddled guiltily against him, his warmth invading her bloodstream, the solid thudding of his heart lulling her unease, his fresh, woodsy scent making her forget the hot stuffiness of the train and think instead of a cool forest.

Finally she closed her eyes. Surely it couldn't hurt to stay where she was until they reached Salt Lake.

"FLAGSTAFF!" the conductor called as the train slowed. "All out next stop that's going to Flagstaff, Arizona!"

Emma gazed out into the glaring afternoon sunlight. This area of Arizona, she knew from teaching geography, was part of the Colorado Plateau—a series of flat plateaus, her book described it, broken by a few mountains and canyons.

Very few, from what she could see. Barren desert stretched on all sides like an enormous, alkaline carpet, dotted here and there with scraggly cactus.

But the mountains in the distance assured her the flat landscape didn't go on forever. Those had to be the San Francisco Peaks, she decided. And Flagstaff sat at the foot of them. "We're here," she said.

Will turned from his window and looked across at her. "What do you mean, we're here? We're where? Where is it?"

"Where's what?"

"The city. Our tickets say Flagstaff. The conductor said Flagstaff. But all I see is desert."

"Oh. Well, I'm afraid the train doesn't run over to Flagstaff. It's not a very important place—not really much more than a lumber camp. The train heads straight down to the capital."

"To Phoenix?"

"Pardon me?"

"To Phoenix. You said to the capital."

"Yes...yes, I did. But the capital of Arizona is Prescott."

"Since when?" He gazed at her as if *she* were being stupid, rather than him.

"Well, let me think. Since about ten years ago, I believe. Tucson used to be the capital but now it's Prescott. In fact, they've moved it so often it's known as the capital on wheels. Heaven knows where they'll stop."

"Phoenix," Will said firmly. "I have a feeling they'll finally decide on Phoenix."

Emma merely nodded. He had a feeling. She'd almost forgotten that Will wasn't quite a normal person, but there he sat, confusing reality with a premonition once again.

He turned back toward the window, and she watched him for a minute, wondering what he thought of her falling asleep against him, last night.

She blushed at the recollection. In the bright light of day, it seemed so terribly wanton. Likely Will had decided she was as loose-virtued as a...well, there wasn't any point in worrying about what Will thought. After all, it didn't really matter a whit.

As soon as they'd visited with John, they'd be heading back to Mountainview. Then Will would go on to take care of whatever business he had in California and she'd never see him again. So what he thought of her didn't matter.

Regardless of that, though, she'd darned well conduct herself impeccably from here on. Last night's behavior had been a...an aberration, that was the word.

"If the train doesn't run to Flagstaff," Will said, bringing her thoughts back to the moment, "how do we get there?"

"A stagecoach. We go the last few miles by stage. It's all part of the tickets."

He stared back out as the train jerked from slow to stop. "But there's nothing here. We're in the middle of Nowhere, Arizona."

Emma scanned their surroundings. "There," she said, pointing to the adobe building about fifty yards from the track. "That'll be the Wells Fargo swing station."

Will's gaze followed her finger. "That's a station?"

"Of course."

"But the stable behind it's three times bigger."

"Naturally. They have to keep changes of six-horse teams in the stable."

He shook his head, gathered up their bags and rose, muttering something she couldn't make out.

She followed him down the aisle and off the train. In those cowboy boots of John's, he stood even taller than he had before. And she couldn't help noticing, for the dozenth time since he'd changed from his suit, how broad his shoulders were.

He was enough larger than her brother that the clothes were a tight fit. Will's back muscles were clearly defined through the cotton of John's blue shirt.

She forced her eyes down and immediately regretted it. There was something about the way his back tapered, something about the way that gun holster rested on his lean hips, something about the way those faded jeans stretched across his . . .

Oh, mercy, what was the matter with her? She'd never before paid a man's body any mind. And aberrations in the middle of the night might be excusable, but this was the middle of the day.

Behind them, with a sharp blast of its whistle, the train began moving again, creating a breeze in the deathly still air. They paused, watching it gather speed and steam on south, until it looked like a mirage in the brilliant sunlight.

Will wiped his brow with his free hand, the movement causing his chest muscles to ripple slightly. Emma swallowed hard and glanced away.

"I don't believe this," he said. "I thought the train was an oven, but it must be two thousand degrees out here."

She bit back the word tenderfoot. She'd promised herself she wouldn't call him that again. Besides, in John's clothes, plus that black Stetson hat he'd traded some drunken cowboy his silk bowler for, he no longer looked the least like a tenderfoot. He looked . . . blast it! She simply wasn't going to think about how he looked.

"It can't actually be hotter than a hundred and ten or so," she offered as they began walking toward the station. "And it'll be a lot cooler inside. Adobe's good that way."

Emma was right, Will decided, stepping into the dim structure after her. It was cooler inside—couldn't be much more than a hundred.

A couple of men, sitting at a small table and obviously in the midst of a card game, stopped to eye the new arrivals with distinct interest. At least, they were eyeing Emma with distinct interest.

Will put down the bags and took her arm. "Well, *wife,* here we are," he said loudly. "Almost to Flagstaff."

The men turned back to their cards and Emma's big blue eyes shot him an "I told you so" message.

Well...so maybe she'd been right. Fine. If she had, that was all to the good. It meant his major problem was solved. He could relax and stop worrying about her.

He shouldn't be feeling so damned responsible for her, anyway. It wasn't his fault she was out here in the middle of Arizona. He hadn't wanted her along.

But now that she was...well, he shouldn't have pulled that dumb joke last night. At least, he shouldn't have carried it on for so long. Grabbing her to annoy her was one thing. She'd deserved it. But he should never have fallen asleep with her in his arms.

Because when he'd woken and found her there— sleeping and looking so darned defenseless—well, holding her like that, even as a joke, had been a downright stupid thing to do.

Looking at her before had been hard enough. But now, every time he looked at her, all he could think about was how soft and warm she felt in his arms.

He forced his thoughts away from her and glanced over at the only other person in the sparse room, an older man—undoubtedly the stationmaster.

"Howdy," the man offered.

"Howdy," Will replied, unable to suppress a smile. He was beginning to feel as if he'd just stepped into an old western series—*Gunsmoke, Bat Masterson, Wyatt Earp,* or maybe even *The Rifleman.*

He'd once idolized the TV western heroes. And this station could be a set on any one of the shows that had been his Saturday morning television fare way back when.

Even then, they'd been ancient reruns. But as a boy, watching them had given him a sense of returning to the 1862 West he'd left. Had given him a sense of returning while remaining in the present . . . or had he been remaining in the future?

Damn. Even after all these years, even now that he'd traveled through time twice, the concept of what was future, past and present could be confusing. Right now, for example, he knew he was in the past. Yet, at the moment, this was his present.

He shook his head. He was no philosopher, so there was little point in trying to sort out the logic.

Instead, he glanced around, taking in details of the adobe brick construction, thinking how unbelievably different these surroundings were from Space Station Freedom.

A trip through time was really an adventure. It wasn't every man who got to spend his vacation in 1887.

"Stage'll be along any time now," the stationmaster said. "Just set a spell."

He'd barely spoken the words when a faint rumble became audible. "There she is, boys," he called to the younger men.

Wordlessly they threw down their cards and headed out.

"Boys'll just change the horses," the stationmaster told Will, grabbing a canteen and following the others to the door. "Then you'll be on your way."

Will and Emma wandered over and stood in the doorway, peering into the distance at the stage. Rather, they peered at the growing cloud on the desert that Will knew was the stage.

It rapidly grew larger and louder, finally thundering up in front of the station.

The air gradually began to clear, but the yellowish dust clung tenaciously to everything. The six horses were covered in sweat, and the sweat was covered in dust. And the red paint of the stage was probably bright . . . under its thick, dusty coating.

The driver leapt down from the near side and wiped a layer of grimy perspiration off his brow. From the far side, a tall, lean man of about forty swung off the coach. He was holding a rifle so easily that it looked like an extension of his arm.

"Clem!" the stationmaster called to the driver, tossing him the canteen. "And I'll be hornswoggled!" he exclaimed, looking across at the other man. "Wyatt Earp! What in tarnation are you doin' back in the Territory?"

Will stared at the tall, lean man in disbelief. Wyatt Earp? The legendary Wyatt Earp standing right here in front of him? Well, hell, he'd just head over and introduce himself. Shake Mr. Earp's hand.

He started for the stage and almost reached it before Emma grabbed his arm and jerked firmly on it. He paused, forcing his eyes away from Wyatt Earp, and glanced down at her. She looked alarmed.

"What?" he demanded.

"He's a killer," she whispered.

"Who?"

"Wyatt Earp."

"Don't be ridiculous, Emma. He's a famous lawman."

"Ha! More like an infamous gunfighter. He and his brothers and that Doc Holliday and Bat Masterson. Haven't you folks back East heard of the Dodge City Gang?"

"Don't be ridiculous," Will repeated, looking toward the stage again, vaguely aware passengers were getting out of it but focusing his attention on Wyatt Earp. He didn't look a whole lot like that TV star who'd played him.

Oh, he was a reasonably good-looking man. And he did have a heavy, drooping mustache. But his hair was blond. And his face was gaunt, and his eyes just a touch small and close-set. In fact, he looked positively... well, he *would* look positively mean, if Will didn't know he was one of the good guys.

By now, the stationmaster had reached Wyatt and was slapping him on the back, raising puffs of dust from his shirt. "You ol' polecat! Never thought you'd be back in Arizona. And ridin' shotgun messenger for Wells Fargo again?"

"Nope. Not officially, at least. I'm just hitching a ride with Clem. Masterson's back in Tombstone, you know. And my brother Warren's there. I'm heading down to see them. There's bound to be a serious poker game just waiting for me."

"Told Wyatt he's liable to find there's a serious necktie party waitin' for him," the driver joked. "But he weren't listening."

"Hell," Wyatt said with a grin, "any folks that's still in Tombstone from the old days must have cooled off by now. After all, it's been years since the OK Corral business. And hell, brother Virgil *was* the city marshall. I was just helping him do his job by killing those cowpokes. Bet nobody even remembers accusing me of murder."

Emma elbowed Will sharply in the ribs.

He ignored her. But maybe he wouldn't be too fast about introducing himself to Mr. Earp.

He turned his attention to the passengers. They were all out standing around the stage now. And either his vision was blurred or a total of nine men had gotten out. But that was impossible. Unless the stagecoach had a false bottom.

"Nine," Emma said. "It's already full."

"You mean all those guys really *were* inside?"

"Of course. There're the two seats that face each other and the bench in the middle."

Will looked back at the coach. He'd seen larger compact cars. "They must ride with their knees locked together in there," he muttered.

"Well, when it's full," Emma explained, "usually each man beside the windows hangs a leg out. But I don't think they fancy doing that in Apache country."

Will reminded himself this was an adventure. "So, since it's full, I guess we have to wait for the next stage, huh?"

Emma shook her head, looking as if she didn't relish having to tell him whatever she was about to tell him.

"What, then?"

"Well...I'll get a seat inside, of course, because I'm a woman. But whoever's seat I take will have to ride up top. And I imagine you will, as well.

"Up top?" Will stared at the coach's roof. "With the luggage?"

"As many as six people sometimes ride up there," Emma said. "It gets a mite dusty, but it's perfectly safe. There's that railing."

Railing? She called that skinny bit of metal a railing? He'd fall off. Those damned horses would get going full tilt and he'd fall off.

"Or maybe, if they wouldn't mind," Emma suggested, "you could sit down front on the driver's bench—between that Clem fellow and Wyatt Earp. One passenger sometimes rides there."

Will nodded slowly, assessing the driver's bench. It couldn't be much more than four feet across.

The tired team had already been unharnessed, and fresh horses were being hooked up. The stationmaster was pointing at Emma, and one of the passengers shrugged and began clambering up the side of the coach, to the roof.

One of them. That meant there would be eight men plus Emma inside. And Will Lockhart would be perched up top with that other passenger and the bags. Or sitting practically on the rumps of the rear pair of horses . . . jammed in between a man with a long whip and a man with a serious rifle...a man Emma claimed was a killer.

"What about you?" the stationmaster demanded, ambling over to Will. "You're packin' iron. Want to sit up front?"

He glanced at the roof again, at that skinny bit of railing, and decided that television writers knew the difference between heroes and killers better than Emma did.

"Sure. Up front's good," he said, climbing in behind the team.

Clem swung onto the driver's bench on Will's right side, and with Wyatt on his left, Will suddenly knew how a canned sardine must feel. He could scarcely breathe, let alone move. Maybe he should have simply gone for the roof and taken his chances.

"Shift yer dang pistol outta the way," Clem snapped, cracking his whip and jolting the team into motion. "I don't need it diggin' in my hip."

Will twisted his gun belt. The Colt ended up practically sitting in his lap, its business end pointing directly between his legs.

He stared nervously down at it as the stage began bouncing along, thankful the hammer was resting on that empty chamber. He might want to have children someday.

Wyatt was holding his rifle flat across his thighs, and its butt began smacking against the side of Will's knee with each jolt of the stage. He refrained from pointing that out. Wyatt didn't seem the sort who'd take kindly to complaints.

They quickly gained speed, the horses' hooves sending up a cloud of sandy dust that stung Will's eyes and managed to creep into his mouth—even though he had it tightly closed. He imagined a darned high percentage of stagecoach drivers died of throat cancer.

They rattled and rolled along, under the broiling sun, until every bone in Will's body was aching. He kept his eyes shut most of the time, trying to protect them, but the occasional peek revealed that the land sweeping by was no longer as flat as it had been.

They had to be nearing those mountains Emma said sheltered Pleasant Valley. And that meant they'd be reaching Flagstaff soon.

He felt the stage slowing and opened his eyes again, hoping they'd arrived. But Clem was simply reining in the team as they reached a sharp bend in the road. A rock formation rose on one side, creating a blind curve.

Just as the horses were completing the turn, Clem let out a string of obscenities and pulled sharply back on the reins. The team snorted and whinnied, skittering uneasily to a stop.

Will peered through the dust... and suddenly felt ice-cold despite the sweltering heat. He'd never before looked into the round muzzle of a rifle.

"Told you, Wyatt, how damn uppity these highwaymen was gettin'," Clem muttered from the side of his mouth.

Three men sat on horseback, blocking the trail. Three men, dressed in dusty black except for the red bandannas that hid their faces. Three men, each training a rifle on the driver's bench.

CHAPTER FIVE

BEHIND THE STAGECOACH, the late-afternoon sun hung low in the sky, elongating the shadows of the highwaymen and their horses, making them look like thin, gray, man-beast monsters on the sand.

But Will was barely aware of either the men or their shadows. His gaze was riveted on the end of a rifle. He'd never realized how terrifying a tiny black hole could be.

They were going to be killed. And what about the passengers inside? What about Emma? Oh, Lord! What would happen to Emma, the only woman aboard?

"Throw us your treasure box," one of the men snarled at Clem.

Involuntarily Will's gaze flickered to the sturdy wooden box that was sitting in the boot, below the bench. The driver's feet were resting solidly on it.

"Now!" the highwayman ordered, emphasizing the command with a jerk of his rifle.

Will's stomach muscles clenched like a fist, but Clem casually leaned over the side of the stage and spit a huge wad of tobacco onto the ground. "Know who this is?" he asked, straightening up again and nodding across at Wyatt.

"It's Wyatt Earp," he went on without waiting for a reply.

Above the red bandannas, three pairs of eyes flickered from Clem to the other side of the bench.

"And this," Wyatt announced, jerking his thumb at Will, "is my brother, Warren."

Oh, geez, Will thought as the eyes shifted to him. He didn't want this trio believing he was one of the Earp brothers. He'd far rather they just figured he was a tenderfoot, like everyone else did.

He realized Wyatt was eyeing him expectantly but couldn't think of anything to say. And even if he could, it would probably catch in his throat. So, instead, he simply forced his hand forward and rested it on the butt of his gun.

The almost imperceptible twitch at the corner of Wyatt's mouth told him Mr. Earp approved. But hell, that didn't mean they weren't about to be killed. He glanced fleetingly at his hand, just sitting there on that gun. Was there even a chance he could get the damned thing out of its holster before he was dead three times over?

"You boys really think you can beat *one* Earp, let alone two?" Clem asked, his voice cooler than Will would have thought possible.

He felt a motion on his left, and by the time his gaze had flashed back to Wyatt, the ex-lawman had his rifle off his knees and was pointing it at the trio.

Will let out a slow breath. They'd just reached show time. Beneath the bottom edge of one of those red bandannas, an Adam's apple bobbed anxiously up and down.

"Why don't you boys run along," Wyatt suggested, grinning.

"And if you got any friends," Clem added, "tell 'em Wells Fargo's got the Earps ridin' shotgun again."

The three highwaymen glanced at one another. Then, in unspoken agreement, they wheeled their horses as one and galloped off.

Wyatt pointed his rifle in the direction of the man who'd spoken.

"Goin' to kill him?" Clem asked calmly.

Will watched in disbelief as Wyatt squeezed the trigger and the rifle erupted with an ear-shattering blast.

"Na," Wyatt said, laughing. "Just want 'em to remember me."

Ahead, the three horses began galloping even faster. One dusty black Stetson hat lay on the sand behind them.

Will couldn't see well enough to be certain, but he thought there was a bullet hole through it. He cleared his throat, barely able to believe the others seemed to think the interruption had been funny. "Ah... that sort of thing happen often?"

"Every couple of days," Clem said. "It's nothing."

Will merely nodded, thinking most stagecoach drivers must not live long enough for the dust to cause them throat cancer. He wondered how many times that sort of thing could happen to *him* before *he'd* think it was nothing. Probably a trillion.

Wyatt turned to him. "Where you from, mister?"

"Boston."

"Yeah? Well, you did all right for an Easterner. What's your name?"

"Will. Will Lockhart."

"Well, Will, let me shake your hand," Wyatt said, extending his own. "You heading on down to Tombstone with us?"

"No. Just going as far as Flagstaff."

"Too bad. The drivers can always use an extra gunman through Apache country."

"We'd best get goin'," Clem said, clicking the reins. "We've got lost time to make up."

The team started forward, raising a fresh cloud of dust, making conversation impossible again. But Flagstaff proved to be only a mile or so farther along.

The sight of its ragtag main street did wonders for Will's sense of well-being. Maybe that little episode hadn't really been as dangerous as he'd thought. After all, here they were, safe and sound.

Clem slowed the horses as they passed the first few roughly constructed buildings, then stopped the stage in front of a marginally more solid-looking structure that bore a Wells Fargo sign.

Immediately two men rushed out to begin switching teams.

"Well, Will," Wyatt said once they'd jumped down from the stage, "if you change your mind and decide to head south, look me up in Tombstone. Try the Crystal Palace Saloon. Or the Oriental. We can always use fresh money at the poker table. And I'll introduce you to my *real* brother Warren."

Will grinned. "I'll keep that offer in mind."

Clem tossed Will's bags from the roof as the passengers began getting out of the stage.

"Thank you," Emma murmured to the man who was handing her down. It took only an instant for her eyes to find Will.

When they did, a wave of relief washed over her, even though she'd known he was fine. The men sitting by the window, who could see what had happened, had assured her that the shot had come from the stage, not from the highwaymen. But seeing for herself that Will was safe made her feel a million times better.

She hurried over to him, resisting the crazy urge to hug him and make sure he was still a solid, live man. After all, she was going to conduct herself impeccably for the rest of their time together. So she stopped just out of arm's reach. "You're not hurt. I . . . I was worried."

"No need to have been," he said nonchalantly. "That sort of thing happens to a stage every couple of days. It's nothing."

EMMA FORCED DOWN the last bite of her dinner and glanced across at Will. They'd been told the Golden Nugget Saloon was by far the best place to eat—which didn't say much for the food anywhere else in Flagstaff.

"Let's get going," Will said, rising and picking up their cases. "We don't want to find the hotel's full."

She wasn't entirely sure she agreed with that sentiment. They'd passed by the town's lone hotel on their way here, and it just might be the most disreputable-looking one she'd ever seen.

If it had been up to her, they certainly wouldn't be spending the night in the Magnolia Hotel. She'd wanted to continue straight on to the Tewksburys'. But there'd been no convincing Will.

"Emma," he'd finally snapped at her, "we've been traveling for well over twenty-four hours straight. I'm tired and hungry and every bone in my body aches. And I'm damned well not renting a rig and heading out for some ranch when it's practically night already. They're not even expecting us. So we'll go and see John tomorrow. Tonight, I just want to get a good night's sleep."

He'd been right, of course. But that didn't make her any happier about staying in that hotel. With a man. Traveling with Will was one thing, but staying in the same hotel wasn't...well, it simply wasn't proper. If her parents knew what was going on she'd be disowned. Just as well they were hundreds of miles away in San Francisco.

Reluctantly she followed Will out of the Golden Nugget and along the dirt street.

Dusk had turned to dark while they'd eaten. Will *had* been right, she told herself again. They could hardly have arrived in on the Tewksburys after dark. Ranchers went to bed when the sun set. And Will certainly did look as if he could use a good night's sleep.

"You seem a mite stiff," she offered.

He glanced down at her and smiled.

For some unfathomable reason, his smile made her feel better.

"A mite," he agreed. "That stagecoach ride was pretty rough."

"Oh?" she teased. "Mark Twain writes about the Concord coach being a cradle on wheels."

"Mark Twain," Will said wryly, "has an extremely warped sense of humor.

"Here we are," he added, pausing as they neared the Magnolia's front door.

Emma tried unsuccessfully to smile. The hotel was nothing more than an overgrown, two-story shack.

Before them, its front door suddenly burst open and a man went flying through the air, onto the street. He got shakily to his feet and began to stagger off.

Will cleared his throat. "Take my arm, Emma. I think we'd better keep right on pretending you're my wife."

Obediently she clutched his arm and they stepped inside. It was even worse than she'd expected. The little lobby apparently doubled as a saloon—a saloon that made the Golden Nugget look positively elegant. This one stank of unwashed bodies, whiskey and beer. And the smoke was so thick it almost choked her.

She tightened her grip on Will's arm as they crossed to the desk. From the corner of her eye, she could see that she was the only woman in the place. And that every one of the men was staring at her as if he hadn't seen a female in years. And that every one of them looked in dire need of a bath, a shave and sobering up.

"The wife and I'd like a room for the night," Will told the clerk.

"Two rooms," Emma corrected him quietly.

The clerk looked from her back to Will. "Two rooms?"

Will glared at her for a moment, then turned to the clerk again. "*A* room. *One.* The *wife* and I simply had a little fight."

"Will, wha—?"

"Quiet," he snapped so sharply she stopped mid-word. He leaned down and whispered in her ear. "Look, Emma, if you think I'm going to spend the night lying awake and worrying about what could be happening to you in this dump, you're crazy. I told you, I want a good night's sleep."

She swallowed hard and thought rapidly. She didn't want to spend the night lying awake and worrying, either. And from the looks of these characters staring at her, she'd have good reason to worry.

Of course, the idea of spending a night in the same room as Will was unthinkable. But so was the idea of spending a night in a room, here, alone.

The clerk, she realized, hadn't taken his eyes off them. She smiled nervously at him. "One room," she managed. "My husband and I simply had a little fight."

Will signed the register and took the key. "I'll go first," he muttered, starting for the stairs. "In case some drunk comes stumbling down."

Emma looked straight ahead, pretending she was oblivious to the male eyes following her. But looking straight ahead, once they hit the stairs, meant that she was looking directly at Will's...

She swallowed hard again. Those jeans of John's were an even tighter fit on Will than she'd realized. Every step he took molded them to the muscles of his...of his legs, she told herself, forcing her eyes down.

They immediately wandered back up—all of their own accord.

She couldn't recall ever having been exposed to a man's body from quite this angle. At least, if she had

been, she'd never noticed. But she was definitely noticing right now. What on earth was happening to her?
And what on earth was she doing? Emma McCully,
spinster schoolmarm, was about to spend a night in
the same room as a man.

She looked up—all the way to Will's shoulders. She
kept forgetting how broad they were. And the way his
dark hair curled slightly, at the nape of his neck, made
her wonder what it would feel like to. . .

Oh, no, it didn't! She had to get hold of herself. Her
immunity to men might have deserted her just when
she most needed it, but she knew right from wrong—
and certain things were definitely wrong, even in the
modern world of 1887.

They turned onto the second floor hall. Will
stopped, opened the door to their room and ushered
her inside.

The dim light filtering in from the hall offered just
enough illumination to see by. She took a couple of
hesitant steps, then simply stood staring at the bed.
Except for the washstand, it took up the entire room.
But how could it seem so large yet so small at the same
time? If two people were lying on that bed. . .

"There's no chair," Will said, sounding amazed.

She glanced back at him.

"In the movies there's always. . . I mean. . . I mean,
I assumed there'd be a big stuffed chair I could sleep
on. I. . . I guess I'll have to make do with the floor."

Emma didn't even ask about *movies*. If she asked
about every strange word Will used, her voice would
be raw.

She gazed at the rough wooden planks of the floor,
then at the bed, the thought she was thinking making

her blush. It wasn't the thought of a woman who was conducting herself impeccably.

But the bed really wasn't *that* small. And Will was so stiff, she'd seen it in his walk. And she trusted him. Last night, on the train, he'd turned out to be a gentleman, after all. She'd lain asleep in his arms and been perfectly safe.

Nervously she crossed to the little shelf that held a lamp. She lit it, then cleared her throat and turned back. "Will...I think maybe it would be all right if you took one side of the bed. I mean, I could sleep under the sheet and you could sleep on top of it and we could share the blanket...and I think maybe that would be all right...given the circumstances, I mean."

Will put the cases down and eyed her uncertainly. "You're sure, Emma? That wouldn't make you feel too uncomfortable?"

Too uncomfortable? Would more uncomfortable than she'd ever been in her life be *too* uncomfortable or not? She didn't know. All she knew was that Will was going through a lot for her and John. And she wasn't about to thank him by making him sleep on the floor.

"It'll be all right, Will. If...if you wouldn't mind just stepping out for a minute, though," she said, gesturing at the pitcher and basin, "I'd like to get the dust off."

"Right. Of course. I'll wait outside the room."

Will backed out, pulled the door closed behind him and leaned against the far wall, thinking Emma was awfully damned considerate. With her 1887 morals, the idea of sharing a bed with a man must scare the hell out of her. And given the way his body was aching, he really appreciated her making the offer.

But whether he insisted on the floor or shared the bed, all he was going to do was lie awake thinking how close Emma was ... close enough to reach out and ... but he wasn't going to.

He might not be up on all the moral standards of 1887, but he knew that women were supposed to "save themselves" for marriage. If he so much as kissed Emma, she might die of guilt. Hell, he merely caught her looking at him and she blushed.

So he wasn't going to so much as kiss her. No matter how badly he wanted to, he wouldn't. After all, he was hardly an uncontrolled sex maniac.

Except that, as much as he didn't want it to be, there was more than simple sexual attraction involved. Hell, he hadn't wanted her with him, and he didn't want to care about her. But something about her had gotten to him—faster than he would have believed possible.

He was damned well going to keep it to himself, though. Because he had no intention of getting involved with a woman from the wrong century. Certainly not a woman like Emma, a woman who'd never even kept company with a man—whatever that meant, exactly.

"Will?" she called through the door. "You can come back in, now."

He took a deep breath, opened the door and stepped into the room.

Emma was lying on the far side of the bed, looking as if she was about to fall off the edge. Her eyes were anxious, and she had the sheet and blanket pulled up practically to her nose.

She'd managed to wash her hair in that darned basin, and her dark, wet locks were strewn across the pillow, making her look as vulnerable as a child.

He turned away. The brown dress and whimsy hat she'd been wearing lay neatly on top of her bag, along with a white, brimmed hat and a blue dress that she must be planning to wear tomorrow.

The dress was the exact blue of her eyes. It would probably make her look every bit as delectable as the brown one did.

He stared at the clothes, wondering what she was wearing right now. He tried forcing himself to think about how the Red Sox were doing, back in the American League East, but it didn't work. All he could think about was Emma, in that bed.

Lord, how could he feel this way about a woman who lived generations before the sexual revolution? What chance could there be that...

None. Absolutely none, he reminded himself firmly. When he went back to 2014, Emma McCully was going to be every bit as chaste as she'd been before he'd arrived. If it killed him. And it damned well might.

He started to unbutton his shirt.

"Will?" she said in an anxious voice.

"Yes?"

"Aren't you going to turn out the light first?"

"Oh, yes. Yes, of course. I can wash up in the dark." He turned down the lamp's wick until its glow died, then stood in the darkness, feeling his desire straining against the buttons of John's jeans.

He probably had to sleep in the damned things. He doubted Emma would be able to handle the sight of him in his Jockey shorts. But he'd never before worn pants with a button fly... wondered how much pressure it took to pop those buttons... wondered whether his odds on a good night's sleep were anything but nil.

SHE WAS HOLDING John's hands as tightly as she could, yet he was slipping away. There was an endless black hole, and he was slipping into it. And his hands were so cold... cold as ice... deathly cold.

She called out to him, but he wouldn't stop pulling against her. Her arms were beginning to ache, but if she let go, something awful would happen to him.

"John," she cried again. "John, don't go."

"Emma... Emma."

He was shaking her. Why was he shaking her?

She opened her eyes, realizing only as she did so that they'd been closed. It was pitch black. And John was gently shaking her. But his hands were warm now. Warm and alive and drawing her up from the fearful abyss she'd been in.

"Emma," he said again. "It's all right. You were just dreaming."

Not John! For a terrifying second, she didn't know where she was or who the man was with her. And then reality came rushing back.

The reality of Flagstaff and the hotel and this bed and Will. Most of all, Will.

She realized she was trembling and her heart was pounding—because of the nightmare or because she was lying in bed with Will? She didn't know which was more frightening.

His hands were resting gently on her shoulders. Warmth from them was seeping through the cotton of her nightdress to her skin. She was intensely aware of his naked chest leaning over her, of his body heat, of his breath on her face. And just as it had on the train, his nearness made her feel safe, yet afraid at the same time.

She tried to pull the sheet up over her shoulders, but Will was lying on top of it . . . so close to her.

"Emma," he murmured, "it's okay." He brushed a lock of hair off her cheek, his fingers cool against her skin, yet his touch sending an unexpected, inexplicable, hot rush through her.

"Yes," she managed. "It's okay. I . . . I sometimes have nightmares, Will. And they seem so real that even after I wake up I'm terrified. I'll be fine. It just takes me a few minutes."

"Emma . . ." Will paused. When he started speaking once more, his voice sounded strained.

"Emma, if you want to cuddle against me . . . for that few minutes it takes . . . it would be all right. I mean, I wouldn't do anything. And I wouldn't think you were . . . I wouldn't think there was anything at all wrong with your doing that. I know how frightening nightmares can be. And sometimes, being close to someone is reassuring."

He shifted away from her, propping first his pillow, then his shoulders, against the wall. And then he reached out to her, inviting her nearer.

She gazed at him through the darkness, uncertain why right and wrong seemed all muddled in her mind, all mixed up with hot and cold and life and death. Because she was still half asleep? Because her mind was too tired to tell her what do do?

But her body seemed willing to decide. Hesitantly she edged closer to Will, into the welcoming circle of

his arm, and tentatively rested her cheek against the
coarseness of his chest hair.

He began lightly stroking her shoulder, his touch so
reassuring, making her feel so protected, that she knew
it was safe to sleep once more, that her nightmare
wouldn't dare return.

It didn't. And when she woke again, sunlight was
filtering in through the thin curtain, sneaking beneath its tattered bottom…and she was lying in Will's
arms.

She tensed at the realization, then gradually relaxed. She was awake, but he was still asleep. Cau-
tiously she shifted a little, so that she could look at
him.

She'd never been like this with a man before. It was
frightening, but not as frightening as she'd imagined.
In fact it felt almost…almost pleasant in a scary sort
of way.

Inside her head, a tiny voice whispered the words
impeccable behavior, and she eased an inch or two
away from Will, trying not to disturb him.

He didn't stir. But his arm was lying across her, and
if she moved any farther he'd undoubtedly wake up.

She lay quietly again, watching him sleep. His hair
was tousled, and his chin and cheeks were dark with
stubble. She felt the strangest desire to touch his face.
To outline his even profile with her fingertips. To trace
his lips.

Years ago, when she'd still been a child but both
Abigail and Hildy had been betrothed, she'd over-
heard them talking about kissing. And she'd been
shocked to learn that her sisters had actually been

kissed . . . that they hadn't minded . . . that Hildy even seemed to like it.

Back then, she'd found it impossible to imagine that kissing a man might be something a woman would enjoy. But right now . . .

Remember who you are, that tiny voice murmured.

Right. Who she was. She was Emma McCully, a woman who suffered from sensibilities, an affliction that could lead to insanity, an affliction that could be passed on to children. She had been told she should never marry because of that, so she had never even kept company with a man, had never put herself at risk of wanting something she couldn't have.

She stared at Will for another minute. Until she no longer felt able to resist her impulse to touch him.

Surely she was allowed one more lapse from impeccable behavior. Surely . . . when no one else would ever know.

Slowly she reached across. Gently she traced Will's mouth with her fingertips. His lips were full and soft and warm. They made her fingers tingle.

She closed her eyes and tried to imagine what it would feel like to touch his lips with her own, instead of with her fingers. And that was when he covered her hand with his.

Her eyes flashed open. He was awake and looking at her.

She tried to pull her hand free of his but he held it fast, and she could feel her face turning crimson.

"Emma," he said quietly. "Emma, don't be upset."

She tried again to free herself, and this time he released her. Quickly she sat up, pulling the blanket around her as best she could. She desperately wanted to run and hide. But there was nowhere to run to. And even if there was, she wasn't dressed to leave this room. Mercy, she wasn't really dressed to be in this room, not to be in here with Will, at least.

He propped himself onto one elbow and gazed at her. "Emma...Emma, it's okay. That was no big deal."

She simply shook her head, certain she was going to die of embarrassment, praying it would happen within the next second.

"Emma, listen to me. Where I come from, it's acceptable for women to be freer with men...physically, I mean," he added, clearing his throat. "Women aren't expected to repress their...their feelings, the way they were in the...*are* in the West."

She swallowed hard and forced herself to speak. "Will, thank you for trying to make me feel better. But I know the world isn't *that* different back East. I don't know...I just don't know what came over me. I've never...I'd never..."

"Emma, I know you'd never. Believe me, I know only too well. But I wasn't merely trying to make you feel better. I was trying to explain that things really are very different where I come from. People think differently. I realize you probably can't believe that, but they do. And that means I don't see anything wrong in what you just did. I really don't. In fact...well, let's just leave it at that. But please try to stop looking so guilty.

"Hey," he said, rolling out of bed and grabbing his shirt off the floor. "I'll go out for a few minutes and let you get dressed. Then we'll have breakfast and find ourselves a buggy to rent. I'll bet we can be at the Tewksburys' before lunchtime.''

THE MARE WAS TROTTING steadily along, demanding no guidance from Will. He took one hand off the reins, pushed back his Stetson and wiped his brow. Beneath the hat, his hair was soaked with perspiration. Not noon yet, but so hot he could see the heat. It shimmered in the air above the sand.

He glanced surreptitiously across the little rig at Emma, unable to keep his eyes off her for more than a minute at a stretch.

Last night, lying with her while she slept in his arms, smelling the sweet, fresh scent of her damp hair, had just about driven him crazy. He must have reminded himself a million times that he wasn't going to do so much as kiss her. But this morning...gawd, this morning had almost done him in.

She was attracted to him, just the way he was attracted to her. If they were in his world that would be wonderful. But in her world it seemed to be a catastrophe—for her, at least.

No, not only for her. This attraction was bad news for both of them. Because, in no time at all, they'd be in different worlds again.

Lord, this situation was so confusing. And telling her that he saw nothing wrong with her touching him might not have been a good idea.

Of course, he'd only been trying to make her feel better because she'd been mortified. But he'd have to be more careful from here on in. He didn't know how 1887 women thought. Hell, half the time, he didn't know how women in 2014 thought.

What if Emma decided that as long as he didn't see anything wrong with her doing . . . well, she probably wouldn't. Her sense of morality was likely a lot stronger than any attraction she might feel for him.

But, just in case, he'd better be darned careful about giving her any come-on messages. Because if she ever decided to take him up on one, he'd never be able to resist her.

Undoubtedly the best thing he could do was get out of her life—the first possible instant he had a chance. Before his feelings got the better of his common sense.

Maybe he could even leave her in Pleasant Valley, with John, and make the trip back to Mountainview alone. If that turned out to be feasible, it would be a damned good idea.

"That must be the Tewksbury spread up ahead," she said, interrupting his thoughts.

For a moment, he gazed through the dazzling sunlight in the direction she was pointing. Then he concentrated on reining the mare to a halt. The owner of the Flagstaff livery stable had assured him she was the gentlest he rented out. But driving a one-horse rig wasn't something he felt comfortable doing.

He peered ahead, toward the base of the mountains, finally picking out what Emma had seen—the distant shapes of a ranch house and out-buildings. Well, that was a relief. He'd been starting to worry about being lost. But the Tewksburys were supposed to have the only ranch for miles. So Emma was right. This must be the place.

He clicked the reins, and the mare obediently started forward again.

Emma continued to gaze at the house as they drew nearer, incredibly glad they'd reached their destination, and that they would be with John in a few more minutes. Because since they'd left Mountainview, her premonition had been growing steadily stronger. And ever more frightening. And that nightmare last night had convinced her that her brother was in real danger. She'd begun to feel that unless he was warned, John was going to die.

She swallowed hard, telling herself that wouldn't happen. They were here now.

She glanced across at Will again, feeling the same strange feeling she'd begun having every time she looked at him. It was partly embarrassment, of course. But it was more than that.

It was something she couldn't define or describe, but that made her heart race and started her breathing faster and set her blushing whenever he looked at her.

He looked at her. She blushed.

"I'd kill for a cold drink," he said. "You figure the Tewksburys are going to be hospitable?"

"Of course," she assured him. "Everyone's hospitable out West. They'll have us stay for lunch and dinner and spend the night if we like." Blast, just the mention of night had started her blushing even harder.

Will grinned at her. "You really figure they'll welcome us with open arms, huh? Even though John's just one of their hired hands?"

"He's actually more than that, Will. Part of his arrangement is to teach Mr. Tewksbury something about accounting while John's learning about ranching.

Ranchers have begun to realize they've got to run their spreads more like businesses."

"John's an accountant? You didn't tell me that."

"I guess you never asked. But that's what he is. He managed Broken Hill's finances. Actually he pretty much managed the entire business."

"Oh?"

She nodded. "Mr. Dursely's a sweet man, but it was luck, not brains, that made him his fortune. He's not terribly smart, and he relied heavily on John. That's why he was so upset when John decided not to go to San Francisco and work for Dursely Oil."

"If Buck's not terribly smart," Will said, "I hope he forgets about that idea of taking on John D. Rockefeller."

They rode a few more yards in silence, then Emma leaned forward excitedly. "Look, Will, they've seen us. Someone's come out onto the Tewksburys' front porch."

She stared through the glare at the lone figure, unable to make out any detail. The man was standing motionless, shadowed by the overhang of the porch and half hidden by a supporting column.

Will clicked the reins again, urging the mare on. "Lord, Emma, I can almost feel a cold drink pouring down my throat. And I can almost taste home cooking. I sure hope Mrs. Tewksbury makes apple pies that are even half as good as yours."

Emma smiled at him, then turned her attention back to the house.

The man on the porch extended his arms, slowly raised them chest high... and the next few seconds blurred together into one.

All in the same instant, Emma realized what was happening, Will shouted something about a rifle, a shot rang out, and she felt death whizz by her head.

CHAPTER SIX

THE MARE SNORTED, lunging forward so suddenly they almost tipped over.

Emma grabbed the side of the rig, her glance darting across to Will. He was scrambling to recover the reins.

A second shot rang out on the echo of the first.

"Get down!" he yelled at her. "Get down!"

She crouched as low as she could and held onto the bouncing rig for dear life.

Finally Will managed to rein in the horse and ease her to a nervous halt. Then they sat staring back, stunned and uncertain. In the distance, the Tewksbury house was almost invisible, lost in the sun's glare. Almost invisible, and silent.

Whoever had been on the porch was gone. And around them the morning was quiet once more—no sign of other people, no sound of further shots.

Will looked across at her, and Emma bit her lip. If he asked whether they'd just experienced an example of the Western hospitality she'd been bragging about, she knew she'd cry.

He didn't. He merely asked if she was all right.

She nodded, certain she couldn't manage words just yet.

"Then let's get back to Flagstaff," he muttered, clicking the reins. "And see if we can get a clue about what the hell's going on out here."

For the first hundred yards or so, Emma watched fearfully over her shoulder. Then she forced her hands to relinquish their death grip on the rig and sat repeating to herself that neither she nor Will were about to be shot in the back.

"Do you think," she finally murmured, her voice quavering, "that could have been the wrong ranch?"

"I suppose it's possible," Will said.

He wasn't, she realized from his tone, any better at lying than she.

"Although," he added, "that livery fellow did say the Tewksbury spread was the only one we'd see out this way."

She nodded slowly. "But what about John? Did he get that reception when he arrived?"

"I don't know. Probably not, though. He was expected. We weren't."

"But... but just shooting at us? Why in heavens would anyone do that?"

"Emma, I have no idea. Maybe the guy thought we were someone else. Hell, I don't know. Maybe we did hit the wrong place. All I know is we'd be crazy to stick around and try to sort things out. We'll ask some questions in town. See what we can learn."

They rode on awhile without speaking, Emma unable to get her mind off her deepening worries about John. Of course, her premonition had focused on late July. So had Will's. And this was only the eighteenth. But still...

"Will?"

"What?"

"Will, what if John *did* get shot at when he arrived?"

"I can't imagine he did."

"But... but your premonition, your feeling that something's going to happen to him on July twenty-fifth?"

"Yes?"

"Could you be wrong about the date? Could something have happened already? Could... could John be dead?" Her final few words came out sounding strangled.

Will glanced at her, then reached over and reassuringly patted her hand.

When he did, she had an insane desire to wrap her arms around his neck and never let go. Instead, she gripped the edge of the seat. She'd already embarrassed herself with him enough to last a lifetime.

"No, Emma. I'm not wrong. I'm absolutely certain John's alive."

"Absolutely?" she whispered.

"Absolutely."

She slipped into silence again and spent the trip back to Flagstaff desperately trying to convince herself that Will was right. By the time they were within sight of the town, she was about half convinced.

They clip-clopped down the main street, to the livery stable, and stopped. Old Tom, the owner, was lounging in the doorway, his skinny frame braced against a timber that was wider than his body.

He watched them get out of the rig, an expression of curiosity on his weathered face. "Thought you wasn't comin' back till late," he said to Will. "Or maybe tomorrow, you told me. I don't give no re-funds."

"That's all right," Will said. "Keep what I paid you."

Tom nodded, took the mare's reins, then looked back at Will. "Find the Tewksbury place okay?"

"Hard to say. We found *some* place. But whoever was there wasn't eager for visitors."

"He shot at us," Emma offered. Maybe Tom could give them an explanation.

He nodded shortly, still looking at Will, as if Emma didn't exist. "That'd be the Tewksbury place you got to all right."

Emma glanced at Will. He cleared his throat. "You...ahh, you mean that's their standard greet-ing?"

"*These days,* it is."

Will simply stared at the other man. "I see," he fi-nally said. "Didn't it occur to you to mention that when we asked for directions?"

"Weren't none of my business, were it?"

A hundred sarcastic responses began dancing on Emma's tongue. She bit them all back.

"What seems to be the problem, *these days?*" Will said more civilly than she'd ever have managed to.

"They's feudin'."

"Feudin'," Will repeated as if it were a foreign word.

"The Tewksburys and the Grahams," Tom said. "Least that's how it started. 'Course, by now, all of Pleasant Valley's feudin'."

"All of Pleasant Valley," Will echoed.

Clearly he thought Tom must be exaggerating. Emma doubted that. Once a feud got going, everyone for miles around was forced to take one side or the other.

"Feudin' over the sheep grazin' in the valley," Tom elaborated. "The Tewksburys rented out a piece of their land to some sheep men. Then some of the other cattlemen begun killin' sheep on it. Then, awhile back, one of them that was workin' for the Tewksburys got himself murdered."

Emma's heart stopped beating. It seemed an eternity before Will spoke again.

"Who was murdered?"

Tom shrugged. "Just some fellow. Not from these parts. They beheaded him."

"His name wasn't John, was it?" Emma whispered. "Not John McCully?"

Tom finally acknowledged her presence. "John McCully? That who you's lookin' for at the Tewksburys'?"

"Yes. He's my brother."

"Shoulda told me. Woulda saved a trip. You won't find him at the Tewksbury place no more. One of the Grahams shot at him a couple of weeks ago and he hightailed it back into town."

"Was he hurt?" Emma asked anxiously.

"Nope. But he said the bullet come so close he heard the angels singin'. Told me he didn't reckon to be the next fellow murdered—not over some fool sheep. Those were his very words to me."

"You know him, then," Emma said, smiling with relief. This old man knew John, and John was safe. Everything was fine.

"Yup, I know him," Tom said. "Sold him a horse the day after he quit the Tewksburys'. Damn fine animal it was, too. Far better 'n the one Tewksbury had him ridin'. Just bought that horse from a fellow passin' through, and the very next day John came lookin' for one."

"But do you know where John is now?" Will demanded.

"Sure. He's gone to Texas," Tom said, slapping his thigh and laughing uproariously.

Oh, mercy, Emma thought. Everything might not be quite so fine, after all. She realized Will was glancing a question at her. He clearly had no idea what was supposed to be humorous.

"Yup, John McCully's gone to Texas," Tom repeated, this time almost managing to contain his laughter.

"He's trying to be funny," Emma whispered to Will. "I'll explain it to you later."

She focused on Tom again. "Do you know exactly *where* in Texas he's gone to?"

The man rubbed his stubbled chin. "Well, he said he was goin' to have a go at another side of the ranchin' business—was aimin' to try his luck as a drover on the Chisholm trail. That's why he needed a good horse. So I reckon he'd head for San Antonio. Or maybe Austin. But he said he'd be stoppin' off in Tombstone for a few days. Lotta fellows do that when they's makin' their way to Texas. Take a break after the ride through Arizona."

"So we could catch up with him in Tombstone," Emma said. "It's not far, Will."

Tom snorted. "That depends on what you think's not far, ma'am. Tombstone's about as far south and east as you can get and still be in the Territory. Set a frog on the main street and he could hop into Mexico in one direction or Texas in the other."

Emma looked at Will again. She didn't at all like the way he was looking back.

He broke their gaze and turned to Tom. "Doesn't Tombstone have a reputation of being sort of...wild?"

"That's what folks say, all right."

"I see. And just exactly how far *is* it from here?"

" 'Bout three hundred miles. John can't have gotten there more'n a day or two ago, ridin' his horse. But it's only three days by stage."

"Three days by stage," Will repeated.

His thoughts were written on his face, and they sent Emma into a panic. He didn't want to go to Tombstone.

"Days and nights, I mean, of course," Tom added. "The coach only stops to change horses. If you don't run into no problems, that is."

Emma had an almost overwhelming urge to pull out that little Remington Mr. Dursely had given her and shoot Tom dead. Next, he'd start elaborating about what he meant by running into problems. And she'd just bet he meant running into Apaches.

"Will?" she said. Despite how hard she was trying to control it, her voice was quavering. With every passing hour, this trip they were making seemed more dangerous. On her own, she'd be terrified. Even Will didn't want to go to Tombstone. She could see that plain as day. And she couldn't blame him.

To him, John was merely a friend he hadn't seen in twenty-five years. But to her...

Old Tom's remark about a frog hopping had brought back a long-forgotten memory. She'd been about six and had been tagging along after two of her brothers, when they'd come across a big old bull frog.

The three crouched down around him and waited.

"He ain't goin' to jump," Clyde finally said. "He's dead."

"He ain't dead," Frank corrected him. "He's just restin'."

"Well, he ain't goin' to jump," Clyde repeated more firmly.

Emma eyed the frog with growing anticipation. Her brothers almost always knew more than she did. But sometimes she knew things nobody else at all seemed to. She rocked excitedly, her arms wrapped around her knees, waiting until it was time. "He's going to jump...now!" she whispered.

The frog leaped clear over Clyde's shoulder, and Emma clapped her hands in glee. Clyde rolled back onto the ground, then punched Frank in the arm, and they both began giggling.

"Emma's a witch," they sang out in unison, pointing at her. "Emma's a witch...Emma's a witch...Emma's a witch...."

Her lip began to quiver, and she bit it still, but they wouldn't stop their singsong.

A tear trickled down her cheek. Seeing it made the boys giggle and sing louder.

Then, suddenly, they were both flat on their backs in the dirt, John between them, pinning them down with his knees. "I ever hear either of you calling

Emma names again," he snarled, "and I'll whup you till you can't move. Understand?"

Clyde and Frank both nodded furiously.

John rose, glaring down at them, then took Emma's hand. "Come on, Emmy. It's almost dinnertime."

Emma realized Will was looking at her strangely, that she was blinking back tears. She shrugged, feeling ridiculous. "Just remembering something about John," she murmured. "I...I love him, Will," she added, almost inaudibly.

Will eyed Emma uneasily. He knew he didn't have a prayer of convincing her to turn back before they caught up with John. But the idea of her going any place as dangerous as Tombstone was crazy. And what if they got to Tombstone and John had already left? What if he'd gone on to Texas? What if he was half way up the damned Chisholm trail?

Emma would want to keep right on going, which would get her killed for sure. And there was an absolute limit, he reminded himself, on finding John. If they didn't catch up with him by the twenty-fifth, it would be too late.

And there was also an absolute limit to how long Will could spend away from Mountainview. It was the only place he could travel back to the year 2014 from, and, according to his calculations, the last date for traveling would be August 1. If he didn't leave by then, it would be three years before the trip would be possible again.

He pictured his father and Erica—seeing the worried expressions on their faces when he'd told them he was coming here. They'd feared something would go wrong. And if he didn't make it home, they'd spend the next three years certain that he was dead. He couldn't put them through that.

He forced their images away and turned to Tom. "How often does a stage run between here and Tombstone?"

"Every day. Passes through around five."

Will nodded slowly. That was about the time they'd arrived yesterday. And their stage had been continuing south. What had Wyatt Earp said?

He recalled word for word: "You heading on down to Tombstone with us? . . . The drivers can always use an extra gunman through Apache country."

Apache country. Three days there and three back—if you didn't get killed along the way. Well, he couldn't dwell on that. He had time to get to Tombstone and back to Mountainview. But Emma making the trip? Maybe, somehow, he could persuade her not to.

"Let's think this through, Emma," he said, pulling their bags out from under the seat of the rig. "Let's catch some lunch at the Golden Nugget and talk about it.

"You were going to tell me," he added as they started walking along the dirt street, "what Tom thought was so funny about John going to Texas."

"Oh . . . well, it wasn't actually his going. It was the phrase—gone to Texas, I mean. Tom was making a joke."

Will glanced quizzically at her. "I'm afraid I didn't see the humor."

"Well...well, a lot of fellows who go to Texas have run away from someplace. Run away because they've committed crimes. They're a pretty rough bunch down there, I gather. So saying someone's gone to Texas is a way of saying he's . . . well, you see.''

Will simply nodded. He saw, all right. In fact, he was seeing a whole lot he didn't want to see in the least.

An hour or so ago, they'd been shot at. And now he'd be heading for Tombstone, which had the reputation of being a wild town. Not to mention a stopping-off place for all sorts of fellows who were *gone to Texas.* Not to mention that getting there would mean spending three days and nights in one of those contraptions of torture that passed for a stagecoach . . . riding through Apache country.

THE WAITER PLUNKED a second glass of beer in front of Will. He took a swig of it and began, once more, to try to convince Emma she should go home.

"Emma, there's simply no point in two of us going."

She shook her head, her expression every bit as stubborn as before. "He's my brother, Will. And you wouldn't even recognize him after all these years. And if I didn't go along, all I'd do would be to worry. So there are all kinds of points to my going."

Damn. This discussion wasn't getting them anywhere. Of course he'd known she wouldn't change her mind. Just as he knew that if they reached Tombstone, and John was already gone, she'd want to keep following his trail. But if they didn't catch up with him in Tombstone . . . well, July 25 would almost be on them.

"Look, Emma," he said, "can we make a deal?"

"What kind of a deal?"

"Well, as much as I want to find John, I can only keep trying for so long. I absolutely *have* to be back in Mountainview by August 1."

"I understand," she murmured. "That business you mentioned having in San Francisco is important. It's something you have to get there in time for."

"Yes. That's it exactly. I have important business. Essential business. It can't possibly wait."

"But... but you don't *really* have to go all the way back north to Mountainview, Will. Not to get to California, I mean. We could spend more time than you think following John. Because there's a main line of the Atchison, Topeka and Santa Fe that runs from someplace in Texas all the way to Los Angeles. Tucson's on the line, so if you went to Tombstone, you could take a stage from there to Tucson. And then a train west to Los Angeles and on up to San Francisco."

Lord, Will thought. If Emma lived in 2014, she'd probably be a travel agent.

She gazed at him silently, the look in her big blue eyes making him want to tell her the truth—to explain how he knew there was a firm time limit on finding her brother. Maybe it would be best if she understood that.

But he really didn't want to come right out and tell her John was facing death on July 25. And making anyone believe that he'd come from 2014, would have him explaining until he was blue in the face. And he wasn't exactly an expert on the theory of time travel. Any explanations he could offer would have a lot of gaps in them. Hell, Emma was more likely to think he was plain crazy than believe that he'd come from the future.

Dammit to hell. How he wished John had stayed at the Tewksburys'. But surely there must be a way...

There was! Hallelujah! Why hadn't it occurred to him before this?

"Emma?"

"Yes?"

"Emma, what if we sent a telegram to Tombstone? A telegram telling John to let us know where he's staying and to wait for us."

A smile lit up her face.

When she smiled, Will thought, Emma McCully was the most beautiful woman he'd ever seen. And suddenly the idea of going to Tombstone didn't seem so dreadful, after all. Not if they knew John would be waiting there for them.

"Who would we send a wire in care of, though?" he asked, thinking aloud. "Could it just go to general delivery? Would someone from the Wells Fargo in Tombstone track down John and deliver it?"

"I don't know. I expect we could get them to try. I mean, yes, I'm sure they would. If we paid them to. Oh, Will, that's such a good idea. And...and you said *us*. You mean you won't be awfully upset that I'm going, too?"

"Well...I guess I can put up with you for a little longer," he teased.

"Oh, Will," she said excitedly, reaching across the table and squeezing his hands in hers.

He stared at them for a second. When he glanced back up, Emma was looking flustered. She started to pull her hands away, but he caught them before she could. "Hey, not so fast. Remember what I told you about people thinking differently where I come from? Back East, we approve of this kind of thing."

Oh, geez! How had those words slipped out? Hadn't he warned himself, only a few hours ago, not to say anything more like that to her?

But damn, he *did* approve. When he'd awakened this morning to find Emma's fingers tracing his lips, and he'd realized she felt something for him, he hadn't been able to think of anything he'd approve of more. Hell, he still couldn't.

Finally he forced himself to release her. She was blushing furiously. And she was as gorgeous when she blushed as when she smiled.

Hell, it seemed to be growing more difficult, by the minute, to keep in mind that he wasn't going to do so much as kiss her.

THE STATIONMASTER who'd greeted their stage yesterday wasn't in the Wells Fargo depot. Instead, there was a young clerk behind the counter. Really just a boy, Emma thought—barely older than some of her students.

"So would that be possible?" Will was saying to him. "If we sent a wire to Tombstone, without an exact address, could someone ask around and locate the man it was for? We're pretty sure he's there—just want to be certain before we head after him."

Emma crossed her fingers.

"Do you think he'd be staying at a hotel?" the boy asked.

Will nodded.

"We could find him, then. There's lots of saloons in Tombstone, but not many hotels. If he's at one of them, he'd be easy to find."

Easy to find. What wonderful words, Emma thought, smiling at Will.

"So," the boy said, picking up a pencil, "what's the message?"

"Family emergency," Will told him. "Am in Flagstaff. Wire me at Magnolia Hotel that you have received my message. Then wait in Tombstone for me. And sign it, Emma."

"Yes sir," the boy said, printing the final words. "And who's it going to?"

"The name's McCully. John McCully."

The boy looked up, pencil poised. "John McCully," he repeated.

"Right."

The boy glanced at the door, as if expecting someone to appear any instant, then leaned across the counter and spoke so quietly that Emma had to strain to hear.

"I don't need to send this, sir. You can save your money. I know that John McCully's in Tombstone. But I'm not sure we could get a wire to him. And I know he wouldn't be able to wire you back."

A tiny chill raced up Emma's spine.

"Oh?" Will said. "What's the problem?"

"I . . . I'm afraid I really can't say, sir. Wells Fargo business is confidential."

Emma stepped closer to the counter and managed an anxious smile. "John McCully is my brother. Has . . . is he hurt?"

"No, ma'am. Not that I know of, ma'am."

She took a deep breath. John was all right. But then why had the boy said they might not be able to get a wire to him? And why wouldn't he be able to wire them back?

She forced another smile. "I'd be terribly grateful if you'd tell us what you know. We've come all the way from Nevada after my brother, and I'm very worried about him."

"I'm sorry, ma'am. I shouldn't rightly have said anything at all."

"We won't repeat a word. I promise you. But anything you can tell us we'd appreciate."

"Well…" The boy paused, glancing uneasily at the door again. "Well, it's just that we had a wire come in a couple of nights ago. Saturday night it was. Came for your brother—to be delivered out to the Tewksbury place. But we'd heard he was gone from there, so we sent a message back, saying that. Then we got a reply, asking us to try and trace him. And we did. Folks said he'd headed for Tombstone, so we wired down to there. And sure enough, he's there."

Emma glanced uncertainly at Will. Who would have been trying to contact John on Saturday night? And why? She'd have liked the answers to those questions, but Will started off on a different track.

"So you've already established which hotel John's at then," he said. "That's good. Because we still have to send him a wire—make sure he knows not to leave before we get there."

The boy glanced uncomfortably from Will to Emma. The look in his eyes told her something was dreadfully wrong. Nervously she inched even closer to the counter.

"What is it?" she murmured. "You're certain my brother isn't hurt? He isn't . . . he isn't . . . ?"

She couldn't force the word out. And she couldn't keep her eyes from filling with tears.

"Ma'am? Oh, no, ma'am, he isn't dead. He . . . he's just in trouble."

"Trouble," Will repeated. "Could you be a little more specific?"

The boy shook his head. "Look, I'm sorry. But like I told you, Wells Fargo business is confidential. I could lose my job for—"

"This isn't really Wells Fargo business," Will tried quietly. "And as I said in the message, there's a family emergency. And you can see that my wife is terribly upset. So we'd be mighty obliged if you could just give us another detail or two."

The boy glanced at Emma.

She bit her lip, feeling guilty about pressing him but desperate to know what was wrong.

He hesitated a second longer. "Well . . . I guess if it's a family emergency . . . ma'am, I'm afraid your brother's in the Tombstone jail."

"What?" she cried.

"In the jail, ma'am. That's why I don't think they'd let us deliver a wire to him."

"But you could try," Will said. "We can't have him leaving Tombstone before we get there."

"I . . . I wouldn't worry about that happening, sir. He'll be there for a spell . . . at least a week or so, I reckon. Until the circuit judge gets there. He won't get no bail 'cuz . . . 'cuz he stole a horse."

Emma stared across the counter, only vaguely aware of the door slamming behind them, of the boy immediately tensing.

"Got everything under control, son?" a man's voice boomed.

She turned, recognizing the stationmaster, but still thinking about John. He couldn't possibly have stolen a horse. If they believed he had, though...

Will had begun speaking, and she looked at him, making herself concentrate on his words.

"Your clerk's got everything under perfect control," he was telling the stationmaster. Casually he picked up the message the boy had written on the telegram form and stuck it into his shirt pocket. "We were just asking about this afternoon's stage. Looks as if the wife and I will be heading down to Tombstone. Think there'll be room for us today?"

"There's most always room."

"Good. Good. Guess we should arrange for the tickets then, huh?" He glanced expectantly at Emma as he spoke.

She couldn't think what he wanted. All she could think about was John.

"Money," he said quietly. "Money for the tickets."

Of course. She dug into her bag and simply handed him the entire wad of bills, then waited anxiously, trying to calm down while he talked to the stationmaster about the trip. But being accused of horse theft...

Will took her arm, smiling at her. "Let's go for a walk. We'll be doing enough sitting in the stage."

He was smiling. Didn't he understand how serious this was?

"What's wrong, Emma?" he demanded once they were outside. "The way I see it, this is the best thing that could have happened."

"The best thing? Will, John's in jail! Charged with horse theft!"

He shrugged. "That means he's stuck in a safe place until we can get to him. Then we'll just bail him out, drag him back to Mountainview with us, and make sure he's cautious as hell on the twenty-fifth. End of problem."

"Oh, Will," she cried, reminding herself he couldn't be expected to know everything about the West. "That boy was perfectly right. We won't be able to just bail John out. It's not nearly that simple. And even if it was, we'd need far more money than we have. Horse theft is an extremely serious offence."

"Oh, come on. Emma. It's hardly murder."

"Will, it's worse." She couldn't keep a tear from escaping down her cheek.

"Emma...Emma..." Will reorganized the bags so he had a free hand, then drew her off the main street, into an empty alley. He put down the cases and rested his hands lightly on her arms. "Look, Emma," he said quietly, "you're just upset. Everything will be all right."

She shook her head. "It won't be, Will. Nothing is making sense. John would never have stolen a horse. And who was looking for him? Who'd have sent him a wire at the Tewksburys'? And his being in jail..."

"Emma, we'll get him out."

Another tear escaped. She brushed at it, trying vainly to retain control.

Hesitantly Will circled his arms around her.

She barely even felt embarrassed about letting herself relax against him. She was just so glad she wasn't alone.

"Everything will be all right," he said once more.

She shook her head against his chest. "Will, it won't be. You don't understand. I meant what I said. Out West, so many men are totally dependent on their horses that horse thieves are considered *worse* than murderers. Whatever happened, whatever mistake there's been, John was lucky he even got taken to jail and wasn't hanged on the spot."

"But he wasn't, Emma. He's safe in jail."

"No, he's not safe at all. There are vigilantes in towns like Tombstone. They might not wait for the circuit judge. They might drag John out of jail and hang him. He could even be dead before we can get there."

"Emma . . ."

"Don't you see?" she cried in frustration. "Will, don't you see? Remember I was worried that you might have the wrong date in mind? That something might happen to John *before* the twenty-fifth? Well, maybe it will. Maybe the awful thing that's going to happen is that he's going to be hung as a horse thief— before we can even reach him."

CHAPTER SEVEN

WILL PRACTICALLY dragged Emma along Main Street to the Golden Nugget, settled her at a quiet table in a corner, then headed over to the bar.

She sat watching him, trying to convince herself John would be all right. She couldn't manage it.

Her brother was going to die—horribly. She'd never seen a vigilante hanging, but she'd read newspaper accounts of them. And just the thought of John...she fiercely blinked back tears.

Will started across the saloon again, a glass of sarsaparilla in one hand and a glass of beer in the other.

"You okay, now?" he asked, sitting down and sliding the sarsaparilla across to her.

She nodded a lie.

He took a large sip of beer, then put his glass on the table and sat gazing at her.

"What?" she murmured.

"John is going to be just fine when we get to Tombstone. I promise you."

"Oh, Will, premonitions are never a hundred percent reliable. You can't know *for sure* he'll be fine. And I'm so frightened for him."

"Emma, I *do* know. For sure."

She merely nodded again, wishing she could believe Will was right.

"Emma," he said after a long silence, "I'm going to tell you something that you'll have trouble understanding. Or believing. It's so incredible I wasn't going to try getting into it, but...well, I've decided I will. Because it'll explain how I know John is going to be safe for a while longer."

"What is it?" she asked curiously.

"Emma, when we were back in Mountainview, I noticed you had a collection of Mark Twain's novels. Have you read one titled *A Connecticut Yankee in King Arthur's Court?*"

"No, I haven't even heard of it."

"Oh. Well, I guess maybe it hasn't been published yet."

She considered questioning the logic of that remark, but didn't. It certainly wasn't the first time Will had said something that made no sense at all.

"At any rate," he went on, "it's a story about a man who travels back through time and ends up living in King Arthur's Court."

"Will...Will, I know you're trying to keep me from thinking about John. And I appreciate the effort. But I'm really not up to a discussion of modern literature."

"No, this isn't a literary discussion, Emma. I'm just saying that this fellow in the book traveled backward through the centuries and ended up in the past."

She forced a smile. "Mr. Twain has an incredible imagination, doesn't he?"

"Emma, we—my father and I, that is—think Mark Twain got the idea for that story from something that actually happened. That happened to us."

"Oh?"

"Yes. You see, when I was a boy in Mountainview, before we moved to...to Boston, my father and Mark Twain were friends. Back then, he was still known as Sam Clemens. And he wasn't a successful writer, yet. He wrote the odd article for newspapers, but mostly he was trying to strike it rich as a prospector."

"Really? That's interesting, Will." She managed a slightly better smile. He was such a kind man, was trying his darnedest to take her mind off her worries.

"You see, Emma, when we left Mountainview, my father told everyone we were going to Boston. And that was true. But Sam was the only one who knew the whole truth."

"For everyone else, your father left out the part about his reason for moving to Boston," Emma murmured. "But people knew about the woman, Will—the one who'd come from there to visit him. I remember my mother telling the story, years ago. And Mr. Dursely mentioned a woman the other day."

"Yes, well, people did know about her, but...well, her name was Erica—*is* Erica. She and my father have been married a long time now."

"And they're happy?"

"Very."

"I'll have to tell my mother that in my next letter. She thought it was so romantic—that your father had pulled up roots and moved to Boston because he'd fallen in love. But even before he left," Emma continued, recalling details as she spoke, "Erica had taken you back to Boston with her. For medical treatment? Is that right?"

"Yes. I needed a specialist."

"And then your father followed."

"That's about it," Will agreed. "Except there's something more...and this is the tricky part...the part my father told no one except Sam ... or Mark, I guess I should call him...."

There was more. Something her mother hadn't known about. Emma waited curiously to hear what it was.

"It's the part we think Mark's story idea came from—the idea about the character traveling back in time, I mean."

"Will, you've got me totally confused. What was it your father told no one except Mark Twain?"

"Well ... in 1862, Dad and I did go to Boston to be with Erica. But Erica wasn't from 1862 Boston."

Emma did her best to smile encouragement. Will's logic was definitely faltering.

"You see, Erica got to Mountainview by accidentally traveling back through time—traveling a hundred and twenty-seven years, to be specific. And it was only because an old Paiute shaman, White Cloud, knew some of the mysteries of time travel, that Erica was eventually able to go home. And when she did, when I went with her, we did go to Boston, but to Boston in the year 1989.

"Emma, for the last twenty-five years, I've been living in the future. That's where the medical specialists I needed were—in the future, where they could cure diseases that there were no cures for in 1862. Emma, back where I come from, today is July 18, 2014."

She simply stared across the table. Will seemed so normal most of the time, that she kept forgetting he had these lapses into insanity. But this one was by far the worst she'd witnessed. Or maybe…maybe he was joshing her.

Of course, that had to be it. She breathed easier again. He was joshing, telling her this fantastic story to make her forget about John's problem.

"It's the truth, Emma," he said, his expression deadly serious. "You see, I don't actually have premonitions the way you do. That's not how I know John will be in danger on July 25, and that he isn't going to be hung within the next few days. I know it because I know what happened in the past. And for me, now, this is the past."

Oh, mercy, he wasn't joshing at all. He honestly believed what he was saying. She'd traveled all this way, and was about to head to Tombstone, with a madman who was convinced he was from the future.

Will gazed across the table at Emma. Her feelings were written all over her face. She figured he was completely out of his tree.

Well, he'd expected that—probably should have stuck to his original plan and not said a word. But she'd been so upset, so convinced that John would be lynched in the next day or two.

He thought, for a minute, about the story Erica had told him a few times, the story of how his father hadn't initially believed she was from the future, of how she'd convinced him by showing him things she had with her and by demonstrating her video camera.

When he'd changed out of his suit, into John's clothes, there'd been no place to put his pocket computer, so he'd packed it. He glanced around. There were scarcely any people in the saloon and none sitting nearby. He leaned over, picked up his bag and sat it on the table.

He opened the case, moved a shirt aside, drew the computer out, and set it down—leaving the bag where it was, as a shield from possible prying eyes.

Emma stared at the little device so curiously that he smiled. As a nine-year-old, when he'd first gone to the future, he'd been absolutely fascinated by the pocket calculator Erica had bought for him. Back then, a tiny machine that could manipulate numbers had been state-of-the-art technology.

But over the years, powerful computers had been shrunk almost to the size of those old calculators.

Emma glanced up, clearly having to drag her eyes away from the computer. "What is that?"

"Well," he said, switching it on, watching its small screen come alive, "it's a gizmo from the future. I used a larger, more complex one to figure out how to get myself here. But why don't I show you some of the things this one can do?"

EMMA WAS CERTAIN that if Will told her just one more fact about life in 2014, her brain was going to explode. Even his profession was inconceivable to her. Not an astronomer but an astro...

"Astro...?" she murmured aloud, wishing she could stop stumbling on the word.

"Astrophysicist," he supplied.

"Astro...phy...si...cist," she slowly repeated, looking across the saloon table at him. "And that's someone who knows all about time and space. And you work in the sky, two hundred miles above ground, on a manmade structure called...?"

"Space Station Freedom," Will told her again.

"And it orbits earth the way the moon does? Without falling down?"

"That's right, Emma."

"And you stay up there for two months at a time?"

"Yes, but I don't have to sign up for full-time duty. I could take a shuttle back and forth each day. If I'm on twenty-four-hour call, though, I get a lot more vacation time."

She simply shook her head. Everything Will had been telling her was too unbelievable to be possible. Yet it had to be. He must have come from the future. This phenomenon he called time travel must be real. Because he had a logical, if incredible, answer to every single question she'd asked him.

And he certainly hadn't fantasized that computer he'd tucked back into his bag. Or the things in his wallet he was showing her.

There was a little card, with his picture on it, that was a license to drive...cars, was the word.

Imagine! There were machines in the future that could go more than ten times faster than the trains they'd traveled on to Arizona. Horseless carriages that didn't need tracks to run on.

And those dozen other brightly colored cards he had, made of...plastic, he called it, could be used instead of money.

She wasn't at all clear how that worked—how he got to keep the plastic but, at the same time, used it to buy things. Or why people needed to have both plastic and money. That strange-looking money he'd shown her. And by sticking one of those cards into a machine, he could get money out. Now that was downright amazing. Better than money growing on trees.

"Would you like to see some photos of my family?" he asked.

She nodded, and he flipped past the cards to a section of pictures. A man and woman, about the same age as her parents, looked through the little clear cover at her. Their images were incredibly lifelike—and colored instead of the brownish tones of daguerreotypes.

The man was an older version of Will—the same dark hair, the same soft, black eyes. And the woman was smiling lovingly at the man, looking extremely happy.

"My father and Erica," Will said.

"Yes, I guessed that."

He turned to the next picture. It was of him, standing with his arm around a beautiful young woman.

Emma simply stared at it, stunned, suddenly realizing Will must be married. But how could that likelihood not have occurred to her until this instant? Just because he'd arrived in Mountainview alone and hadn't mentioned a wife? Why hadn't she even thought about whether...but now that she was, why did she care? Why was there a ridiculous lump forming in her throat?

"Your wife?" she managed to ask, certain she already knew the answer.

"No, that's my sister, Cheryl."

Emma glanced from the picture to him, praying she'd heard correctly.

"My half sister, technically speaking," he was saying. "I just never think of her that way. My father and

Erica had two children after they were married. First Cheryl, and then," he added, flipping to a picture of a fellow who was about twenty, "my brother, Craig."

Emma gazed blindly at Craig's image, knowing there could still be a picture of a wife coming up, aware she desperately didn't want Will to be married.

But that made no sense. He'd be going back to the future in no time at all. He'd explained how he'd intended to stay only one day and absolutely had to go back by August 1. And... and even if he didn't belong in another time, she could never marry him, anyway.

Marry! Had she actually been thinking, deep down, about the possibility of marriage? No, she could never—*would* never—even consider such a thing.

"That's it," Will said, snapped the wallet closed.

"That's it?" she repeated. "No... no wife or children?" Oh, had she really asked that? Out loud?

The way Will was staring at her told her she had. She could feel her cheeks starting to burn.

"No," he said quietly. "No wife or children."

Frantically she tried to think of a way to change the subject. "No hats," she finally said inanely.

"Pardon?"

"No hats. Neither Erica nor your sister was wearing a hat."

"No, hats went out of style long ago. In the 1940s or '50s, I think."

"Mercy." She sat thinking she would feel naked without a hat, until another, far more important thought popped into her mind. "Will, you haven't told me how you know something's going to happen to John on July 25. I mean, you said you don't actually have premonitions—that you know because, in your world, it's something that happened in the past. But exactly how did you learn about John?''

Will stared at Emma uncomfortably. He'd been afraid she would wonder about that, but had been counting on her being so amazed by everything he told her that she wouldn't think about it.

''I . . . I was in Mountainview, Emma. The Mountainview of 2014, I mean.''

''The town still exists?''

''Well, kind of. Years ago, in the 1970s, I think, it was restored as a tourist town.''

She eyed him quizzically.

''It was turned into a replica of what it was in the 1800s,'' he explained. ''And people visit it to see what life was like in the past. It would be like you visiting a town that looks exactly as it did in the 1700s.''

''Oh.''

He smiled, hoping she'd forgotten her original question.

''So you went to the Mountainview of 2014,'' she persisted, dashing his hope. ''And exactly how did you find out that something had happened to John?''

He tried a shrug.

''Will?'' she pressed.

''I . . . I saw some records.''

''What records?''

When he didn't answer, she repeated her question. And he couldn't think of anything to tell her but the truth.

''Dammit, Emma,'' he muttered, suddenly wishing he'd never opened his mouth about the future, ''I saw

John's tombstone. And it said he was killed on July 25, 1887.''

Her response was a sharp intake of breath and a horrified look. "His tombstone?" she finally whispered. "Then my feeling is right? My nightmare was a premonition? He's going to be killed?"

Will reached across the table and took her hands in his. "No. That's why I'm here. That's why I came. To prevent John from dying."

Emma gazed at Will, desperately trying to think her way through this situation she could barely believe, let alone understand. The effort only left her more confused.

"You can do that?" she finally asked. "You can actually prevent John from being killed?"

He shrugged again, looking uneasy. "I hope so. That's why I came. To try."

"But you're not sure you can?" she pressed.

"Emma...Emma, I *think* it must be possible to change the past. It seems to me I've already done that, as far as my own life is concerned, by going to the future. But I can't do better than saying I believe it's possible, because I don't really understand how time travel works."

"But, Will! You've traveled through time. And you told me you figured out how to do it with your computer. So how can you not really understand how it works?"

"Emma, I didn't figure out a whole lot. Time travel is an incredibly complex phenomenon. Somehow, every so often, time holes form in the universe. And when they do, people can move from one given time to another. But exactly how and when is a major mystery. Remember I told you about that Paiute shaman who helped us get back to the future?''

Emma nodded.

''Well, White Cloud used blue moons to tell her when traveling through time was possible. And rudimentary as her theory was, it's basically right. Blue moons are involved. Their gravitational pull does have something to do with when time holes open up. But when and where they'll open, and for how long, is almost impossible to calculate.''

''But you *did* calculate it, Will.''

''Emma, I was only able to ascertain times for one hole—the one that occasionally opens at Broken Hill mine. Because that's the one Erica accidentally fell through. So I knew exactly where it was. And I had the time she came and went to use in arriving at my predictions. Then I just went into Broken Hill at the right time, followed the same mine shaft Erica had followed, and ended up where I wanted to be in the past. But that doesn't mean I know everything there is to know about time travel. Far, far from it.''

''So if you don't know everything...if you don't know for sure that you can change events of the past, then John could be killed, after all,'' Emma whispered. ''You might not be able to prevent it. And that boy at Wells Fargo said the circuit judge would be getting to Tombstone in a week or so. Will, that judge might find John guilty of horse theft...and he could be hung on the twenty-fifth.''

Will squeezed her hands. ''Not if we can prevent it, Emma.''

EMMA STOOD OUTSIDE the Flagstaff station beside Will, watching for a sign of their stagecoach.

He glanced down at her, his dark eyes radiating concern. "You okay now?"

She nodded, grateful for his reassurance. It had calmed her considerably. And it had her believing John was going to be all right. She and Will would do whatever they had to and John wouldn't die.

Not that she even vaguely understood how someone could travel to a different century, let alone influence events once he got there. But clearly, Will's coming to 1887 had changed *her* recent past from what it would have been.

If he hadn't arrived at her door, her past few days would have been completely different. And if her "history" could be drastically altered, then so could John's. Will had convinced her of that.

She peered down Main Street again, this time seeing the cloud of dust that would become the stage. "There it is, Will."

He shaded his eyes and watched it grow nearer. "Doesn't look as if there are any passengers riding on top today. Maybe I'll get a real seat."

"I hope so." Yes, she would feel far better if there was room for Will inside the coach, where it was safer... and where he would be with her. She'd never relied on a man before—not since she was a child, at least. But she didn't know what she'd have done, recently, without Will.

Just an hour ago, when she'd been so upset, he'd calmly sat in the Golden Nugget with her and they'd talked things through.

"Emma," he'd said, "this isn't nearly as bad as you think. Maybe it's even good, because until now, we didn't know what sort of danger John was in. But now we do know. He's at risk of being hung as a horse thief on July 25. So as long as we prevent that from happening, he'll be fine. That's the tiny bit of history we have to change. We've got to get him out of jail and out of Tombstone. And I really believe we can do it."

That made sense to her. They weren't fighting blind anymore. And convoluted as it was, the rest of Will's logic made sense as well. As long as John hadn't stolen a horse, he was innocent. And if he was innocent, arresting him had been a mistake. And if that was the case, they would be able to get him out of jail. That was the way the American justice system worked.

She just hoped the system worked that way in the Territory of Arizona, as well.

But Will had to be right. They'd have all kinds of possible approaches to straightening out the problem.

Tombstone was a mining town, which meant there'd be a whole slew of lawyers there, getting rich off the miners' land claim problems. So getting legal help would be easy. Maybe one of the lawyers could even resolve John's difficulty without waiting for the circuit judge.

Or they could ask Wyatt Earp for help. Of course, she didn't think that was one of Will's better ideas. Mr. Earp would probably recommend John shoot his way out of jail or something.

Will had come up with several other possible options, though. He was a darned intelligent man. Brilliant, probably. She had a suspicion not just anyone could be an astrophysicist.

So her initial impression of him had been all wrong. He didn't suffer from sensibilities and wasn't verging on any serious disorder of the mind. Despite all those peculiar words he used and strange things he said, he wasn't crazy, at all.

He was simply from the future.

She'd have to be careful not to say anything about that. If she let anything slip, people would think they were both insane.

The stage rolled to a halt in front of them, horses breathing hard. Before the dust had even begun to settle, the driver and guard leapt down from the bench and three men started unhitching the tired team.

The coach's doors opened and the passengers swung out into the sunlight to stretch their legs.

Emma glanced at them fleetingly. There were just two—two men. Not only would there be room inside for Will, but they'd actually be able to breathe.

She focused on the first man out. He was a preacher, a man in his mid-thirties with a full mustache and curly brown hair peeking out from beneath his black bowler. His black suit was shiny with wear, and his white clerical collar was frayed. Even the bible he clutched was well-worn.

The other passenger... the other passenger was grinning at her, revealing a set of gleaming white false teeth, and her brain registered that she was seeing a familiar face in an unexpected place. "Mr. Dursely!"

His grin broadened as he marched over. "Hoped I'd catch up with you two. Didn't fancy riding all the way to Tombstone on my own."

Will shook Mr. Dursely's hand. "What are you doing here, Buck?"

"Like I said, I'm going to Tombstone. Got me a problem," he added, his grin vanishing. "Got me a real serious problem, and I need John's help. Tarnation, I should never have let him go ahead with his fool ranching idea. Now he's sitting in a danged jail, and I've got me a real serious problem."

"You know he's in jail?" Emma asked. "In Tombstone?"

While Buck nodded, she tried to figure out how he'd heard. "Was it you who was trying to send him a wire?" she guessed. "Then had Wells Fargo track him down?"

Buck nodded again, setting her mind at ease about that little mystery.

"Did you know he's charged with horse theft?" she asked.

"Yup. And when I heard that, I figured he had about as serious a problem as me. So," he added, patting the case he was holding, "I brung along enough money to bribe the entire Arizona Territory."

Will grinned. For all he'd managed to reassure Emma, he hadn't been the least bit certain they'd have an easy time getting John out of jail. But from anything he'd ever heard about Tombstone, citizens who wouldn't take a bribe would be few and far between. So Buck's bankroll improved their odds immensely.

"See, Emma," he offered as if he'd truly never had a doubt, "I told you everything would work out. Buck will solve John's problem, then John will solve Buck's."

"I sure hope he can," Buck muttered. "I sure do hope he can." He glanced questioningly at Will. "Say, did your pa get you a good education back East?"

"Ahh . . . yes. Yes, he did."

"You read good? You know much about numbers?"

Will nodded. "I can read just fine, Buck. And I know a fair bit about numbers." Hell, if he told Buck how many number-crunching courses it took to get a Ph.D. in astrophysics, Buck would faint. But, of course, he wouldn't know what astrophysics was.

Buck was patting his case again. "Got my problem in here, Will, along with the money. Got me a loan agreement from the First Coastal Bank of California. John helped draw up the original draft and said I was guaranteed safe.

"But a wire came from one of my men in San Francisco. Got delivered on Saturday. If I'd read it before you left, I might have asked for your advice then. But it said something's gone wrong. That this loan's going to make me lose Dursely Oil. That the bank's going to take it away from me."

"What's the problem, exactly, Buck?"

"I . . . I can't rightly figure that out. See, I don't read so good. John always looked after the reading and the numbers. I've tried to get through this agreement a hundred times. But the letters start blurring after a while. I never yet made it even to the middle. And I can't see what's wrong. But my man says if the value of Dursely Oil stocks drops much lower, the bank's going to take my company."

"I'll look at it if you'd like, Buck. See what I can figure out. I can read it on the stage."

"I'd appreciate that, Will. I'd appreciate that mightily. Maybe, if I understand what the problem is, I'll know what to do. Just can't get it, though," he muttered, shaking his head. "I was danged worried about borrowing so much money. But John said I couldn't possibly lose the company."

Buck glanced over at the preacher, who was hovering by the stage, and beckoned him over. "I met the Reverend on the train," he explained as the man started toward them. "He got on at Marble Canyon this morning, and we been keeping each other company since then.

"These here are old friends of mine," Buck told the preacher. "Reverend Christian, this is Miss Emma McCully and Mr. Will Lockhart."

Will managed not to smile when he heard the man's name. "Pleased to meet you, Reverend Christian."

"Just call me Reverend Bill. I'm not used to formality, living out in the middle of the desert."

"Reverend Bill," Buck explained, "spends most of his time on Apache reservations, bringing them Indians religion."

"The Apaches are on reservations?" Will asked. "You mean everything I've been hearing about them causing problems in Arizona is just talk?"

The preacher shrugged. "Depends what you've been hearing. The Warm Springs Apaches are none too friendly. But only the Chiricahua Apaches are really on the warpath. Ever since Cochise died, they haven't spent much time on their reservation. And they've made things a mite unsafe."

Will glanced uneasily at the stagecoach, wondering how many Chiricahua Apaches there were—not spending much time on their reservation. That coach didn't look as if it would stand up to an avalanche of arrows.

"Then, of course, there's the Apache Kid," the Reverend added. "Wherever he's at, things are more than a mite unsafe."

"He's the one I told you about," Buck interjected. "The one that's terrorizing Arizona."

"He's a mean one, all right," the preacher agreed. "Makes Geronimo look like a saint."

Will simply nodded. The last person he wanted to hear about, right before they started on a seventy-odd-hour trip through the wilds of Arizona, was that damned Apache Kid.

CHARLES K. MATTHEWS sat behind his desk in the First Coastal Bank of California, a deep frown creasing his forehead.

He read the message a final time, then shredded the paper into minuscule pieces and dropped them into the garbage basket. He didn't like this turn of events. Didn't like it in the least.

It wasn't the money it would cost him. The job had to be done, and someone had to be paid to do it. But murder was not his cup of tea. He would have preferred not going to extremes.

And he wasn't at all happy about relying on a man he didn't know. Particularly, he thought with a shudder, a man who was known as Butcher Knife Bill. The Territories were apparently populated by the most unsavory men imaginable.

But there were limits to how far personal contacts could reach . . . and limits to what his own men would do. There was a point at which he had to accept third-party arrangements.

He opened a file and tried to concentrate on the financial details of the Concklin purchase. But an image of Buckingham Dursely's face superimposed itself on the page.

The man was behaving like a fool. He'd left no choice. But still...

Charles closed his eyes and conjured up an image of the bank president's office. The nameplate he saw on the door read Charles K. Matthews. And he saw himself sitting in the enormous black leather chair. He'd keep that chair. And the mahogany desk, as well. Perhaps he'd leave the entire office as it was—initially, at least. John D. Rockefeller thoroughly disapproved of profligate spending.

CHAPTER EIGHT

THE CONCORD ROCKED along, jolting its passengers back and forth. Outside, twilight had fallen, and the combination of motion and poor light made reading difficult. But Buck was clearly desperate to know exactly what the loan agreement said.

"Find the problem yet?" he asked when Will glanced up.

"Not yet, Buck. Just resting my eyes."

The stage hit a particularly rough bump, almost sending all four of them to the floor.

Next to Buck, Reverend Bill silently curled himself back into the corner and closed his eyes again. For a man of the cloth, Will thought, the preacher was far from sociable.

Emma resettled herself beside Will, her hand brushing his thigh as she adjusted her skirt.

Her touch sent a bolt of lightning through him. With every passing hour, he found it more difficult to remember that involvement with her was out of the question.

Different worlds, he silently told himself. Emma wasn't actually part of his life. He was temporarily living in a time warp, but he'd soon be going back to his real life and leaving her behind.

So in the meantime... well, it was probably a good thing Buck had appeared. Because without a chaperon...well, it was *undoubtedly* a good thing Buck had appeared.

Will forced his eyes back to the agreement and finally managed to force his thoughts back to it, as well. He continued reading to the end, reread the wire Buck had received from his man in San Francisco, then looked up once more.

"Well?" Buck demanded.

"You said something about the value of Dursely Oil stocks dropping recently?"

"Will, them shares have been downright plunging. A few weeks ago they were trading for ten dollars apiece. Now they're down to five. Don't make no sense to me. Company's worth just as much as it was before."

"Well, I think I know where your problem is, Buck—what your fellow's referring to in this wire."

"Yeah?" Buck leaned forward.

"You see, in this agreement, you've put up your shares as collateral."

"That's right, I did."

"And there's a clause near the end—"

"I never got that far, Will."

"Well, I'm afraid there's a clause that says if the market value of your collateral falls below the amount of this loan, the bank is entitled to assume ownership of the shares in lieu of payment."

"In lieu of?"

"Instead of payment, Buck. Instead of you repaying the loan, the bank would take your shares."

"You mean...you mean, instead of me having to pay back the money, the bank would own my company?" Buck said slowly, clearly hoping he'd misunderstood.

"I'm afraid that's it."

"But I'd get the shares back when their price went up again, wouldn't I?"

"Not unless the bank wanted to sell them back to you—at the higher price."

"But...but that can't be."

"Sorry, Buck. That's what the agreement says."

"But...but I wouldn't have near enough money to buy them back with. The only real cash I got left is right here in this case. I put almost all the money I had, and that borrowed money, into the company. If the bank took those shares I'd be busted. I'd even have to sell Mary Beth's new house. I'd be poorer than a damned church mouse."

Reverend Bill opened one eye.

"Sorry," Buck mumbled. "Didn't mean no offence.

"But John told me nothing like that could happen," he went on, turning his attention back to Will. "He said he made sure of that when he helped draw up the agreement."

"John helped *who* draw it up?" Will asked.

"The bank's vice president. He came all the way from San Francisco to talk to me about the loan. And he and John agreed on the terms. And John told me there was no way the danged thing could possibly make me lose my company."

Will fleetingly wondered whether his childhood friend had grown up to be an idiot. He realized Emma was leaning toward him and glanced at her.

"John never saw the agreement in its final form," she said quietly. "Mr. Matthews, from the bank, took it back to San Francisco to have it officially typed before Mr. Dursely signed it. But as soon as they'd worked out the terms, John left for Tewksbury's."

Will nodded, telling her he caught her implication. The 1887 banking profession undoubtedly had it share of crooks.

"So, Will?" Buck said anxiously.

"I think you'd better have John take a look at this when we get to Tombstone—make sure it's exactly what he and the banker agreed to."

"And if it's not?" Buck asked uncertainly.

"Well, I'm not a lawyer, Buck. But I'd say you might be able to do something about it."

"Might?"

"Well, as I said, I'm not a lawyer. And you *did* sign this. But we'll start by seeing if John says there's anything in it that shouldn't be."

"Like that part about the share prices dropping," Buck said slowly.

Will nodded. "That'd be my guess."

"So . . . so, Will, how much farther could they drop before they'd be worth less than the loan amount?"

Will gazed at the figures again, wishing he could pull out his computer. Back in his student days, when he'd been a numbers fanatic, he'd have calculated in his head. But now he was a little rusty, so he used a pencil. "You'd run into trouble at a little over four dollars," he finally said. "You'll be okay unless they slide to about four dollars and ten cents."

Buck nodded, then smiled a forced-looking smile. "I'll be okay, Will. Them shares'll never drop to anywheres near four dollars. Ain't no reason in the world for them to have dropped as low as they are now."

"Then you'll be fine," Will said, trying to sound reassuring. He couldn't see any point in explaining the process of stock price manipulation to Buck. Not yet, at least. It would only make him more worried.

But odds were high that someone at the First Coastal Bank of California knew exactly how to manipulate stock prices—just as low as he cared to.

Buck carefully refolded the loan agreement, opened his case and slipped the papers in.

Will caught a glimpse of the stacks of bills inside and decided Buck hadn't been exaggerating by much. There just might be enough money in there to bribe the entire Territory of Arizona.

"THERE SHE IS," Reverend Bill said, pointing out the stagecoach window. "That's Tombstone in the distance."

Emma peered into the late-afternoon sunlight, across the expanse of desert, scarcely able to believe their destination was finally in sight.

The second day out, midway between two stations, the Concord's thoroughbrace had broken. Repairing the massive contraption of belts and springs had cost them an entire day, so they'd been four days getting here instead of three. But they'd still arrived in time to save John. Today was only Friday, and the twenty-fifth wasn't until Monday.

She glanced at Will, knowing the lost day had made him uneasy—had started him worrying about what would happen if he was delayed getting back to Mountainview.

Not that he would be. Not past August 1, at least. But if by the tiniest chance he was, he'd have to stay in this century for the next three years. And then what would happen?

But it was silly to even wonder about that. After all, this was only July 22.

She smiled ruefully at how easily the date came to her. Normally, during the summer, she paid no mind to the calendar. Yet lately...it was because she couldn't stop envisioning the date on that gravestone Will had seen.

And...and it was also because every day that passed meant Will's departure was growing closer.

He'd been here a week now. And they'd been together almost every moment of it. Day and night. It was almost like being married to him.

She snuck another peek across the seat. Will was gazing out toward Tombstone, his rugged profile softened by several days' growth of dark beard, his hair curling at his neck—perceptibly longer than it had been a week ago.

One week. In only one week she'd come to know him so well. Had come to rely on him so much. Had come to...

She tried to block out the word, not wanting to admit, even to herself, how she'd come to feel about him.

Almost like being married to him, an unbidden little voice repeated inside her head, refusing to let her ignore it. Almost like being married...right down to the strange fact that every single morning, starting that very first morning on the train, she'd awakened snuggled in Will's arms.

No matter that she'd been going to sleep, these past nights, in her own corner of the coach. By morning, she was always cuddled with Will—as if her body had decided that's where she belonged. And the most frightening thing was that she believed her body might be right. But that . . . well, that could simply never be.

He turned from the other window and grinned at her. "You know, I think everyone's been pulling my leg. Four days through Arizona, and we didn't even catch sight of a renegade Apache."

"You never will," Reverend Bill said, reminding them of his presence. "Not until there's at least one arrow stuck in you, that is. Apaches are the sneakiest warriors alive. A war party could have been watching us all the way from Flagstaff without our knowing it."

Emma eyed the Reverend uneasily, wishing that if he'd finally decided to begin offering comments, he'd pick a different topic.

"But no sense worrying about the Apaches now that you're here," he went on. "Where are you three planning on staying, anyhow?"

"Don't rightly know," Buck told him. "Got a suggestion?"

"Best place for the lady would be the Grand. It's at the corner of Allen and Fourth. The food's no good in the restaurant, but if you just slip on down the little alley behind the back door, you'll get to a good place—Molly's Café."

"Thanks. And say," Buck added, "do you know anything about the sheriff in Tombstone?"

The preacher shrugged. "Last I heard, they were between sheriffs. Bob Hatch got himself..." he paused, glancing at Emma. "Bob Hatch left kinda sudden."

Her stomach muscles tightened. It wasn't difficult to imagine what had happened to Mr. Hatch.

"I hear," the Reverend continued, "that the sheriff of Cochise County is basing himself in Tombstone just now. Fellow by the name of Slaughter."

"And what's he like?" Buck pressed.

"He's a tough old guy—real law-and-order sort. I hear he tells outlaws to get out of Cochise County or get killed. He'd just as soon shoot them as look at them."

"So..." Will ventured, "I guess a real law-and-order sort would be pretty honest, huh?"

"Sure is," Reverend Bill replied.

"Wouldn't be the type to take bribes, then?" Will asked.

"Nope. Not Mr. Slaughter."

Emma's stomach muscles tightened even more at that news. She wondered if there were any deputies who might not be so honest, but the preacher prevented further questions by turning to the window.

"Don't you worry," Buck told her. "We'll figure out something. And you know, a good meal is bound to make us think better. I can't wait to eat."

"Not me," Emma said. "All I want to do is see John, then soak in a tub for at least an hour."

"Me, too," Will agreed. "I just want a shave and a long, hot bath," he added, glancing at her then looking quickly away.

"Hell," Buck said. "After that pig slop they've been serving up in the swing stations, I'll worry about a bath later. Once we've seen John and checked into the Grand, I'm heading straight to Molly's Café."

The coach began slowing, and Emma peered back out. On the trail ahead sat a mounted man, a rifle held loosely in one hand and the reins of a second horse in the other.

"This is where I get out for now," the preacher said, shoving the door open as the stage creaked to a halt. "Might see you in town in a day or two. Meantime, the Lord keep you safe," he added, turning toward the lone rider.

"Guess he's heading back to the reservation," Buck said. "Sure was a quiet one, wasn't he? Must come from spending so much time out there with those Indians."

The Concord started rolling again, and Emma turned away from the window.

"The Reverend forgot his bible," Will said a few minutes later.

She glanced across the rocking coach, and sure enough, the worn bible was wedged into the corner where the Reverend had been using it as a pillow.

"I'll just stick it in my bag." Will reached over for it. "In case we do see him in town."

Emma nodded and looked out the window once more. Across the final quarter mile, Tombstone could be any mining town—a collection of tents and one-story buildings, with a few larger structures in the center. The only difference was that most mining towns she'd seen were in mountainous regions. The Tombstone mines must be underground.

"Danged flat, huh?" Buck muttered, his words echoing her thoughts.

She nodded. Even the few low hills outside town looked as if they'd been ironed. At first sight, Tombstone struck her as a place they'd want to leave just as quickly as they could—the minute they got John out of jail.

"THERE SHE BE," Buck said, pointing ahead.

Emma stopped and stood looking along Tough Nut Street. In contrast to the predominantly frame construction of most of Tombstone's buildings, the jail had been built of rough-hewn stone. Its two small front windows were secured by metal bars.

The day was just slipping into evening. The sun still hung low on the horizon. But even in the warmth of its lingering rays, the little building struck Emma as cold and ominous.

"Come on," Will said, taking her arm, "John's going to be darned glad to see you."

"I won't talk to him about Dursely Oil right off," Buck told them, patting the case he never let out of his grasp. "Can't do much about it over the weekend, anyway. And we'd best relieve John of his own worries first."

"Thanks, Mr. Dursely," Emma said, managing a grateful smile. She knew how concerned he was about his company. Before they'd left the Wells Fargo office, he'd wired New York to check the closing price of Dursely Oil shares. And the news that they'd slipped from five dollars to four dollars and eighty cents had clearly upset him.

She took a deep breath as they neared the jail's door. It was standing ajar, revealing a dirt floor inside. That made her feel even worse. John wasn't accustomed to all the comforts in the world, but...

Will stepped through the doorway, drawing her inside after him. Buck followed.

Vaguely she realized there was a man sitting to their right, his chair tipped back and his feet crossed on top of a desk. But it was the rear of the one-room jail that claimed her attention—the area that was divided into two cells. There was a man in each. And one of them was John.

Her heart sank at the sight of him. Apparently prisoners weren't even allowed to clean up. He looked as if he'd been dragged for miles through the dirt. His brown hair and dark clothes were almost gray, and his shirt had several tears in it.

Even with his ragged growth of beard, she could see a large bruise across his cheek—purple, shading to yellow. Judging by its severity, it had been made with a gun butt. She winced at the sight.

John glanced over, then leapt to his feet. "Emma! And Buck! How did you two get here?"

"Oh, John!" Emma tried to rush forward but Will grabbed her, jerking her back. As he did so, she realized the man on their right had jumped up... and was leveling a rifle at them. Her heart began pounding.

Will cleared his throat. "Mr. Slaughter?"

The man nodded curtly. "And you?"

"Will Lockhart. And this is Buck Dursely. And this lady is Miss Emma McCully, your prisoner's sister."

Emma tried to quell her fear and assess the sheriff. Reverend Christian had called him a tough old guy, and the description fit. He was in his late fifties or maybe sixty, with the weathered brown face of a man who'd spent most of his life outdoors.

His hair was graying, and his neat beard was almost entirely white. But he certainly did look tough. He was standing straight and tall, and she couldn't imagine he'd hesitate to use that rifle.

"Mr. Slaughter," Will said, "we were hoping we'd be able to visit with John."

The sheriff gestured, with his rifle, to the far wall. "Hang your weapons over there."

Will and Buck unstrapped their holsters and hung them on two of the pegs. Emma was suddenly very aware of the little Remington pressing between her breasts, but she certainly wasn't about to unbutton her dress and dig it out.

"You've got five minutes," the sheriff said, sitting down again but keeping his rifle trained on them.

"You," he called to Buck as they started toward the cell. "Leave that case in the corner."

Buck hesitated. "You two go ahead," he said after a second. "You don't need me to find out what's going on." He nodded across to the sheriff, then leaned against the wall. "I'll just wait over here, Mr. Slaughter."

Emma hurried the last few feet and reached through the bars to take John's hands. They bore recent cuts. "John, are you all right? I've been so worried about you."

"I'm okay, Emma," he said, gazing past her at Will, a question on his face.

"It's Billy," she explained. "Billy Lockhart. He . . . he came to visit you in Mountainview."

John continued staring for a moment, then almost smiled. "Billy? You're really Billy?"

Will nodded, gazing back at his old friend. Those smoky-blue eyes could belong to only one man. And there were several other traces of the young Johnnie McCully he remembered. A warm feeling deep inside him tightened his throat with emotion. For the first time, he was absolutely certain that making this trip through time had been the only thing to do.

"Yes, I'm really Billy," he said quietly. "Do you remember saving my life? All those years ago?"

"I sure do."

"Well, from what we've heard, you might be needing the favor returned. Is that right?"

John glanced at Emma, as if he was wondering exactly what they'd heard.

"Have you really been charged with horse theft?" she whispered.

"I'm afraid so."

She swallowed hard. "John, I know you can't be guilty."

He almost smiled again. "Thanks. You're the first one with even a doubt about it."

"What happened?" Will asked.

"Well, back in Flagstaff, I bought a horse."

Will nodded. "From old Tom, at the livery stable there."

"You talked to him?"

"Yes."

"Well, it turned out the horse was stolen. I doubt Tom knew that. He probably bought it in good faith himself. At any rate, the fellow who owned it and a couple of his friends caught up with me not far from here and...well, I'm just lucky that one of them didn't hold with lynchings. He convinced the others to bring me into town. They took all the money I had with me, but at least I'm not dead."

Emma's heart began racing. She'd heard an unspoken "yet" at the end of John's statement.

"What did Slaughter say when you told him your side of the story?" Will demanded.

"His exact words," John muttered, "were 'I've heard that one before, fellow'."

"Oh, John," Emma murmured, biting her lip. "What's going to happen now?"

"Now I wait for the circuit judge. And hope to hell he believes me."

"And if he doesn't?" Will said.

"*If* he doesn't?" snarled a sarcastic voice from the other cell.

Emma glanced into it. The man inside was about twenty-five, with stringy brown hair, pale eyes that seemed to look right through her, and an angry scar that ran from the corner of his left eye all the way to his chin. He was lounging on his cot, watching them with interest.

"Your brother, ma'am," he said, "is goin' to swing into eternity at the end of a rope."

"Shut up, Rafe," John snapped.

The younger man merely grinned a yellowed grin.

Emma turned back to John, trying not to show how terrified she felt.

"Emma...Emma, it'll be okay," John said.

Rafe snorted. "Okay? Hell, Judge Wallace don't know but one verdict for horse thieves. And that's guilty."

"Emma," Will said, "we can verify John's story—repeat what Tom told us. And the only evidence against John is circumstantial."

The comment brought a laugh from Rafe—a laugh so cold it sent shivers through her. Her brother couldn't die. He simply couldn't.

"'Course," Rafe said, "could be, McCully, you won't even have to wait for the good judge to arrive. Could be the Law and Order League might decide to save the Territory the cost of a proper trial."

"Who are the Law and Order League?" Emma whispered, afraid to hear Rafe's answer.

"Oh, I guess in some towns, our Law and Order League would just be called vigilantes," Rafe told her. "But they're a little more organized here. Have what they call trials. Hell, last week they tried Russian Clem just for being a damned nuisance—then hanged him for it, while Deputy Haslett stood by and watched."

"That's enough, boy!"

The sheriff's roar sent Emma two feet into the air. She wheeled around as he spoke again.

"What happened last week," he snarled to Rafe, "only happened 'cuz I was up in Tucson. Ain't no vigilantes running the law in Tombstone when I'm around. And I aim to be around for the next little while."

Emma gazed at that rifle of Mr. Slaughter's. The way he was aiming it at Rafe made her wonder just how safe John was, even under the law's watchful eye. Hadn't Reverend Christian said the sheriff would just as soon shoot outlaws as look at them? Not that her brother was an outlaw, but people obviously believed he was.

She realized Will was whispering to John and edged nearer.

"What about jumping bail?" he was saying, his voice barely audible. "Buck has enough money with him to bail you out of this hole and get you safely out of Arizona."

John shook his head. "There's not a chance I could get out on bail. Not with a horse theft charge and not with Slaughter."

"All right, then, we'll have to try something else. I'll talk with him before we leave and see if that gets us anywhere. But don't worry. We're not going to let you hang. That's for damned sure."

"Your five minutes are up," the sheriff called over.

Emma glanced at Will. How could she leave John here when her mind was racing with thoughts of Mr. Slaughter's rifle and the Law and Order League and a hanging judge on his way?

Will shook his head. "We've got to go for now, Emma."

"Just give me a minute more."

He nodded, then strode slowly over to the sheriff, buying Emma time. "His sister's just saying good-bye. That okay?"

"Damn good idea," Rafe called out. "She might not be seeing him again. Not alive, anyways."

Sheriff Slaughter trained his rifle on Rafe once more. "I like my jail quiet, son. And one way or another, I keep it quiet."

Rafe grinned insolently, but slouched lower on his cot and didn't reply.

"Mr. Slaughter," Will said, "John McCully is innocent. What he told you was the truth. He bought that horse at a livery stable in Flagstaff. From a man named Tom something. Miss McCully and I talked to the man ourselves. I . . . I don't expect Tom would go for the idea of a trip down here to testify, but I'm sure he'd be happy to send a wire or something."

"You're sure, are you?" the sheriff said sarcastically. "Well, let me tell you a few things. First off, I hardly get a prisoner in here who doesn't claim he's innocent. And second off, McCully was riding a horse with someone else's brand on it. And third off, a wire ain't going to convince nobody of nothing.

"And fourth off, even if I figured this Tom fellow really existed, in these parts, a man doesn't voluntarily stick his head in a noose. And if someone was to admit to having that stolen horse to sell to your friend, then we just got us a different horse thief, right? So if you think your friend Tom would be happy to help, you're loco. He wouldn't even admit to knowing McCully."

Will nodded slowly, feeling naive as hell. He'd assumed that testimony from Tom would be the obvious solution. But, like it or not, he could see the sheriff's point. He glanced back at Emma. She was deep in conversation with John. He knew she'd appreciate more time.

Several Wanted posters were tacked onto the wall behind the desk. One picture was of a defiant-looking young Indian with high cheekbones, thick black hair that reached below his shoulders, and a mouth that slashed across his face in a straight, cruel line. The name beneath the face came as no shock.

"So that's the Apache Kid, huh?" Will said. "I keep hearing about him."

"Just hope you don't get to seeing him," the sheriff said.

"Right...right. A fifteen thousand dollar reward. That's awfully high, isn't it?"

"The Territory wants him awfully bad. He's a vicious one. Strange story, though. Son of an Apache chief—of Geronimo's brother, in fact. But he was raised by a white man. The Kid used to be an army scout. Then went wild and started killing folks." Slaughter looked over at Emma as if he was about to interrupt her.

"That circuit judge," Will said quickly. "When do you expect him to get here?"

"Monday."

Monday...which was July 25. Will swallowed uneasily. "I see. And how long will John's trial take?"

"Maybe ten minutes."

"Ten minutes," Will repeated. If he'd had any lingering doubt that the verdict was a foregone conclusion, it had just vanished. "Well, I guess Buck and I'd better collect our guns now."

He glanced at Emma again as he strapped his Colt back on. She was backing slowly from the cell, as if finding it physically difficult to tear herself away from her brother.

Lord, they simply *had* to come up with a plan to get John out of here. A plan that would change that tiny piece of history they had to change.

Because it was crystal clear that as the universe stood now, on July 25, 1887, John McCully would be hung as a horse thief. And to prevent that from happening, they had to get him out of jail and out of Tombstone. If they could do that, he'd be safe.

"I feel so awful, having to leave John in there," Emma murmured as they left the jail.

"We all do, Emma," Buck said.

Will tried to think of something reassuring to say, but he was just too tired to feign optimism. Apparently so were the others. They headed along in silence. Evening was rapidly closing in, its gathering gray reflecting their mood.

They stopped to pick up the bags they'd left at the Wells Fargo station, then proceeded along Tombstone's main drag.

From Sixth Avenue over to Fifth, Allen Street consisted mainly of wooden, false-fronted buildings that leaned over the boardwalk toward the wide dirt street—a post office, a hardware store, the office of the *Tombstone Prospector* newspaper.

But at Fifth, Allen turned into a saloon strip. Activity was just getting underway for the night, and lights, piano music and the sounds of male voices filtered from windows and through doorways.

Toward the end of the block, they passed the Maison Dorée Restaurant, then the Cosmopolitan Hotel, then yet another saloon. Finally Will spotted their destination. Across the street stood the Grand Hotel.

He could see absolutely nothing grand about it. But it did look less disreputable than the Cosmopolitan. They trudged over and registered for three rooms.

"There you are," the clerk said, giving Will the keys. "Second floor—rooms seven, eight and nine."

"Can we get baths?" he asked.

"Yes, sir. There's a bathtub at the end of your hall. I'll have the first batch of hot water sent up right away. You going to want three baths?"

"Just two," Buck said. "I'll arrange for mine later."

They climbed the stairs and headed down the dim hall.

"Emma, you take the middle room," Will told her, unlocking the door and handing her the key. "And have the first bath. Just tap on my door when you're through with the tub. Then, after I'm done, we can get some dinner. That Maison Dorée Restaurant we passed looked fairly decent."

She gave him a weary smile and turned to Buck. "You're sure you don't want to wait and eat with us?"

Buck shook his head. "My stomach's been rumbling for hours. Tell you what, though. Don't you two go out until I get back. I'll eat quick, then go along with you. We can talk while you eat—decide what we'd best do about John."

"All right," Will agreed. "We'll wait for you in Emma's room."

"Good. Good. And we're going to come up with something, Emma. Don't you fret."

"I know we will," she said.

She was, Will thought, about two seconds from bursting into tears. He had an almost overwhelming impulse to take her in his arms and hug away her unhappiness. And the impulse didn't surprise him in the slightest.

Sometime during that damned stagecoach trip, he'd developed a permanent desire to have her in his arms.

He might have been telling himself, from the first moment they'd met, that Emma was off-limits. But waking up beside her each morning, feeling her warm softness against him, had made him realize he wanted to spend the rest of his life waking up beside her.

Somewhere along the trail between Flagstaff and Tombstone, he'd fallen irrevocably in love with Emma McCully. And what on earth was he going to do about that?

CHAPTER NINE

BUCK GOT HIS HANDS and face reasonably clean, then turned from the washstand and stood eyeing the case that held the bank agreement and his money. Maybe he should just hide the danged thing beneath the bed, instead of toting it along to the restaurant.

That, he decided, glancing at what passed for a lock on the door, wouldn't be smart.

He headed downstairs once more, recalling Reverend Bill's directions—Molly's Café was just along the alley that ran behind the Grand.

He crossed the main floor to the back door and stepped outside. Night had completely fallen now, and the darkness made him hesitate.

There were no windows in the rear of the buildings, nothing to throw light into the alley. It was pitch black except for the few shadowy places where scattered rays of moonlight were creeping down.

From nowhere, an image appeared in his mind— Mary Beth's train pulling out of Mountainview, bound for San Francisco. She and the children were all smiling through the open windows at him.

"Take good care of yourself, Buck," she called. "We'll be waiting for you. We love you."

"Bye, Pa," Buck, Jr., shouted, waving furiously. "Come soon."

Without thinking, Buck patted his holster, then grinned nervously to himself. What did he figure? That he'd absently taken off his gun and forgotten to strap it on again? Hell, he was hardly *that* tired.

He started along between the buildings, hoping the back of the café was easily identifiable. If it wasn't, he'd have to—

In the blink of an eye, one of the alley's shadows became a man.

Buck grabbed for his Colt, but the fellow spoke up quickly.

"Relax, Buck, it's just me—Reverend Bill." The preacher struck a match and held it to illuminate his face. His clerical collar glowed eerily in the faint light.

"Tarnation, Reverend! You scared the blazes out of me. What are you doing here?"

And then it caught his eye...revealed by the match's flicker...the glint of steel. In his other hand, the preacher was holding a gun.

Buck glanced at the man's face once more, trying to see his expression, but the flame died, making him almost invisible again.

"Reverend?" Buck said uncertainly.

"Sorry, Buck, I'm not really a preacher man. And I got me a job to do."

The click of a gun being cocked split the darkness and sent icy chills down Buck's spine. He thrust his case in front of him at arm's length and quickly stepped back. "Here," he managed despite his fear. "This is what you want. No need for shooting."

"Sorry, Buck," the voice said again from the darkness. "That bag you take such good care of's just going to be a lucky bonus for me. It's killing you that's my job."

Buck heaved the case forward into the night, whirled and ran. He stumbled a step. An explosion of noise sent pain searing through his skull. Bright orange pain that crumpled him to the ground.

A sudden shaft of light fell onto the dirt before him. A man shouted something. Another shot rang out. Then all was black . . . deathly black.

WILL PACED ACROSS Emma's room, wishing he felt more confident. He didn't know how this mess with John would turn out, or even how they should be tackling the problem. It was damned hard to play a game when you didn't know the rules.

Emma sat in the room's one chair, watching him, absently toying with an errant lock of her still-damp hair. He was doing his best to ignore how delectable she looked, but it was impossible.

He couldn't figure out how she affected him so strongly when her dresses covered almost every square inch of her—from neck to feet to wrists. But simply looking at her turned him on more than seeing a hundred naked women would. And right this moment, when she was still glowing from the bath and wearing a pink dress that clung enticingly. . .

He tried to concentrate on the issue at hand. "Emma, Wyatt's definitely our best starting point. You don't know anything about how things work in Tombstone, and, hell, I scarcely know anything about how things work in this century."

"Will, you know a whole lot more than you did when you arrived in it. I . . . I don't know what I'd do without you right now . . . what I'd have done without you for the past while."

He tried not to smile, but the way she'd come to rely on him made him feel ten feet tall. He only prayed he could make things turn out right for her and John.

"And I guess you're right about talking to Mr. Earp," she continued. "After seeing John in that dreadful jail . . . well, I'll go along with absolutely anything that might get him safely out of Arizona."

"Good. First thing tomorrow, I'll look for Wyatt. He shouldn't be hard to find. He mentioned frequenting a couple of saloons."

"What do you think he'll suggest?"

"Well, now that we've met the sheriff, I doubt it'll be bribery. Maybe he'll figure there's something a lawyer could do. But I suspect it's more likely we'll end up hiring a couple of guys to pull a commando raid."

"Pull a what?"

"A . . . it's not important. But one way or another, we'll pay someone, and they'll get John out of jail."

"You mean . . . you mean we might *break* him out?"

Will nodded.

"I never in my life imagined," Emma said slowly, "that I'd be involved in plotting a jail break. I've never even broken a minor law before. Have you, Will?"

"Not really. The closest I came was back in my younger, wilder days, when I was a university student. I counted cards in Vegas."

"You did what? Where?"

"Las Vegas, Nevada."

Emma nodded. "It's a mining town."

"Well, it eventually becomes a famous gambling town—wall-to-wall casinos. And what I did there is called counting cards. I used to be a numbers freak, and I could remember which cards had already been played out of a Blackjack shoe—increased my odds on winning by a whole bunch. But when the casino caught on, I got thrown out of town." Will grinned, recalling how much money he'd won before that happened.

"Counting cards is breaking the law, then?" Emma asked.

"No, it's actually just having a darned good memory for numbers. But casino people don't look at it quite that way. At any rate, in John's case, it seems as if breaking the law might be the only way we're going to get justice done. And I'm sure Wyatt will help us out. I'll just tell him all the details, and he'll suggest what to do. I bet he'll know exactly who we should talk to and how much it'll cost us."

"Thank heavens for Mr. Dursely and his money," Emma murmured.

"Right this minute, I'd be a darned sight more thankful for him if he'd show up. I'm starving. We shouldn't have said we'd wait for him—should have gone out for our own dinner as soon as we got cleaned up. The three of us could have talked later."

Emma shrugged, then cleared her throat. "Will?"

"Yes?"

"Will . . . if you're going to tell Mr. Earp all the details, there's something you should know."

"What?"

"John has a gun. I gave him mine."

Will gazed at her as her words sunk in.

"That little Remington Mr. Dursely lent me back in Mountainview, remember?"

"Of course I remember. But how the hell did you get it to John without anyone noticing?"

"I did it just before we left the jail. When you were talking to Mr. Slaughter. I . . . well, I was so worried about that Law and Order League and the way the sheriff looked as if he'd barely need an excuse to use his rifle, and I thought . . . well, I just dug the gun out from . . . from where it was hidden and slipped it to John. I made sure Rafe couldn't see what was happening. I know it's not a very big gun, but at least . . .

"Will, I guess I lied a few minutes ago, didn't I? When I told you I'd never broken even a minor law, I mean. I guess giving John a gun wasn't exactly a law-abiding thing to do. But you don't think I did wrong, do you? Not under the circumstances?"

Will shook his head ruefully. "What I think, Emma, is that you are really something."

"Really something?" she asked, her tone uneasy. "Does that mean you think I'm good or bad?"

He gazed at her for a moment, wondering how much longer he could last without telling her precisely how good he thought she was . . . how absolutely terrific he thought she was. Probably, he decided, he'd be doing well to hold off for as long as three more seconds.

Emma eyed Will anxiously. She'd grown to care so much about his opinion of her that, if he lectured her when she was already upset, she was going to dissolve into tears. But the warm smile that gradually appeared on his face assured her there was no lecture coming. It also sent a whole series of little tingles racing through her.

"Emma, in this case—in your case—really something is very, very good."

He stood watching her for another minute, the look in his dark eyes making those tingles race even faster. Then he crossed the few steps to her chair, leaned down and drew her up into his arms.

She swallowed hard, her pulse leaping erratically, her heart pounding. He was going to kiss her. And she was going to let him.

And then someone knocked on the door.

Will continued gazing at her, clearly willing the someone to go away.

"It's Mr. Dursely," she finally forced herself to whisper.

Will nodded and turned to the door, leaving her feeling sadly alone.

She glanced in the mirror and watched him walk across the room. He'd put on his suit jacket, with his jeans, to go out to eat. It looked a strange combination, but he said that in his world it was ... trendy was the word. In the glass, she could see him opening the door. But the man in the hallway, carrying a rifle, wasn't Mr. Dursely.

"Sheriff Slaughter," Will said. "Ahh ... come in, sir."

Emma turned, suddenly unable to breathe, certain the man had come to tell them something had happened to John. "My brother?" she managed.

"Your brother's fine, ma'am."

She felt so relieved she actually smiled at the sheriff, but he was no longer looking at her.

He glanced around the room, focused on her bag, then turned to Will. "That case your friend was carrying earlier. I don't suppose either of you two have it, do you?"

"No," Will said. "What's the problem? What's happened?"

"Well, I've just been in his room and that case ain't there," Slaughter said, ignoring the questions. "You know what he had in it?"

Emma bit her lip as her relief evaporated. What was this about?

Will glanced at her, apparently uncertain what to tell the sheriff.

She shrugged anxiously. Will had been right. She didn't know anything about how things worked in Tombstone, wasn't even sure she could differentiate the good guys from the bad.

"Ahh . . . there were some papers in the case," Will finally said. "And some money. Look, Sheriff, has something happened to Buck? Is he all right?"

"'Fraid he ain't. Someone shot him—just out back of the hotel here."

"He isn't . . . isn't . . . ?" Emma couldn't force the rest of the question out.

"He'll be okay, ma'am. Someone heard the ruckus, opened his back door to investigate, and whoever shot your friend ran off. Reckon he grabbed that case before he did, though."

"But you're sure Buck's not seriously hurt?" Will demanded.

"He'll be fine. He was taken to Doc Goodfellow's, and the Doc says he was real lucky. There was a lot of blood. Always is with head wounds. But the bullet just tore a line across his scalp. That missing case, though—that's my only clue to who did this. Anyone besides you two know he had money in it?''

Will shook his head.

"There was the Reverend," Emma murmured.

The sheriff swung around to face her. "Who, ma'am?"

"Reverend Bill Christian. A preacher who was on the stage with us. Mr. Dursely mentioned having money with him. And he had his case open a few times. But a preacher wouldn't—"

"What'd the *Reverend* look like, ma'am?"

Briefly she described him.

"I'd lay odds that weren't no preacher," the sheriff muttered angrily when she finished. "I'd say it was a murdering sidewinder by the name of Butcher Knife Bill, alias Bill Christian, alias Bill Christie, alias Bill Christianson and the Lord only knows who else."

"Now that I think about it," Will said, "it was *Reverend* Bill who suggested Buck use the alley out back."

"That no good son of a..." The sheriff paused, glancing at Emma. "Did that skunk come riding right into my town on the stage?"

"No. Another man met him with a horse. About a quarter of a mile out."

"Yeah, I've heard he's taken to holing up in the desert, someplace near here," Slaughter said. "With a bunch of other varmints I'd love to get in my gun sight. I haven't been able to find their hideout yet, but damn, I won't be resting now until I've got that Butcher Knife in my jail. He's been a burr under my saddle for too damned long. And coming into town!

Even at night. Coming into town when he knows I'm plumb itching to get him. Must have been a heap of money in that case to tempt him."

"I think there was a fair bit, all right," Will said.

Slaughter nodded, started to the door, then stopped. "Reckon you two will want to head over to Doc Goodfellow's. He's on Fremont Street. But don't bother going till morning. He treats head wounds with some drug that'll keep your friend knocked out all night."

The sheriff pulled the door closed behind him and Will turned. "No wonder the *Reverend* knew so much about Slaughter. Sounds as if they're arch enemies."

Emma merely nodded, gazing unseeingly across the room.

"What are you thinking?" Will asked quietly.

She shrugged, not certain she could speak over the lump in her throat. "I was thinking," she finally said, "that now we have no money to get John out of jail with. Oh, Will, now John..."

It was impossible to continue. She and Will had come all this way, had tried so hard, and it was all going to have been in vain.

Will stepped forward and wrapped his arms around her, reassuring her with his nearness. Wordlessly he was telling her she wasn't alone in this, that she had someone to rely on. Someone wonderful, she thought.

"We'll figure out something," he murmured. "I promise we'll make sure John comes through this just fine."

Emma pressed her cheek against Will's chest, feeling his warmth and strength, listening to the solid thudding of his heart, until she regained control.

Somehow, they *would* make sure John came through just fine.

"I'm okay now," she whispered, glancing up.

He looked at her for a long, motionless moment, then spoke. "I'm not, Emma. I'm not okay at all. Could we sit down for a minute? I have to talk to you."

She nodded, wondering what was wrong but not putting her question into words. That strange, exhilarating feeling she got when Will was very close to her made speaking difficult. Her heart was racing, and she was breathing far faster than normal. Being in Will's arms made her positively dizzy. Sitting would probably be wise.

He led her across to the bed and drew her down beside him, still holding her hands in his.

"What . . . what is it, Will?"

"Emma, it's kind of about how confusing it is to try thinking of the present as the past. Or the future as the present. Or the past as the future . . . part of the past as the future, I mean."

She nodded. It seemed the appropriate response, although she didn't have the slightest idea what Will was trying to say.

"Emma, the thing is . . . well, hell, it must be plain as day to you without my even saying it. Emma, I've fallen in love with you. I didn't mean to and I know it makes our situation even more confusing, but I couldn't help it. And I can't keep pretending that you're nothing more than a traveling companion when I love you."

She simply stared at him. He loved her. He hadn't meant to, but he'd fallen in love with her. The same way she hadn't meant to, but had fallen in love with him.

"Emma?" he murmured. "Emma, I don't know what would normally happen next in your world, but in my world you'd tell me how you feel about me."

She swallowed hard. If she told him the truth, wouldn't that just make things more difficult? For both of them?

The silence lengthened... she could sense him tensing.

"I see," he finally said stiffly, releasing her hands as he spoke. "I thought...well, I guess I misread your feelings."

She should leave it at that. But something wouldn't let her. "I love you, too, Will," she whispered.

Relief washed across his face, followed by the warmest smile she'd ever seen.

"Then everything's going to work out," he said, stroking a stray wisp of hair from her cheek. "Somehow, we'll make everything work out."

He took her face in his hands and gazed at her. Then, ever so slowly, he leaned forward. Until the warmth of his breath was caressing her skin. Until the scent of shaving soap, mingled with his own personal scent, filled her nostrils. Until his lips were so close to hers she could almost feel them.

She closed her eyes and he brushed her mouth with a kiss. It was more delightful than she'd imagined possible. His lips felt heavenly—full and warm and moving ever so softly against hers.

He smoothed his hands down her back, drawing her closer, fitting her body perfectly to his as if they were two halves of a whole, and kissed her more firmly. Then he gently began tracing her lips with his tongue.

The unexpected shock of what he was doing sent a strange sensation rushing through her. But it was an exciting sensation that made her want him to continue... that made her wonder if maybe she was supposed to...

Tentatively she touched Will's lips with the tip of her tongue.

"Oh, Emma," he whispered, telling her she was definitely supposed to, making her more bold.

His mouth tasted deliciously salty-sweet. She couldn't get enough of it. And then he slipped his tongue between her parted lips and began exploring their inner surfaces. She almost moaned, instinctively pressing closer against him, loving the solidness of his body next to hers.

"Oh, Emma," he finally whispered again, drawing away from her a fraction, "Emma, I want to just keep on kissing you forever."

She gazed into his soft black eyes, wanting to keep on kissing him forever, too. But rational thought, driven away by his nearness, was returning. No matter how much they might want it, there couldn't be a forever for them.

It probably would have been better if there hadn't even been a just now. Not that she'd give it back. Not for anything. And she'd never forget it. If only... if only so many things were different.

"I mean that," he murmured. "I mean forever, Emma. I... look, I think we should talk about what's going to happen to us when I go home. What would you think about coming with me? What...what would you think about marrying me?"

Marrying him? She felt tears forming, beginning to spill down her cheeks. This wasn't fair. Simply wasn't fair. How could he be offering her something she wanted so badly when she knew she couldn't have it?

"Don't cry," he said gently. "I know everything has happened awfully fast, but we don't have very long to decide. So let's just start thinking about it, okay?"

"There's nothing to think about, Will," she told him, making herself say the words that almost choked her. "I can't marry you."

"Emma...Emma, I realize there'd be problems to work out and that it would be hard for you in a lot of ways. And I know the idea is scary but—"

"No, you don't understand." She took a deep breath, then tried to explain. "Will, I can't marry anyone. I can't..." Embarrassing as it was, she went on. "Will, I can't bear children. I absolutely adore them. And I'd give anything to have a family. But I can't, Will. I just can't."

He sat watching her closely. Through her tears, his face was blurred. But it was still the face she'd come to adore. And sitting here looking at him now was making her heart break.

"Emma," he finally said, "back up for a minute. You *do* love me."

She merely nodded, fearing that if she said the words again, the hurt might grow worse. Although that hardly seemed possible.

"You love me a whole lot?" he pressed.

She nodded another admission, and he smiled broadly at her, as if her loving him made everything all right. He didn't realize what—

"Emma, think back to the story your mother told you about my father and I leaving. Remember that Erica took me to the future even before my father could go?"

"Yes," she whispered.

"Emma, that was because I needed medical treatment that didn't exist in 1862."

She just kept nodding, feeling like an idiotic toy someone had wound up. She tried breathing deeply, tried to get her emotions under control while he spoke.

"Emma, there are all kinds of disorders that can't be cured now but can be in the future. You could probably have children just fine. And if you couldn't, it wouldn't matter. Not to me. I'm not desperate to have children. But I *am* desperate to have you."

"No, Will, you don't understand. It's not something medical treatment could cure. It's not physical... it's my sensibilities."

"It's your what?"

"My sensibilities. The feelings I get. My premonitions."

"What about them?"

"Well, you know," she elaborated, fighting to retain the thin veneer of composure she'd managed. "They could be indications of future insanity. I might... Will, I might end up crazy. And if I had children, they'd be at risk, too."

He stared at her with a positively incredulous expression. "Emma, where on earth did you ever get an idea like that?"

"I've always known it, Will," she explained, blinking back fresh tears. "My mother told me as soon as I was old enough to understand. Then, when I was living in San Francisco, I visited a specialist and he explained it scientifically."

"And . . . and you seriously believe this?"

"Of course."

"And that's why you've never kept company with a man?"

"Yes."

"Oh, Emma," Will said, drawing her to him and hugging her so tightly she thought she'd faint.

"Emma, darling," he whispered into her hair, "there's no truth in what your mother said. She must have believed some old wives' tale that goes back to witch burnings. And that specialist in San Francisco must have been a quack. There's no relationship between insanity and . . ."

He released her from his bear hug and took her by the shoulders. "Emma, remember the day we met? Remember I mentioned something called ESP?"

She simply nodded again, her mind whirling. What he'd just told her couldn't possibly be true. Not when she'd always known, always believed . . . and yet he'd told her so many other incredible things that she'd come to accept. She tried to concentrate. He'd asked her a question. Something about . . .

"ESP," she murmured dazedly. "Yes, I remember. It was one of the first things you talked about that I didn't understand."

"Well, Emma, ESP is something that's been extensively studied in the future. The letters stand for extrasensory perception. That's what you have—just a strong sensitivity to the paranormal."

"The what?" she asked.

"The paranormal. That simply means things outside the range of ordinary experience. But being sensitive to the extraordinary isn't an indicator that you might end up crazy. Or that there might be any problems with your children. Oh, Emma, having ESP doesn't mean there's anything wrong with you. On the contrary, it means there's something special about you. But, hell, I knew there was something special about you the first instant I saw you."

She sat staring at him in stunned silence, wanting desperately to believe there was nothing wrong with her.

"Do you know what I'm thinking?" he asked. "Right this minute?"

She gazed into the depths of his eyes and read his thoughts. "You're thinking you'd like to kiss me again," she whispered.

"See," he said, drawing her to him once more, "all that was, was a great example of ESP. There's absolutely nothing wrong with you. In fact, you just might be perfect."

CHAPTER TEN

EMMA GLANCED guiltily at Will's door, knowing she should go back to her own room, go to bed. It was late, and they'd be busy tomorrow. They had to check on Mr. Dursely, then Will would have to track down Mr. Earp.

But she was feeling so contented she didn't want to move. Will had puffed the pillows against the wall, turning his bed into a giant sofa. Sitting here, cuddled against him, she recalled the time, years ago, when her sisters had been courting.

They'd sat in the parlor with their beaux, and, even though she'd only been a child, seeing them in love had made her wistful. She'd always been certain she'd never know what it was like to love a man. But now she did. And the feeling made her happier than she'd ever dreamed she would be—so happy that she was certain Will was right. Everything *would* work out... for John... for them... everything.

"Tell me more about the future," she said.

Will smiled at her. "Well, let's see. If we were in the future now, there'd be a telephone in this room. And instead of having gone across the street for dinner, we could have just picked up the phone and asked room service to send up whatever we wanted."

"Room service," she repeated, memorizing yet another new term. "And there'd be telephones in every house, you said. Connected all over the world. So I could even call my parents in San Francisco. Any time I pleased. Except...oh, Will, that's the thing that makes me most unsure. If I went with you, I'd never see them again."

He leaned closer and kissed her neck. "I know, Emma. I know how hard that would be."

"Never see them again," she repeated quietly. "Or John. Or anyone. I...it frightens me, Will. I'd miss them so much. I'd feel so alone."

"You'd have me, Emma. And my family. And you'd meet other people. And soon, you'd be busy with those children you want."

The thought of having a baby made her smile. "But you said you weren't desperate to have children," she teased.

Will grinned at her. "I'm not. But I really like kids. And I'd especially like ours...yours and mine."

She nodded slowly. *Their* children. By choosing to go with Will, she'd lose everything in her life here. But by choosing to stay, she'd lose Will. And their future together. She didn't think she could bear that.

"But my parents," she said again, thinking aloud. "Even though we live in different places now, we're so close, Will. I write them every week. And I visit as often as I can. Abigail and Hildy and my brothers are scattered all over the country. Only John and I have ever even been to San Francisco. And, oh, Will, my mother and father would be so terribly, terribly upset if I simply vanished."

"I know, Emma. I understand perfectly, because if I didn't make it back to Mountainview by August 1, if I didn't make it home until the next time hole opens at Broken Hill, Dad and Erica would be just that upset. They'd spend three years not knowing what had happened to me. But in your case, you could explain. You could write a long letter and tell your parents all about me."

"They'd never believe any of this, Will. You know what my mother would think if she got a letter telling her I was going to live in the future? That I was going to marry a man who works in the sky? A man who used to spend two months at a time up there but, once we're married, will be hurtling through space every night, taking a shuttle home?"

Will grinned again. "What would she think?"

"She'd think," Emma said, forcing a smile, "that my sensibilities had gotten the better of me and I'd gone insane, just as she always feared I might."

"Well, we could tell John the truth. And he could go to San Francisco and explain everything to your parents."

She nodded slowly. "Maybe. Maybe he could. If we can get him out of jail. Oh, Will, I don't even want to think that maybe we can't. And my mind's spinning in circles. Tell me more about how the world works in the twenty-first century. Tell me . . . remember in that hotel room in Flagstaff when . . . ?"

She could feel herself beginning to blush and was glad the little kerosene lamp was so dim. But her curiosity drove her on. "Will, that night, before I knew you were from the future, you told me that where you came from women were freer with men. Physically," she added, forcing herself to say the word. "I didn't understand exactly what you meant by that."

He cleared his throat. "Well, relationships between men and women are different."

She waited. He didn't go on.

"I know," she finally pressed. "I mean, you've told me about women working at men's jobs and being well-educated and about equal rights and all. And about those women rocket scientists being on Space Station Freedom with you. But...but what exactly did you mean that night?"

"Well, I meant that in the future, if a woman loves a man, she usually expresses that love physically. Even if they aren't married to each other."

"Expresses it. Physically. By kissing him, you mean."

"Ahh ... partly."

"But that doesn't sound different, Will. I've been kissing you."

"Well, actually, it's more than kissing, Emma. When a woman loves a man she...well, she usually does what a wife in 1887 would do with her husband...in bed, I mean. In the future, people don't have to be married to...it's considered perfectly acceptable."

Emma inched away from Will, suddenly dreadfully uncomfortable about sitting on his bed. Surely he wasn't trying to tell her...but he'd said "do with her husband...in bed." And she was darned sure he hadn't meant sleep. But he couldn't possibly have meant the other. Could he?

She sat silently, drawing circles on the bedspread and pondering. But blast it, the only way she was going to find out, for sure, was by asking. She screwed up her courage and looked at Will. "You mean they make love? Virtuous women? When they're not married?"

He nodded. "It's the norm."

"The norm?" she repeated uncertainly.

"It's what most people do, Emma."

"But... but what if the woman wasn't married and got...?" Oh, mercy, it was even harder to force this one out than *physically*. "What if the woman got pregnant?" she finally blurted out, rushing all the words together.

"She wouldn't," Will said firmly. "Not if she didn't want to. Birth control's been perfected in the future."

"Birth control?"

"Ahh... contraception?" he said hesitantly.

"Contraception?" Rats! All the words she didn't know sometimes made conversing with Will awfully frustrating.

"Emma, they know how to prevent women from becoming pregnant."

"How?" she demanded, her curiosity besting her embarrassment.

"Various ways. The easiest is a drug that's been developed. Its effect lasts for a year. So you only need an annual inoculation."

"You mean women are just given a needle? Once a year? And that works?"

"Actually it's often the men who are inoculated. In fact, it's one of the standard shots I have for working the long stretches on Space Station. Not that...I mean I don't...but being up there for months at a time they assume that maybe..."

Emma swallowed hard. "It's all right, Will. I didn't expect you'd never... I mean, I hadn't really thought about it...but you would have here, too. Only it would have been with a soiled dove, not a virtuous woman." She sat staring at the bedspread, hating those unknown female rocket scientists who worked on Space Station.

Will tucked a finger under her chin and tilted her face up. "A lot of things have changed in the future, Emma."

She nodded slowly. "I think that's a good example of what you told me was called an understatement, Will." But mercy, how many other inconceivable facts were there to learn about life there?

"Look, I didn't mean to upset you," Will was saying. "And I certainly wasn't trying to imply that I expect you to...I realize you've been taught differently. I was only explaining about sex because you asked. I think you should get some sleep, now," he added quietly. "Come on. I'll walk you down the hall."

He took her hand, and she followed him out of his room and along to her own, her thoughts in a tangle. She'd realized that *things* would be awfully different in the future, but she hadn't considered that people's ways of thinking would have changed so drastically.

She paused, her key in her door, and gazed up at Will. "What about your father, Will? You were just a little boy when you went to the future, but he was an adult—like me. Did he make out all right? Did he have problems with everything being so strange?"

Will rubbed his jaw thoughtfully. "He had *some* problems."

"Like what?"

"Well...he lost a lot of the gold he'd brought along. Got ripped off by a scam artist pushing a phony investment."

Emma shook her head. "Will, I don't even understand half the things you say. I'd feel as if people around me were speaking a foreign language. I don't know what ripped off means or what a scam artist is. But I'd probably get ripped off by one, too."

Will draped his arms around her waist. "Emma, I was simply saying that Dad got fleeced by a flim-flam man. And anything you didn't understand you'd only have to ask me about. It would just seem strange for a while. In the long run, Dad made out fine. He had a few sticky patches in the beginning, but today, he's a famous writer—writes books about the Old West. He and Erica worked through the problems he ran into. That's what we'd do."

Emma nodded slowly. That's what they would *try* to do. But what if...?

"Emma," Will said as she opened her door, "I love you." He bent and kissed her softly on the forehead. "Hey," he added teasingly, "the last inoculation I had is only good for another month. So, if you like, we could get started on those children you want as soon as we're married. And everything else will work out. I promise."

"Yes...of course," she whispered, stepping into her room and closing the door.

She sank onto the bed, trying to sort through her fears. What if...?

What if she went with Will and found she couldn't work out the problems that faced her? What if she couldn't manage to fit in with the people there, all those millions of people who thought so differently from the way she did? What if she made both herself and Will unhappy because of it? What if she gave up her life here and that turned out to be a dreadful mistake?

"MAKE SURE he stays bedfast for a while," Dr. Goodfellow told them at the door. "He's not in any danger. He was lucky—the bullet really just grazed him. But he needs rest. All he's going to feel up to doing, for three or four days, is sleep. I'll stop by the hotel later and check on how he's coming along."

"Bedfast," Buck muttered, tapping the brim of his tetson nervously against his thigh as the three of them started slowly down Fremont Street. "How the hell does he figure I'm going to track down that imposter of a preacher from a bed?"

Emma glanced at Will and he nodded, knowing exactly what she was thinking. Buck could barely walk, let alone track anyone down. And going after a man who'd already shot him once, a man the sheriff had called a murdering sidewinder, would be dangerous at the best of times.

"Buck," Will said firmly, "there's so much bandaging on your head that you look as if you're wearing a turban. You're in no shape to do anything but sleep."

"I just slept a whole night. I can't waste any more danged time sleeping. That guy tried to kill me. I'm going to have to find him. Catch him by surprise, before he learns I'm still alive and tries again."

"Buck, he won't try again. He just wanted your money and he got it."

Buck stopped walking and turned to face them. "Will, someone hired that skunk to murder me. He told me my case was just a lucky bonus. 'It's killing you that's my job,' he said. That's the last thing I remember."

A cold shiver seized Will. He glanced at Emma. Her eyes were as big as saucers.

"Who...who would want to kill you?" she asked.

"I don't know. I don't know who and I don't know why. But I do know I have to get the Reverend. Because if he's been paid to kill me, he's going to try again."

Will shook his head, trying to organize his thoughts. "Look, Slaughter says the Reverend is actually a lowlife who's going by the name of Butcher Knife Bill. And he holes up in the desert someplace, so he probably won't even be back in town before we're ready to leave—won't find out you're not dead."

"Will, even if that's true, he's got my money. And we need that to get John out of jail. And he's got that blasted bank agreement. It was in my case, too. I have to get it back to show John."

"Buck, you can't go after a killer. You wouldn't know where to start looking and you wouldn't stand a chance against him if you found him. Your best bet has to be just staying in your hotel room, out of sight. That way, he won't learn you're still alive."

"But the money," Buck insisted. "How are we going to help John out without any money? I could wire Dursely Oil for some. But with tomorrow being Sunday, I reckon we'd have trouble getting it soon enough."

"Well, we're not flat broke," Will said, patting what was left of the wad of bills Emma had given him back in Flagstaff. "We don't have enough for any major bribes, but...well, we're going to get John out of that jail somehow. As soon as we get you to the Grand, I'm going to find Wyatt Earp and see what he thinks our best plan would be. Then I'll go and talk to Slaughter—let him know about someone hiring Butcher Knife to kill you. And I guess, while I'm at the jail, I could ask John about that bank agreement. I remember the details clearly enough that he and I can figure out what's going on with it."

"Dammit, Will, I should be involved in all this. I can't be lollygagging in bed while you're out doing everything. It's me that someone wants dead."

"Buck, just take the doctor's advice."

He shook his head. The movement caused him to stagger.

"You see?" Will said. "You aren't fit to go anywhere but to bed."

Buck muttered to himself during the remainder of their walk to the hotel.

"You take my room," Will told him as they started up the stairs. "Then, on the off chance someone does come looking for you, they won't find you where they expect to. And keep your gun in the bed with you. I'll leave a message at the desk for Dr. Goodfellow, so he'll find you all right."

Once they got Buck inside the room, he collapsed onto the bed as if he couldn't walk another step.

"Why don't you go next door while I help him out of his clothes?" Will said quietly to Emma. "Then...oh, hell, Emma, I don't know what you should do while I'm gone. Maybe you should sit in the lobby. At least Buck has a gun, but you don't. And I don't like the idea of your staying up here."

"I wasn't intending to stay up here. I was intending to go along with you."

"Ahh ... Emma, *I'm* going to talk to Wyatt Earp, remember? If we end up planning a jail break, that's strictly men's business."

She eyed him without speaking. He couldn't tell what she was thinking but her expression made him uncomfortable.

"You know what I mean," he said. "You've never even broken a minor law let alone a major one."

"I gave John my gun," she pointed out.

"Well...well, you've already done your part, then."

"Will, I think ..." Emma paused, glancing over at Buck.

Will followed her gaze. The older man was already asleep, clothes and all.

"I think," she continued quietly, "it would be a good idea for me to go with you. I admit I feel peculiar about it. After all, Sheriff Slaughter does seem like a good man. But he's made a mistake, arresting John. And you said yourself, just last night, that breaking the law is likely the only way we're going to see justice done. And if you plot an escape, I *should* be in on it. It's *my* brother in that jail."

"Emma, Wyatt and I could be talking about brandishing guns and maybe knocking people out."

"Well, you told me that in the future, there are women policemen. And women serve in armies. And—"

"Emma, we aren't in the future. And I don't think Wyatt would figure it was appropriate for you to be along."

"Will, from what I've heard about Mr. Earp, he's hardly an arbiter of proper behavior. But that isn't the point."

"Emma, exactly what *is* the point?"

"Well, it's that I've been giving a lot of thought to everything you've told me about the future. Especially since we talked about me maybe going back with you. And one of the serious problems I see is that it's impossible for me to know how I'd cope with all the changes I'd have to face. So the point is that I've decided the best thing to do is try acting differently here—acting as if I were in the future, I mean."

"Ahh...Emma...that just wouldn't work. The reactions you'd get here would be altogether different from those you'd get in 2014."

"I realize that, Will. I know other people won't understand why I'm acting strangely. But regardless of how they react, *here* is the only place I'm going to have a chance to see how I feel about acting differently, isn't it?"

"Ahh..." There was a definite flaw in her logic, but he couldn't easily put it into words. And the last thing he wanted to do was discourage her from gearing herself up to go to the future with him.

"I guess maybe you do have a point, Emma. But not as far as going with me right now is concerned. Even in the future, women don't plan jail breaks."

"Oh? How many jail breaks have you helped plan?"

"Well...none."

"Exactly. So you don't really know who's involved in planning them, do you?"

"Well, it's *mostly* men. I'm damned sure of that."

Emma shrugged. "It won't do any harm for me to go along. If I'm going to learn about being equal to men . . . well, I've never even spoken to a man of Mr. Earp's reputation. So I'd better see how I feel conversing with one. Maybe I should even call him Wyatt. Or do you think that would be far too bold?"

"Ahh . . . why don't you wait and see whether he calls you Emma?"

"Yes, that's a good idea. But I think it's important I get a sense of this sexual equality. All I know about it is what you've told me. And what women like Susan B. Anthony say, of course. So I really do think I'd better have a crack at acting more like the women in your world, doing more things that men do, and see how I make out. So . . . so what do you think, Will?" She smiled uncertainly at him.

He managed to smile back reassuringly. And managed not to say he thought he might have created a monster.

THEY FOUND WYATT EARP in the Oriental. It was easily the most ostentatious saloon Emma had ever seen—ornately flocked red wallpaper, gilt-framed mirrors and a polished mahogany bar that stretched for a mile.

Behind it, a barkeep was wiping glasses. At its far end stood the saloon's only customer, Mr. Earp, his foot resting easily on the bar's brass rail, a glass in his hand and a bottle of whiskey in front of him.

He certainly looked a different man from the one who'd ridden shotgun on their stage. His blond hair had been neatly trimmed, and, instead of dusty trail clothes, he was wearing what had to be a typical gambler's outfit. Of course, Emma didn't know much about gambler's wardrobes, but she doubted many men wore red paisley vests beneath their suit jackets. Or had such heavy gold watch chains.

Will, in jeans and a checkered shirt, struck her as being far more suitably dressed for high noon in Tombstone.

Earp spotted them and raised his drink in a salute.

Emma eyed him surreptitiously as they walked the length of the bar. His mustache was so long and full that his lips were barely visible. She was glad Will was clean-shaven. She couldn't imagine she'd enjoy being kissed by a man with a mustache. But then, she couldn't imagine she'd enjoy being kissed by any man except Will.

"So, Will, you decided to visit Tombstone after all," Earp said when they reached him.

Will nodded. "Got here yesterday. I'm traveling with an oilman named Buck Dursely and Miss Emma McCully, here. I'm a long-standing friend of her family."

"A pleasure, Miss McCully," Earp offered, tipping his hat politely.

Emma smiled at his formality, relieved that she wouldn't feel obliged to try calling him Wyatt. Using Will's Christian name had seemed the natural thing to do because he'd been John's childhood friend. But calling most men anything but mister would cause her discomfort.

"What'd you fancy to wash the trail dust out of your throat?" Earp asked Will.

"Beer's good."

"And you, ma'am?"

"Ahh . . . sarsaparilla, please." Of course, Will had told her that even virtuous women drank alcoholic beverages in the future, but there was no sense in rushing headlong into this experiment.

"Dakota?" Earp called to the barkeep. "One beer and one sarsaparilla."

Will dug into his pocket, but Earp shook his head. "It's on the house. I'm part owner of this place—from back in the old days, when my brother Virgil was marshall down in these parts."

"It . . . it's a very elegant saloon," Emma said, glancing at Will to see if he was impressed that she'd spoken up. She felt disappointed that he didn't seem to think anything of it.

"Why, thank you, ma'am. We did our best. Imported this bar here all the way from London, England. Cost us a hundred-and-twenty thousand dollars."

"Mercy," she murmured as Dakota slapped their drinks onto the bar.

Will took a long sip of beer, then gestured toward the tables. "Mind if we sit down, Wyatt? I'd like to talk to you about something."

Earp picked up his bottle, led them across the room and settled himself with his back to the wall.

"It's about Miss McCully's brother," Will began.

Emma watched the other man as Will told the story. From beginning to end, there wasn't the slightest change of expression on his face.

"So," Will concluded, "between the Law and Order League and Judge Wallace, I figure waiting in jail and standing trial on Monday could be darned hazardous to John's health."

"I'd say your friend's got a heap of trouble all right," Earp agreed. "The more horse thieves Wallace can rid the Territory of, the happier he gets."

"But John's innocent," Emma protested, unable to keep quiet another second. Surely being innocent was what mattered.

"Could be he is, ma'am."

"So shouldn't we hire a lawyer?"

"Ma'am . . . ma'am, I'm afraid you'd just be wasting your money. A man caught riding a stolen horse doesn't have a defense in Arizona. Not that people believe, anyhow. Slaughter just did his job by locking your brother up, and the judge'll do his by stringing him up. 'Fraid that's the way things are."

Emma could feel tears forming. If even Mr. Earp didn't think there was any hope . . .

Will reached across the table and covered her hand with his. "Hang in there, we're not done yet," he murmured, then turned his attention back to Earp. "If John isn't going to get a fair trial, then we have to break him out of that jail. And I figured you'd be able to tell us how to do it."

Earp slowly stroked his mustache with his fingers . . . then shook his head.

Emma's spirits sank even further.

"You don't break anyone out of Slaughter's jail, Will. At least, I don't. And if I don't, there's not many would. Now, if your friend Dursely still had that case full of money... well, we'd probably be able to find someone who'd help you. But not without it."

Will nodded slowly. "All right. If I have to get the money back first, then maybe you can give me some idea about how to find this Butcher Knife Bill."

Earp initially looked surprised at the suggestion. Then he grinned.

If she still had the little Remington, Emma thought, she'd pull it out and shoot that grin right off his face. Didn't he understand how serious this was?

"Will, giving you *some idea* wouldn't help at all. You ever hear of a place called Hole-in-the-Wall?"

"I recall reading something about it. It's a famous hideout. Butch Cassidy and the Sundance Kid used to use it, didn't they?"

"Used to?" Earp repeated. "You hear about something happening to LeRoy and Harry?"

Will sat staring blankly at Earp for a minute, then said, "Ahh ... no. No, I expect they're just fine."

Earp nodded. "Good. Anyhow, the hideout Butcher Knife's using is even better than Hole-in-the-Wall. You could ride right by the entrance without seeing it. And I sure as hell can't draw you a map. Not unless I want the Butcher and a dozen other outlaws gunning for me.

"I'd like to help you out, Will...and you, ma'am," he added to Emma. "But if I told you how to find that place, I'd have to make a damned fast trip out of Tombstone. And hell, I just got here."

"But you *do* know where the hideout is?" Emma pressed.

Earp grinned again. Fleetingly she wondered if she could manage to kill him with her bare hands.

"Ma'am, me and my brothers have taken refuge with some mighty unsavory polecats over the years. And people have been using that hideout for a long time."

"But...but then why doesn't Sheriff Slaughter know where it is?"

"That," Earp said, looking at her as if she were feebleminded, "is why it's called a hideout. So," he went on, turning back to Will, "sorry I can't help. But now that we've discussed your business, how about we pass some time with a game of cards? Like I told you back in Flagstaff, we can always use fresh money at the table."

Emma shook her head, then realized neither man was looking at her. "No, we have to go," she said, starting to rise.

"Not so fast," Will said, glancing at her, his gaze saying to sit back down. "I wouldn't mind some cards. And I've got enough money to pass a fair amount of time."

"What's your game?" Earp asked. "Poker... faro...twenty-one?"

"Will...," Emma said, dragging out his name.

"Twenty-one," he said, ignoring her. "Let's play a little twenty-one."

Earp shoved back his chair and rose. "I'll just get a couple of new decks of cards from Dakota. And you'd like another beer, Will?"

"Sure. Thanks."

"Will," Emma hissed as Earp started for the bar, "what do you think you're doing?"

"I think I'm going to play a little twenty-one with Wyatt Earp," he said. And then he grinned at her.

"Will, don't be ridiculous! We have to go and talk to the sheriff about Mr. Dursely. And we still have to figure out how we're going to save John. Will, my brother's rotting in jail, in danger of being hung the day after tomorrow. And you're going to waste time drinking beer and playing cards? With a gambler like Mr. Earp?"

"That's what I'm going to do, all right, Emma."

"Will, have you lost your mind?" She was, she realized, one vocal tone away from screaming. She made a gigantic effort to control her anger and argue logically. "Will, that man's card playing is legendary. It's all he does these days. And even when he was a lawman, he made more money at poker than at his job. And we can't risk losing our money on top of Mr. Dursely losing his."

"Trust me, Emma. I know what I'm doing."

"Will—"

"Dammit, Emma, will you just trust me? Maybe Wyatt makes his living at poker, but I'm not going to play poker with him, am I?"

"But, Will—"

"Emma, remember what I told you about counting cards in Vegas? Well, twenty-one is just a different name for blackjack. It's my game. I can win against a six-deck shoe and Wyatt's only going to play with a *couple* of decks. So just keep quiet and trust me."

She opened her mouth to object again, but Mr. Earp reappeared at the table, handed Will a fresh beer and settled back into his chair. "House minimum's generally five dollars. That okay?"

Will took their money from his pocket. "Why don't we make it ten?"

"Ten it is. First cards down?"

Will nodded. "Fine with me."

Emma closed her eyes as Mr. Earp began shuffling the two decks into one. She couldn't bear to watch this. She recalled precisely what Will had said about being thrown out of Los Vegas. It had been back in his university days, ten or twelve or even fourteen years ago. And he'd said he *used* to be a numbers freak. He *used* to be able to remember which cards had already been played. But a lot of years had passed. And if he'd lost his knack for remembering, they'd be left with no money. They'd be even worse off than they already were.

She opened her eyes again and glanced across at Mr. Earp, focusing uneasily on the gun strapped to his hip. His reputation didn't stop at his gambling prowess. He was also known for shooting fast and straight. And for having a quick temper.

What if . . . what if Will *hadn't* lost his talent for remembering? If that proved to be the case, they still might find themselves in an even worse predicament.

CHAPTER ELEVEN

MR. EARP REACHED INTO yet another pocket, but this time, his hand came out empty. His face expressionless, he stared across the table at Will—for what Emma was certain was eternity. There was an enormous stack of money in front of Will. Almost all of it had originally been Earp's.

Finally, he spoke. She breathed again at his words.

"Thought I had more with me, but I guess we're going to have to call it a game. How about coming by tonight and giving me a chance to win that back?"

"I'll give you a chance right now, Wyatt."

Earp shook his head. "I'd like to take you up on that, but it's against house rules. Players can only bet what they can put on the table. And being an owner and all, I can hardly break the rules."

"There's something else you could put on the table, Wyatt."

Emma glanced at Will uncertainly, but he was gazing directly at Earp.

"What's that?" Earp asked.

"A map to Butcher Knife Bill's hideout . . . winner takes all." Will pushed the pile of money before him into the center of the table. "And, if I happen to win," he added, "I burn that map before the day's out. And neither Miss McCully nor I ever admit to having gotten it from you."

Earp sat gazing at the money, then his eyes flickered to Emma.

"Never, I'd never say a word," she said quickly, before she could think better of it. She wasn't at all certain she wanted him to agree to Will's bet. Just the thought of them going to that hideout, of trying to get Mr. Dursely's money back from Butcher Knife Bill, frightened her half to death. But if that's what it was going to take to get John out of jail . . . except that . . .

Except that Will had just won all this money. So why did they need to get Mr. Dursely's money back? Mr. Earp had said that if they had enough money they'd be able to find someone to help them. And now they had *this* money. So, mercy, what was Will doing, offering to risk it all? If he lost, they wouldn't have either the map or any money. He hadn't thought this through carefully enough.

"Will?" she whispered urgently.

"Later," he said, his voice barely audible but firm. "Trust me."

She swallowed hard and looked back at Mr. Earp. He was gazing at the pile of money again, a deep frown creasing his forehead.

"All right," he finally said. "Winner takes all. And if you win, you burn the map before the day's out."

"Right," Will agreed. "Have you got a piece of paper, Emma?"

She dug anxiously in her handbag, wordlessly produced paper and a pencil, then watched as Earp drew the map.

He printed instructions here and there on it, folded it closed and put it in the pot. Then he picked up the unplayed cards.

Emma held her breath as he dealt two of them facedown—one to Will, one to himself. They each checked their own, then Earp dealt two cards face-up...a four to Will and a Queen to himself. She simply stared at that four. She'd been watching long enough to know it wasn't a good card.

"Hit me," Will said quietly.

A two fluttered down on top of his four. *Six,* she added silently. She'd give anything to know what his other card was.

"Again," he said.

This time it was a five. *Eleven.* But Will wasn't smiling. Clearly his down card wasn't a ten-count. No magic twenty-one. She bit her lip, almost able to hear him thinking.

"Again," he said.

An eight fell. Emma closed her eyes. That made nineteen points faceup. Unless his first card had been an ace or a two, he was over twenty-one and they'd just lost everything.

"That's fine," he said.

Relief swept her. He hadn't gone over. She opened her eyes again and gazed at Earp. He was staring at his queen, knowing as well as she did that he couldn't stand on less than twenty—that Will had either twenty or twenty-one.

Finally he turned over the next card. A seven. "I'm bust," he said quietly.

Will flipped over the first card he'd been dealt, showing it was an ace.

Earp put down the remainder of the deck, slowly leaned forward and pushed the pot toward Will. "I do believe," he said, "this is the first time I've been bettered by an Easterner."

"Guess I just got lucky," Will said, gathering up the money and stashing it, and the map, away. "I know you seldom get bettered by anyone."

He shoved back his chair, rose and shook Earp's hand. "The map won't be around after today."

"Let's go visit your brother," he added, turning to Emma.

She managed a polite goodbye to Mr. Earp and followed Will out of the saloon.

"Will?" she said when they reached the street. "Will, could you have lost?"

He glanced down and tucked her arm through his own. "I couldn't have busted on the final card I took, if that's what you're asking. I knew the queen Wyatt was showing was the last ten-count. We had a run on them and there were only lower cards left."

"But...but what if he'd drawn a lower card than he did? What if he'd made twenty-one?"

Will grinned at her. "I thought you were trying not to worry about what-ifs, Emma."

She trudged silently along beside him for a minute, a thousand different questions still racing around in her mind. But the ones concerning what would happen when they got to Butcher Knife Bill's hideout were far more frightening than any of the others.

"Will? Exactly what do you have in mind about that hideout? I...I'll help you, of course. We can get me another gun, and I'll go along. But I'm not much of a shot. And Mr. Dursely can't ride in his condition, so there'd only be the two of us."

Will stopped mid-stride, jerking her to a halt, and stood staring down at her. "You don't actually think we're going to that hideout, do you? Lord, Emma, I'm not suicidal."

"But if we're not going there, why did you gamble everything for the map?"

"Because we might be able to get John out of jail with it. And if we can get him out legally, we won't find ourselves with a damned posse on our tails. Emma, just think about how much Sheriff Slaughter might like a look at this map before I burn it."

BRIGHT AFTERNOON SUNLIGHT had replaced San Francisco's usual morning fog. Charles K. Matthews stepped out onto California Street, smiling with satisfaction. The sunshine suited his mood.

This was one Saturday he wouldn't have to listen to his wife complain about his staying late at the bank. There was no need to. The message he'd been hoping for had arrived. In Tombstone, Arizona, one Mr. Buckingham Dursely lay dead. And one Mr. John McCully would shortly be hung as a horse thief.

Now that, Charles reflected once more, his smile growing broader, was a genuine stroke of luck. He'd never have imagined a man as intelligent as McCully would have been stupid enough to steal a horse. But apparently he had been. And that meant the only man who could possibly cause a problem wouldn't be alive to do so.

Charles locked the front door of the First Coastal Bank and began his walk home, absently wondering how long it would be before Mrs. Dursely learned she was a widow.

It could be quite a while, he thought hopefully. Despite his offensive, idiotic name, Butcher Knife Bill had proven intelligent. According to their intermediary, he'd had the brains to cut the Tombstone telegraph wires after sending his own message. Charles smiled again. He appreciated a man with initiative.

And it would certainly be preferable if the bank was able to assume the Dursely Oil shares before news of its president's death reached San Francisco. Seizing control of a company from the estate of a grieving widow would look bad. And it was just the sort of story those newsmen at the *Chronicle* and *Examiner* loved to print.

But if the bank had taken over just *before* the news of Dursely's murder broke, the reporters would probably slant their stories to focus on Mrs. Dursely, rather than First Coastal—portraying her as the sympathetic victim of a terrible patch of ill fortune.

Charles mentally pictured the woman. With her blond hair and blue eyes, she'd undoubtedly look attractive in mourning dress. When he'd met her, during his visit to Mountainview, he'd been surprised at what a handsome woman she was. Dursely's death was unfortunate for her, what with those five children and all....

Maybe the bank should establish a pension for her. Yes, yes, that was a brilliant idea. It would offset any bad publicity about First Coastal taking over Dursely Oil. And they'd be making so much money, when those company shares went back up again, that even setting aside funds for a generous pension wouldn't cause objections from the board of directors.

Another minor problem solved, before it had even arisen, Charles turned his thoughts from Mrs. Dursely to his own wife. It would be pleasant to arrive home early for a change, and not be greeted by a whining voice and suspicious gaze.

"Now that we know where that hideout is, you sure we shouldn't hire horses and head for it?" Buck asked for at least the tenth time.

"I'm certain," Will told him again. "I doubt you should even have exerted yourself to the extent of coming back to your own room."

"I wanted to change my clothes. And I sure didn't figure on you two arriving back and hustling me into bed again—before Doc Goodfellow even left."

"Try to relax, Mr. Dursely," Emma said. "You just stay right there and relax."

"Emma, I don't need to relax no more. Doc Goodfellow told me I was doing fine. You heard him yourselves. He said just to be sure to take those pain pills he left."

"I hardly think he meant you were ready to go chasing outlaws," Will said. "I'm not even sure he should have taken those bandages off so soon. The flesh around that bullet wound is all raw and swollen."

"He said it needed air," Buck explained.

"Well, it doesn't need wind or sun or trail dust. And I thought we agreed that the best thing for you to do was lie low in the hotel."

"I ain't agreed to nothing all day," Buck muttered. "You just keep ordering me around. And I hate like hell to think of that Butcher Knife varmint being out there, knowing he might come after me again. And him getting to keep my money."

"Buck," Will said wearily, "your money wouldn't do you much good if you got killed, would it? For all we know, there are a dozen crooks holed up in that hideout. So let's just leave the action to the sheriff."

"But what if he doesn't come by? I mean, if you didn't tell his deputy about the map, maybe Slaughter won't bother checking to see what you want."

"He'll come," Emma said. "We told the deputy it was the preacher we wanted to talk about. Sheriff Slaughter will know who we mean. And we said it was urgent. And the deputy told us he'd pass the message on the minute Mr. Slaughter got back to the jail."

Buck adjusted his pillow, then looked unhappily at Will once more. "Maybe I should head on over there and talk to John myself."

"Dammit, Buck, will you take it down a thousand? I've told you sixty-three times. The safest thing for you to do is to stay right here. And I've also told you sixty-three times that John and I discussed the loan agreement."

"Humph," Buck snorted. "Sounded to me like you mostly discussed how you won all that money off Wyatt Earp."

"We discussed the loan agreement, too. *In detail.* And John says there's absolutely no way that clause was in the original draft. There was nothing at all about the bank being able to seize your shares. It was exactly what you and I suspected. Someone inserted that before the papers were typed up. Inserted it and hoped you wouldn't notice, I guess."

"And I didn't! How could I have been such a fool dunderhead?" Buck muttered a string of obscenities, then glanced guiltily at Emma and apologized.

"Look, Buck," Will said, "things might not be nearly as bad as they seem. If we...*when* we get John out of jail, the two of you can go directly to San Francisco and see about sorting this out with the bank."

"John said he'd go with me?"

"Hell, he said he never wants to see another horse or cow as long as he lives. After what's happened to him in the past few weeks, he wants nothing more than to get away from the Wild West. So the two of you head straight for the coast. And once you're there, confront the bank officers with the truth. Inserting that clause was probably just one person's bright idea."

Buck shook his head slowly. "I can't imagine it was that Mr. Matthews—the bank fellow who came to Mountainview. He was a real gentleman, Will."

"Well, maybe it was someone else. But I'd be willing to bet it was just one person. I can't believe an entire bank management would go along with that sort of thing. So when John tells them what's happened, I expect you'll be okay."

"You really think so, Will?"

He nodded. "A man who's president of an oil company could cause quite a stink, Buck. You're an important businessman. The newspapers would be happy to run your story. And a major bank can't afford a scandal."

"So all we gotta do then," Buck said, looking hopeful, "is get John outta that danged jail. Think we can manage it, Will?"

Before he could answer, someone knocked on the door. "It's Sheriff Slaughter," a deep voice called from the hall.

"I think," Will said, "we're about to get the answer to your question."

MR. SLAUGHTER was positively itching to see that map. Emma just knew he was. Learning that Butcher Knife Bill hadn't simply set out to rob Mr. Dursely, but had been hired to kill him, had turned the sheriff's face purple.

"I'll get me that son of a bitch if it's the last thing I do," he'd sworn when Mr. Dursely had finished his story.

But it was clear the idea of releasing a prisoner, in exchange for a look at the map, didn't sit well with the sheriff.

He paced across Mr. Dursely's room once more, past Emma's chair to where Will was standing by the window. "This is bribery, Lockhart. I should arrest you for even suggesting it."

Will shook his head. "It isn't bribery, sir. With your reputation for honesty, only a fool would try to bribe you. I'm simply offering to trade you the chance to get Butcher Knife, and whoever else is in that hideout, for the freedom of an innocent man."

"Innocent according to you," Slaughter snapped.

"I wouldn't even suggest this if John were guilty," Will said. "That's why I wanted you to hear what Buck had to say about John's character. And explain again that Miss McCully and I met the fellow who sold her brother the horse—back in Flagstaff. Maybe someone stole that animal, but it wasn't John. He paid good money for it."

The sheriff turned to the bed and eyed Buck. "And you say you trusted McCully to handle your money?"

"Every cent of Broken Hill Mine's finances."

"And how long'd you say he worked for you?"

"Ten years. But I've known him since he was just a whelp. Him and Will here, too. And they's both honest as men come. John would never steal no horse. And if Will says someone told him that John paid for it, then that's what someone told him. And Emma here's a schoolmarm. You can believe her, too," he added, glancing over at her.

"Emma, didn't they make you swear on the bible, at that teacher's college you went to, that you'd never tell even a little white lie?"

She nodded a little white lie to the sheriff.

He began pacing again, then wheeled back to face Will once more. "Why didn't you tell me last night that you had this map?"

Emma flinched at the question, but Will merely shrugged. "I wanted a chance to think things through. And I didn't know, until this morning, that Butcher Knife meant to kill Buck. I figured the same as you did—that it was just a robbery. But now that I know that's not the case... well, we've got a lot stronger reason to care about your getting him behind bars."

Slaughter considered that, then asked another question. "When you won't tell me where you got the map, how do I know it's what you say it is?"

"Fair-enough concern," Will said slowly. "So...if I tell you where I got it, do we have a deal?"

Emma gazed at him uncertainly. Will had given his word that he wouldn't tell where the map had come from. What if he did, and Butcher Knife Bill learned it was Mr. Earp who'd drawn it?

But what if going back on his word was the only way Will could convince the sheriff the map was authentic, the only way to get John out of jail alive?

Slaughter rubbed his jaw. "You understand that the lone reason I'm even considering this is because you three have me believing McCully *is* innocent."

"I understand that," Will said.

Emma realized she was holding her breath. Her eyes were glued to the sheriff. He was considering setting John free!

"All right," he finally muttered.

They'd done it! They'd saved her brother. Emma bit her lip to keep from cheering out loud.

"We'll start with you giving me the map," Slaughter told Will. "And telling me who you got it from."

"That's not quite the offer I made," Will said. "I'll tell you where I got it. But I won't give it to you. I can only let you look at it. As I said before, I'm going to burn it once you've seen it."

"That don't make no sense, son. And I'm not making a deal for just a look."

"Then you aren't making a deal."

Emma stopped silently cheering midcheer and her heart began racing with anxiety.

"Because if I gave you that map," Will went on, "there's always the chance Butcher Knife might end up seeing it—if things went wrong for you at the hideout, I mean. And if he saw it, he'd know it was me who gave it to you. And then things would go wrong for me."

Emma's brain began racing every bit as fast as her heartbeat. Frantically she tried to puzzle out what Will was up to. The sheriff had been ready to set John free, but now Will was throwing obstacles in the way. And what he was saying didn't even make sense. There'd be no reason for Butcher Knife to connect the map to him.

The sheriff stood silently, gazing out the window, then finally turned and nodded. "All right. Just tell me where the map came from, and let me have a good long look at it. And I'll let your friend go. If, when I see the map, I figure it's the real McCoy."

"Oh, it's the real McCoy, sir. It came from Butcher Knife, himself. I'll just go get it out of my room."

Emma's eyes followed Will into the hall. The tight pain that had seized her throat was relinquishing its hold. John was going to be safe, after all. But she still hadn't figured out why Will was playing this game. The map was in his pocket—where he'd stuck it back in the saloon. So what in mercy was he doing?

In two minutes, she knew. He strolled back into the room carrying the worn bible that *Reverend* Bill had forgotten on the stagecoach, flipped it open to the center, and took Mr. Earp's map from it.

"I imagine Butcher Knife drew this for one of his friends," Will said. "But he left his bible on the stage and . . . well, here you are, sir."

The sheriff grabbed the map and stared at it so intently Emma suspected the pencil marks might evaporate under his gaze. She could practically hear his mind memorizing the details.

Finally, with obvious reluctance, he handed the paper back to Will. "Okay, I expect that's authentic, all right."

"So...?" Will pressed.

"So, I'll keep my side of the deal. But I want all of you out of Tombstone five minutes after I set McCully free. In case that damned Law and Order League decides it knows better than I do. And you write down your address for me, Dursely. I just might be getting your money back."

"You feel well enough to travel, Buck?" Will asked.

"I feel just fine. Don't worry none about me. The sooner John and I are on our way to San Francisco the better I'll like it."

"San Francisco?" Slaughter said.

Buck nodded.

"You'll want to take the stage up to Tucson, then, I reckon. And catch the daily train to California from there."

"I reckon," Buck agreed. "How long's the trip?"

"A couple of overnights from Tucson to Los Angeles. Then one more to San Francisco. Now, there's a late stage to Tucson. That'll get you out of Tombstone fast and into Tucson tomorrow morning. So I want you all at the Wells Fargo depot by eight."

Buck checked his pocket watch, then glanced at Will. "That'll give us time to pack and have some dinner first. We can eat right downstairs," he muttered when Will looked as if he were about to object. "Have some of that no-good hotel food."

"Get four tickets to Tucson," Slaughter told them. "I'll bring McCully over just before the coach leaves. Then," the Sheriff added, smiling the first smile Emma had seen on his face, "I've got to get me a posse together. Come morning, I've got a hideout to see about." He nodded to them and strode out, pulling the door shut behind him.

Emma grinned at Will. "You did it! Oh, I'm so happy I'd like to dance around the room." With her eyes, she told him she'd also like to hug and kiss him, if Mr. Dursely weren't watching. "What made you think of putting the map in Butcher Knife's bible? The sheriff didn't doubt for a second that's where you originally got it."

Will shrugged, but he looked mighty pleased with himself. "Well, Slaughter obviously wasn't going to make a deal unless he learned where that map had come from. And I certainly couldn't tell him where we really got it. Aside from having promised Wyatt I wouldn't, I'd hate to have *him* after me almost as much as I'd hate to have Butcher Knife after me. But when Buck dropped that line about you swearing on the bible...well, I heard the word bible and the idea just popped into my mind."

"We make a danged good team, Will," Buck said. "Maybe we should stick together. Like I told you before, I can always use good men. Why don't you think about coming along to San Francisco with John and me?"

"Sorry, Buck, but I've got to be getting back to Mountainview. I have unfinished business there."

A flicker of disappointment crossed Buck's face, but he quickly replaced it with a smile and turned to Emma. "What about you, gal? You could come along with us. This'd be a good chance to visit with your folks for a spell."

"I'll think about it Mr. Dursely," she said, then went back to her room and quickly packed, still considering the suggestion.

A few minutes later, she hurried along the hall.

Will was putting the last of his things into his bag when there was a quiet knock.

"Will?" Emma called from the hall.

He grinned, still amazed that the mere sound of her voice made him happy, and opened the door. She scurried in, shoving it closed again and wrapping her arms around his waist.

He gave her a long, loving kiss, then stood holding her and smiling down. "You know, I really do like the new, modern Emma McCully."

Her face flushed pink, making him smile even more broadly. He hoped she never grew so modern that she overcame her tendency to blush.

"We did it, huh?" he murmured into her hair. "We managed to change history for John. In a couple of hours, we'll have him on his way out of Tombstone. And Buck thinks *he* and I make a good team. Lord, *you* and I make the best team the world's ever seen."

"Which world?" she teased quietly. "Yours or mine?"

"Oh, Emma, aren't we going to make my world ours? Don't you think—"

She reached up and silenced him with her fingertips. "Will, I have to ask you something about that. Now. Before we join Mr. Dursely for dinner."

"All right," he said, wishing she didn't have a million questions, wishing she could just see her way clear to say yes. He reminded himself this was difficult for her, but if she decided not to go with him...oh, Lord, he didn't even want to think about that possibility.

She disentangled herself from his arms and stood holding his hands. "Will...Will, you still have more than a week until August 1."

He nodded. It was nine days away. And if he thought for just an instant, he'd be able to tell her exactly how many more hours he could possibly spend in 1887, exactly how many hours he had left to convince her.

"And going back to Flagstaff will take three days. Or longer, if we had a delay on the stage, again."

"You trying to make me nervous, Emma?"

"No. But that's at least three days, Will. And then another one from Flagstaff to Mountainview makes four."

"And?"

"And...and I have an idea. Will, what if, instead of going back the way we came, we went to San Francisco? It's only three overnights from Tucson. Sheriff Slaughter said two to Los Angeles and one more to San Francisco. And it's only two days by train from San Francisco to Mountainview. I've made the trip several times. So the total would only be one more day's traveling. And all by safe, reliable trains instead of an awful old stage. And I could see my parents that way. They could meet you and...and I could explain, Will. About you . . . about the future . . . so that if I did go back with you they'd realize what had happened to me . . . they wouldn't worry."

He closed his eyes and offered up a prayer of thanks. Emma might be willing to come home with him!

"Oh, Emma," he said, folding her into his arms once more. "Oh, Emma, you make me so happy. I want us to be together more than anything in the world."

"Whose world?" she asked softly.

"Ours. I love you, Emma," he added, capturing her lips in another kiss, thinking that if it weren't for Buck and John, he'd simply stay here and kiss her for the rest of the night. She was undoubtedly the most kissable woman in any world.

Finally, reluctantly, he forced himself to draw away a little.

"Did that kiss mean," Emma whispered breathlessly, "that you'll come to California with me?"

"Emma, if you can consider traveling a hundred and twenty-seven years with me, the least I can do is go to California with you. Besides, I like the thought of safe, reliable trains. Slaughter's got a Wanted poster of the Apache Kid on the jail's wall. I keep seeing his face in my dreams—and getting a mite anxious about making that stagecoach trip all the way back up to Flagstaff."

CHAPTER TWELVE

OUTSIDE THE TOMBSTONE depot, twilight had fallen. The stagecoach was late arriving, but there was still no sign of the sheriff with John.

Beside Emma, Will was tapping the tickets absently against his leg. Mr. Dursely sat on the bench across from them, half asleep, his face pale and drawn.

He jerked awake and shook his head. "Damn, I've got the worst headache of my life. And all I feel like doing is sleeping."

"The doctor said that's all you'd feel up to doing for a few days," Emma reminded him.

They lapsed back into silence. Minutes later, a faint rumble became audible. The sound of a distant stage.

Emma looked at Will, her anxiety turning to panic. "They're not coming. The sheriff changed his mind."

"That isn't it," Will said firmly, taking her hand. "He's just waiting till the last minute—so nobody from that darned Law and Order League realizes he's setting John free."

The words were barely out before Mr. Slaughter was standing in the doorway, his rifle in one hand and Emma's brother beside him. John still looked every bit as dirty and bedraggled as he had in the jail cell. But he was alive and a free man—wearing his gun and carrying his bag.

Emma rushed across the room and threw her arms around his neck. "Oh, John, I'm so glad you're safe." She pressed her face against his chest, tears she couldn't control streaming down her cheeks.

"Hey, Emmy," he murmured in an embarrassed voice, putting his arms around her and patting her back. "Hey, Emmy, cut it out. You're drowning me." Then he bent and whispered in her ear. "Thanks, Emmy. Thanks so much for coming after me."

She simply clung to him, barely listening, while Will and Mr. Dursely slapped him on the back and John thanked them for saving his life. Her brother wasn't going to die. In a few minutes they'd be leaving this horrid town behind. Everything was going to be fine.

The instant the stagecoach rolled to a stop, Sheriff Slaughter hustled them into it. In minutes, the tired horses had been replaced with fresh ones and the stage was departing. They fastened down the curtains, and Emma sat in the darkness between Will and John, certain there was no place on earth she'd rather be. If only she could stay with both of them forever. If only she didn't have to choose between the people she loved.

Before they were two seconds out of Tombstone, Mr. Dursely had curled into the corner across from them and begun snoring.

John reached into his boot and pulled out the Remington. "Here, Emma," he said quietly, "you should take this back. I'm glad I didn't have call to use it, but, sitting in that jail, I was mighty grateful for its company."

Emma tucked the tiny gun into her handbag.

"Hell, Will," John was saying, "I want to hear all about what you've been doing since we were boys. But I'm half dead. Jail's no place to get a decent night's sleep."

Will grinned at his old friend. "After we've waited twenty-five years to catch up, I guess we can wait another night."

"I reckon we'll have to," John said, grinning back. "'Cuz I can hardly keep my eyes open." He pulled his hat low over his forehead and slumped down in the seat.

Emma waited until he began breathing deeply, then snuggled against Will. Last night, in the Grand, she'd felt incredibly lonely in that room of her own.

"What are you thinking about?" Will murmured.

"Oh . . . I'm thinking how amazed John's going to be when you tell him about the future. And when we tell him about us being more than just friends."

"More than just friends," Will repeated. "You know, you have a definite gift for understatement, Emma. You're the farthest thing beyond just a friend that I've ever had."

She smiled at him, and he nuzzled her neck. The sensations that caused made her immensely glad she was far beyond just his friend . . . and made her doubt she could possibly live without him.

"You going to get some sleep, now?" he asked.

She nodded, taking a final, reassuring peek at John, then relaxing against Will. She sat listening to his heartbeat, smiling to herself. And the next thing she knew, daylight was creeping beneath the Concord's window curtains and the stagecoach was slowing. Half asleep, she snuggled more comfortably against Will.

John stretched awake beside her, then unfastened the curtain. "We're here," he announced as the coach jerked to a halt. "This is Tucson. I stayed here a night on my way to Tombstone." He turned from the window and his gaze settled on Emma—his expression a mixture of uncertainty and alarm.

Quickly she escaped from Will's arms and straightened her dress. The very first moment Mr. Dursely wasn't around, they were going to have to explain everything to John. Before he decided his childhood friend was an unprincipled sidewinder and his spinster sister's honor needed to be avenged.

"I should go into the depot, here," Mr. Dursely said as they climbed out of the stage. "If I send a wire to one of my managers in San Francisco, he can have money waiting for me at the train station in Los Angeles. We can't keep spending your money the entire trip, Will."

Will laughed. "Don't worry about it. I've been thinking of it as spending Wyatt Earp's money. Besides, it's Sunday. There'd be no one at the offices to receive a wire."

"Humph," Mr. Dursely muttered. "I've been sleeping so danged much I can't even remember what day we're at."

The four of them made their way through the quiet town to the Tucson station. This early in the morning, it was almost empty.

"I'll go check the departure time and buy our tickets," Will said. "Then we can get some breakfast. I imagine we'll have a fair wait for the train."

He headed off, and Emma followed him with her eyes, watching while he talked with the man behind the ticket counter.

Finally he started back, clutching the tickets, his face grim.

"What's wrong?" she asked uneasily when he reached them.

"What's wrong is that today's Sunday. And the *daily* train Slaughter told us about is only daily six days a week. We're stuck here until tomorrow."

"Today's only the twenty-fourth," she murmured, trying to sound reassuring. "But...but if you think it would be cutting things too close, I'll understand," she forced herself to add.

Please say you'll still go, though, she prayed silently. She didn't know if she could go with Will into the future if she couldn't see her parents first. She needed more time to think. She loved him so much, but what he was asking of her would change her life entirely.

He gazed at her, then finally shook his head. "No, there's enough time, Emma. We'll just get to San Francisco on the twenty-eighth, instead of the twenty-seventh. But that's still four days before August 1."

She smiled her relief, wordlessly saying how grateful she was.

"Having to stay over here's not real terrible, is it?" John said. "Hell, I'd sure like to get a bath. And spend tonight in a real bed."

"Damnation!" Buck swore. "It *is* real terrible, John. Those danged stocks could start dropping lower again tomorrow, and we're going to be wasting another day."

"Buck," Will said, "like it or not, we're stuck here overnight. So we may as well get hotel rooms. I guess," he added, turning to John, "this'll give us plenty of time to catch up on the past twenty-five years."

"JOHN," WILL SAID, grinning across to where his friend was sitting on the edge of the bed, "if you keep shaking your head every time we tell you something more, your neck'll get so stiff you won't be able to move it."

"Tarnation, Will, how can you expect me to be anything but plumb amazed at all these things you're saying? Just this computer alone would have been enough to astonish me."

"You can keep it when I go back."

"Really?"

"Sure. You use the sun's rays to recharge the batteries, so they'll last a lifetime. And it'll give you and Buck an edge when it comes to taking on Rockefeller."

"When? You mean *if*, Will. If there's still a solvent Dursely Oil by the time we get to San Francisco."

"Oh, I think things will work out. All it'll take is your testimony about what was and wasn't in the original bank agreement. Then it'll be Dursely Oil taking on Standard Oil. Sort of like David taking on Goliath. You know, I really envy you the prospect of that excitement."

"Well, I wish I was looking forward to it more than I am. But I'm a mite tired of running a business. That's why I wanted to try something different. Arizona didn't exactly give me the kind of adventure I wanted, though."

John gazed back at the computer, ran another calculation, then chuckled. "I sure understand why you didn't try explaining time-travel to Buck. Even if you showed him this...well, he doesn't know enough about numbers to realize how incredible it is."

Will shrugged. "Initially I didn't intend to tell anyone. But when Emma and I...well, I had to tell her."

"So help me, Moses, that's mighty hard to believe, too. I mean, my sister has nothing to do with men for her entire life, then falls in love with one who's living in a different century. Imagine spending the rest of your life in the future, Emmy. Lord, now that's exciting. But...you know I'm not good at saying this sort of thing...but if you decide to go, Emmy, we'd really miss you."

"And I'd miss you," she said quietly, glancing down at Will from her perch on the stuffed arm of his chair.

He took her hand, squeezed it reassuringly, then looked back across the room. Now that John had cleaned up and shaved, it was easier to see young Johnnie in the adult face. Not only those familiar, smoky-blue eyes and his pronounced jaw, but also that faint scar on his chin. He'd gotten the gash that had become that scar when they were boys. They'd been climbing a cliff, and Johnnie had fallen on a jagged rock.

"Hell, even if Emma doesn't go, I'm going to miss *you*, Will," John said. "After all these years you show up, and you'll be gone again in only a few days. Doesn't seem right."

"I'm just glad I could come at all."

"Hell, you can't be half as glad as I am. You know sometimes, sitting in that jail, I could actually feel a rope around my neck. And then, when you told me about seeing my gravestone, I could feel it again. Lord, I sure wasn't looking forward to dying of hemp fever."

"Well, you're perfectly safe from dying now, John," Emma told him. "We changed your history."

John shook his head again. "Damn, but this time-travel is hard to puzzle out. I was hung tomorrow, on July 25. But according to Will, tomorrow was a hundred and twenty-seven years ago. Just can't get the logic of that to set right in my brain. Strange, though..."

John rubbed his jaw thoughtfully, then looked over and caught Will's eyes. "Will, you understand exactly how all this works, huh?"

"Well, no, not exactly. I mean, I haven't got a handle on all the details. But I understand it well enough. You don't have to worry. If Emma goes back with me, she'll be perfectly safe."

"Ahh...that wasn't actually what I was thinking about. I was just kind of wondering...wondering about the wording on that gravestone. *Killed,* I mean. Strange that's what it would say when I was strung up as a horse thief."

"That occurred to me, too," Will admitted. "I thought about it when we first learned you were in jail, when we first knew you faced hanging. And I decided that whoever wrote the inscription figured *killed* sounded better than *was hung.* Kinder to your memory—that might be the best way of putting it."

John nodded slowly. "I guess that could be it. But when you say you understand how this works *well enough*... I mean, with tomorrow being July 25, you're absolutely certain something can't still happen? That maybe I wasn't actually hung at all...in the past...the past that's really tomorrow, I mean? You're sure I couldn't have died some other way?"

Emma's hand tightened on Will's, and the words *absolutely certain* began echoing uneasily in his mind. But no, nothing would happen tomorrow. He and Emma had thought this through carefully, before they'd even gotten to Tombstone.

And they'd worked out the logic. In the course of history, John had been hung as a horse thief. Hell, he'd been locked in that cell and charged with horse theft, with a hanging judge on the way. How much more obvious could the situation have been?

So, by preventing the hanging from taking place, they'd saved his life. They'd changed a tiny piece of the universe when they'd persuaded Slaughter to free him.

"Will?" Emma asked, gazing at him with troubled eyes. "Will, it isn't possible that we figured this out wrong, is it? Is it possible there *could* be something tomorrow? That John didn't actually die by hanging?"

Will slowly shook his head, not wanting to consider that possibility. But the words echoing in his mind had changed from *absolutely certain* to *absolutely uncertain*.

"Will?" Emma said again. "It isn't possible something else could happen, is it?"

He tried to admit he didn't know, but the sentence stuck in his throat.

"Maybe," Emma murmured uneasily, "we shouldn't take that train tomorrow. Maybe we should stay right here in the hotel."

"I doubt that would help," John said. "If fate intends something to happen, it's going to happen. I could get killed in a hotel as easily as on a train."

"Look," Will finally managed, "I'd say the odds have to be that we've already got this beat. But...well, we all have guns. So, just in case, it might be a good idea to stick together from midnight on. And stay alert."

"What...how are we going to explain that to Mr. Dursely?" Emma asked. "If we tell him we're worried, if we tell him why, I mean, he'll think we're crazy."

Will glanced at John.

He shrugged anxiously. "If something *were* to happen, Buck's in no shape to be much help. So I reckon the easiest thing would be just not to say anything to him. Besides, I'll probably be fine."

John's eyes said he wasn't at all convinced that was true. So did Emma's. And Will didn't need a mirror to tell him what his own eyes reflected.

THE FOUR OF THEM stood at the far end of the platform, watching the train approach. Emma eyed it nervously as it chugged the final distance to the station. They'd made it safely through the night, through the early morning hours of July 25. But was there evil lurking on this train? Something that could kill her brother?

The locomotive drew abreast of the platform and slowly continued on toward them, a lazy, charcoal haze from its smokestack drifting back over the mountain of coal in the tender. Behind that was the baggage car...the diner...four Pullman Palace Cars...finally, a string of unreserved coaches and the caboose.

When the locomotive reached the stretch of rail beside them, the wheels finally squealed to a halt. Arriving passengers began getting out. Someone opened the baggage car, and porters started unloading luggage. A pile of bags sat nearby, waiting to be loaded on.

Inside the locomotive's cab, a fellow wearing soot-covered overalls began shoveling fresh coal into the firebox. Another man, whose cap identified him as the engineer, was fiddling with something. He glanced out, gave Emma an appreciative look, then turned his attention back to whatever he was doing.

"Everything seems to be under control in there," John said. "But let's stay out here for a bit and watch what's going on."

Mr. Dursely glanced at him. "You don't want to get our seats, first thing?"

"How about you going ahead and doing that?" Will said.

"Sure."

Mr. Dursely started off, and Emma watched him until he stepped onto the little platform of the first Palace Car and disappeared inside. Then she turned to Will and John. They were both surveying the activity.

"Exactly what are we looking for?" she asked.

Will shrugged. "Anything that seems unusual, I guess."

"Like those soldiers?" John said, nodding at four men in cavalry uniforms who were pulling a large wagon. They stopped and began loading wooden crates and boxes from the wagon into one end of the baggage car.

John headed over to them, Will and Emma on his heels.

"We got the cavalry riding along to Los Angeles with us?" John casually asked one of the men.

"Wish you did," he said, wiping his brow. "Hear Californy's nice." The man glanced past John as he spoke and suddenly snapped to attention.

"Sir!" he said, saluting sharply.

The other soldiers immediately followed suit, almost dropping one of the crates in their haste.

Emma turned and saw a man who seemed vaguely familiar, a distinguished gentleman with a hawklike nose, a neat white beard and a ramrod-straight back. She guessed he was in his sixties. She also guessed that he would happily take on most men in their forties—and best them.

He was wearing an army uniform covered with more gold braid, medals and general's stars than she'd ever seen in one place. She glanced at his face again and realized who he was. He had frequent speaking engagements these days, and his picture had probably been in every magazine in the country.

He returned the soldiers' salutes, then stepped nearer. "Springfield repeaters?" he demanded, gesturing at the crates.

"Yes, sir!" one of the men replied.

"Where they bound for?"

"Fort Yuma, sir!"

"And a whole passel of ammunition."

"Yes, sir!"

The general smiled slightly. "Good. I'm traveling to Yuma myself. And arriving on the same train as these supplies will make my visit there more pleasant. General Crook gets tetchy as a teased snake if he runs low on ammunition. Carry on, men," he added, starting off along the platform once more.

"Yes, sir!" they chorused, saluting again.

"Hell," one of them muttered once the general was out of earshot. "Who'd ever have figured to see the old man himself?"

"Who *was* that?" Will asked the soldiers.

They shot him looks of pure disbelief. "That's General Sherman," one of them finally said.

"Really?"

Will, Emma realized, was grinning the same amazed-looking grin he'd worn the first time he'd seen Wyatt Earp.

"You mean General William Tecumseh Sherman?" he demanded. "Of the Atlanta campaign? Of the march to the sea?"

"I mean," the soldier replied stiffly, "General William Tecumseh Sherman who was general in chief of the army until he retired."

"Yes," Will said quickly. "Yes, of course."

"Let's move on," Emma murmured, taking his arm.

"I didn't know he ended up general in chief of the whole army," he was muttering. "In *Gone with the Wind,* he was only a major general."

John shot a final glance at the baggage car, then started along with them. "I just wish," he said, "I knew what might go wrong."

"Hell," Will offered, grinning again, "I've decided to stop worrying. Nothing's going to go wrong when we've got the retired general in chief of the army on our train."

Emma managed a smile, wondering how much of Will's newfound confidence was real and how much was an attempt to make John less anxious.

They walked down to the first Palace Car and boarded it. It was about a third full—mostly men, only a couple of other women. From the doorway, Emma couldn't see anyone who seemed the least suspicious-looking. And, sitting near the far end, was General Sherman himself.

"See," Will said to John. "We've even got him in our coach. That had to be a good omen. Hell, we're going to be perfectly safe—and comfortable to boot. This sure beats the devil out of those unreserved coaches we took to Flagstaff, Emma. Even a bathroom in this one," he added, looking through the partially open doorway.

"Even two," she told him. "One at each end of the coach. And at night, the porter turns each pair of seats into a bed. Those panels between the windows have curtains stored behind them that draw around to form walls."

When they reached the seats Mr. Dursely had saved, they found him sleeping again, his jacket balled against the window as a pillow.

Emma absently thought that Mrs. Dursely was going to have the vapors when she saw that head wound.

And she'd have Mr. Dursely visiting a San Francisco doctor within the hour.

They sat quietly, waiting for the train to leave, John checking his pocket watch every minute or two. Emma could see how desperately he wanted the entire day to fly by.

He noticed her eyeing him and shrugged. "It's a long time till midnight."

"We'll make it," she murmured. "All of us."

Eventually the conductor shouted "boooaard," and the whistle shrilled. A minute later their coach jerked into motion. The train chugged along slowly, then gathered speed as they reached the outskirts of Tucson and started off across the desert.

Emma gazed out into the glare but soon found herself watching John again, praying their worries were groundless.

They rocked along for miles, the coach as peaceful as a church, its passengers lulled by the rhythmic clickity-clack of the wheels, baked into drowsiness by the sunshine streaming through the windows.

Next to John, Mr. Dursely was still dozing. Beside Emma, Will was quiet. She knew he was fully alert, though. She sensed the same tension in him that she was feeling.

John's gaze slowly and regularly swept the coach, but everyone except the three of them seemed at least half asleep. He caught Emma's eye and smiled at her. "Calm as toads in the sun," he murmured. "Sure hope they all stay like—"

His words were lost in the explosion of a million sounds—a screeching whistle, the squeal of metal against metal, the shouts of people being jolted from sleep, being hurled from their seats as the train swayed wildly, threatening to tip, skidding along the rails, trying to stop but forced to fight its own momentum.

Mr. Dursely was pitched to the floor between the seats. Will threw himself across Emma, pinning her safely. Her gaze flew to John. He was clutching the armrest, braced against the seat, his eyes darting everywhere at once.

Men yelled. Bodies thudded. Wheels keened against rails. The whistle blasted again—the long, piercing wail of a wounded beast. And finally the train shuddered to a halt.

A last quiver and the coach was still. For a split second all was deathly silent. Then the air filled with shocked expletives and shouted questions. Somewhere, a woman was sobbing.

Will and John were both on their feet, looking around. Mr. Dursely pulled himself up from the floor, muttering.

Emma slid quickly across to the window and peered out. Nothing. Nothing but sun and sand and heat so hot it was dancing in the air.

"It's a tree trunk," a man shouted from the other side of the coach.

Emma turned. The man who'd spoken was staring out a window, gazing toward the front of the train.

"A tree trunk's fallen across the tracks," he elaborated. "That's why we stopped."

"There isn't a tree growing around here for miles," John snapped quietly, drawing his gun. "If there's one across the tracks, someone dragged it there."

Will stared at his friend, seeing his own horrified thoughts on John's face. The train had become a trap. A death trap. *This* was how John got killed.

No! Will swore silently. John wasn't going to be killed. Not after everything they'd gone through to prevent it. Somehow, they all had to get out of whatever this was alive. He eased his Colt from its holster, glanced at Emma, and motioned her down between the seats.

She'd barely sunk to the floor when the door at the front end of the coach burst open. Someone shoved the engineer inside. He stumbled against a seat, grabbing it to keep from falling.

Behind him, in the doorway, stood a man—young, dressed in a blue cavalry uniform, a yellow kerchief tied rakishly around his neck, an ammunition belt slung on his hips, a rifle in his hand, pointed at the engineer's head.

Will stared, his heart pounding. He recognized that man. Straight black hair past his shoulders, held with a headband. High cheekbones, a defiant expression and a mouth that slashed across his face in a straight, cruel line. This time, though, the man's face was in burnished, copper color—not the black-and-white it had been on the Wanted poster in Slaughter's jail.

Will glanced sidelong at John. "The Apache Kid," he said quietly, his throat tight.

John's expression grew even more tense.

A second Indian appeared behind the Kid, also brandishing a rifle, then a third.

Murmurs of fear rippled through the coach.

"Those are repeaters they've got," John murmured. "Don't try anything. They could kill everyone in here without reloading."

"Guns off!" the Kid shouted. "Take your guns off and lay 'em in the aisle. Then your valuables. Fast!"

The men quickly began unstrapping their gun belts.

Will bent down and put his Colt in the aisle, then glanced back at Emma. She was still crouched on the floor, looking as terrified as he felt. His stomach muscles were clenching and reclenching like crazy.

"Valuables!" the Kid shouted. "Money. Watches. Rings. Everything."

Emma fumbled with her locket, hands trembling, and finally passed it to Will. He put it, his money and his signet ring onto the floor, adding them to one of the little piles. Buck and John tossed over their watches.

The Apache Kid started down the aisle, using his rifle to prod the engineer ahead, focusing a cold, black stare on each passenger in turn.

Following, the second Indian tucked his gun under one arm and began shoving the hand guns and valuables into a large sack. The third Indian took a few steps, then turned and began easing along backward, covering their rear, training his rifle from side to side.

The passengers stood motionless, frozen with collective fear.

The Kid reached Will and John . . . glanced down between them at Emma.

"You," he said, pointing his gun at her. "You come with me."

"No," Will protested, starting to move. Instantly the Kid's rifle barrel was pressing into his stomach. He stopped breathing, waiting for death.

Behind him, Emma scrambled to her feet. She pushed between him and John, trembling.

The second Indian scooped the last of the loot into his sack, then trained his gun on Will. The Kid shifted his to Emma, motioning her forward.

She shot Will a quick, terrified glance, then started down the aisle.

"Nobody move," the Kid snarled over his shoulder. "We have men posted outside the train. Anyone sticks his head out gets it blown off."

With his gun, he forced Emma and the engineer the final few feet to the end of the coach. The other two Indians continued walking backward, covering the remaining passengers.

Will thought frantically. The Remington was in Emma's purse. That was the only weapon they had left. Slowly, praying neither Indian facing him would notice, he began sliding his foot across the floor to where her bag was lying.

"Don't!" John hissed from the corner of his mouth. "You'll be no help to her dead."

CHAPTER THIRTEEN

THE THREE INDIANS disappeared into the next coach with their hostages. Instantly the air was alive with shocked murmurings.

Will grabbed Emma's handbag from the floor and began searching in it for Remington, swinging into the aisle as he dug through her things. But before he could take a step forward John grabbed his arm, twisting him back.

"Will, we have to think first."

"There's no time," he said frantically, pulling away and whirling toward the end of the coach again. His fingers found the gun and he yanked it out, tossing the purse aside and breaking into a run, vaguely aware John was right behind.

"Hold it!" an authoritative voice boomed. Six feet ahead, General Sherman stood solidly blocking their path. "You don't go after Indians with a peashooter! Especially not after the Apache Kid. You need a plan."

Will stopped, his mind racing. He couldn't think of a plan. All he could think was that he had to save Emma. "What?" he demanded. "What plan?"

"First you calm yourself, boy, or you'll be dead quicker than a dose of salts works."

"All right. All right," he managed, desperately trying to control his panic. "All right, I'm calm. Now what?"

"Now you listen. There's only three of those Indians—plus likely one more, watching their horses. So—"

"General!" a passenger interrupted excitedly. "The Kid said there were others posted outside the train."

Sherman shot the man a smoldering glare. "You believe *me,* not some renegade Apache. If there were more, one of them'd be guarding the engineer up front. They wouldn't have brought him along with them. You two with the lady?" he demanded, his gaze flashing back to Will and John.

"And me!" Buck called out from behind them. "I'm with her, too. I can help."

Sherman's gaze swept the three of them, clearly assessing. "All right," he said to Will. "Give your friend at the back there that .22.

"Now!" he snapped when Will hesitated. "Dammit, boy, don't you know who I am?"

"Yes, sir!" Will wheeled around and passed Buck the little gun.

"Good," Sherman said, glancing around at the other passengers. "I need a volunteer—a man who knows horses."

Several men spoke up.

"I was born on a horse," said a tall young man, stepping into the aisle.

Sherman nodded. "All right. You, me and these two," he said, gesturing at Will and John, "are going to get off this train and see what we can do. And you," he added to Buck. "When those Indians come back through, you come after them. Keep your distance. Don't even go into the dining car till they're already out the far end. And when you get up front, you'll just have to see what's happening. But we might need the element of surprise that a shot from behind them would give us."

"There's more of us'd come with you now, sir," someone called to him.

"No, I need your help in here—so the Kid doesn't realize any of us are missing. Once they've finished in the car behind this one, I want some of you to go back there. And send some of those folks up here. I saw a couple of cavalry officers getting on that coach. Make sure they come up here in case the Kid remembers seeing my uniform. And some of you go into the diner. Nobody be where they were five minutes ago." Without another word, the general pushed past Will and John and started for the front of the coach.

Will simply stared after him, unable to make his legs follow. The Indians had taken Emma in the other direction. That was the way he wanted to go. He had to get to her. He turned.

"For God's sake," John snapped, jerking him roughly around again. "You can't do it alone. And if anyone can help us save her, he can."

John started after Sherman, and Will forced himself to do the same, trying to banish the image of Emma's terrified expression from his mind. He had to get a grip. He had to do exactly what the general told him to. That was his only hope of saving the woman he loved.

But each step was taking him farther away from her. And she needed him. She was in mortal danger. And she'd once told him that Apaches loved to torture their victims. He began praying she'd be all right.

Sherman reached the end of the coach and glanced back at the other three. "We'll go through the dining car, rather than outside just yet. Keep an eye out either side for the Indians' ponies. They'll probably be right up near the locomotive."

They hurried, single file, through the diner, past several frightened-looking waiters and passengers who weren't touching their food.

The closer they drew to the front of the train, the louder the hissing sounds from its steam engine. But Will was certain his heart was pounding so loudly it could be heard above the noise. "There they are," he said, adrenaline surging as he spotted horses waiting to one side of the engine.

The general stopped in his tracks and hit the floor as if he were twenty years old. The others followed suit. "All right," he said quietly, peering out the bottom of a window. "Just what I figured. One Indian on horseback holding three other ponies. And he's watching to the back of the train."

Yes, Will told himself. Just what the general had figured. Maybe, just maybe, there was a chance.

Sherman reached into his boot and pulled out a long, gleaming knife. "You," he said, pointing to the tall young man. "Stick with me. We'll round the front of the locomotive and surprise him from behind. I'll take him. You make sure none of those ponies run off. The Kid would see them for sure.

"And you two," he ordered, nodding at Will and John, "follow us along until you reach the door of the baggage car, then get inside." He paused, slipping his hand up onto a table and retrieving a dinner knife that he handed Will. "You'll have to take care of the lock with this. There are Springfields in that coach I want uncrated. Get as many as you can loaded for action. The engine noise should cover you, but be quiet. And when you hear a knock, open the door on the far side of the car."

They crept through the final few yards of the dining car on hands and knees, below window level, then out onto the sand and along the opposite side of the train from where the waiting Apache sat.

Will had never been so terrified in his life. One mistake and that Indian would sound an alarm. One mistake and a horse would go racing off across the desert, alerting the Kid. One mistake and Emma would die.

His throat ached with fear. He told himself not to think about her, to concentrate on the job he'd been assigned. But if anything happened to her... *don't think!* he began silently repeating.

They reached the door of the baggage car, and Will started digging at the lock with the knife. Sweat was pouring from his body and his hands were shaking. He was certain he wouldn't be able to break the mechanism.

Incredibly he did.

John shot him an anxious grin when the lock gave and the door shifted a few inches. Slowly they slid it open a couple of feet. The rumbling noise it made sounded like thunder, while the hiss of the engine suddenly seemed as quiet as a snake's warning. But there was no alerting cry from the Indian.

Will and John scrambled up into the car. Tools were fixed to one wall—among them, a crowbar. Using it, they quickly opened a crate of guns, then a box of ammunition.

"You know how to load these?" Will whispered.

John nodded and silently demonstrated how the cartridges went in. "You got any idea how to fire them?"

"No," Will admitted.

John moved the lever under the stock, demonstrating the proper motion. "You get about twelve shots a minute."

They had a dozen guns loaded and were prying the top off another case when there was a tap on the far side of the car.

"He's done it!" John said. "That's the signal."

Will leapt across a crate, unlocked the door and slid it open. General Sherman and the younger man were waiting outside, the front of the general's navy tunic stained almost black with perspiration.

The four ponies stood quietly, their leads disappearing into the space between the tender and baggage car. Will glanced a question at the young man.

"Tied 'em to the connection link," he explained. Then he bent down and, from beneath the train, dragged out the blood-drenched body of an Indian.

Will felt ill. He looked at Sherman again and realized it was blood, not perspiration, that had stained his uniform.

Wordlessly the two men picked up the body and heaved it into the baggage car.

"Get it out of the way," the General snapped, starting to scuff sand with his boot, rapidly covering bloodstains on the ground.

Will swallowed his revulsion, then grabbed the dead man by his arms and tugged him along to the end of the car.

When he turned back, Sherman and the younger man were inside, clutching rifles. The door on one side had already been closed and John was sliding the other one shut, sealing them into a dark grayness that was broken only by light filtering in through the odd crack.

"Now what?" Will demanded of the general, trying to keep both his eyes and thoughts from wandering back to the dead body.

"Now you and your friend grab a couple of guns. Then we sit tight. If we hear any shots, we hightail it back along the train. If not, we just wait. Those Indians won't leave without having a look-see at what's in here. And they'll come up on the horses' side and shoot that lock open. So take cover behind something and stay there."

Will's heart began hammering even more fiercely. "What about the hostages?"

"Boy, we'll do our best not to get them killed. If I can, I'll give the Kid a chance to surrender. But we just got to wait and see what happens when the time comes."

Oh, God, Will thought in horror. That meant wait and see if the Apaches killed Emma. He glanced at John and remembered the date. Oh, God, it meant wait and see if the Apaches killed Emma *and* John.

THEY'D BEEN WAITING forever, crouched tensely in the dark baggage car.

Will had tried to keep his thoughts from Emma, but it was impossible. He'd never loved anyone the way he loved her. If Emma was killed, he didn't want to live. He'd rather die avenging her death.

But... but what if she were already dead? What if the Apache Kid had...? No! They'd have heard shots.

He pictured Sherman's silent knife, the Indian brave lying dead at the end of the car, and felt sick. What if...?

And then his speculations exploded in a deafening barrage of gunfire. Close. So close he could smell the powder. So close the car's door was shattering under the rain of bullets. He could feel the air move as they whizzed by his head, could hear the soft thud of flying wood chips landing around him.

The suddenness of it stopped his heart for an instant. By the time it started again, daylight was streaming through the splintered lock area. Then someone shoved what remained of the door along its track and sunlight blazed into the dimness of the car, blinding him.

"Throw up your hands!" Sherman screamed, leaping to his feet, a dark figure against the bright light.

Only half his words were shouted before guns began blasting again. From outside. From inside. Will frantically began pumping his rifle at the open doorway, knowing it was insane. Emma was probably out there, maybe in the line of fire. But he didn't know what else to do and didn't stop firing until the gun had ceased its furious vibrating and was silent in his hands.

He grabbed a second rifle and spun halfway back toward the door before he realized all was quiet.

He tore across the car, skidded to a stop against the far wall and peered out the side of the opening, terrified what he might see.

Two bodies lay motionless on the sand. Two Indians. Their bag of loot was spilled around them.

The engineer was a few feet to one side—half lying, half sitting. One of his shoulders was drenched in blood, but he wasn't dead.

Will's gaze swept away from them, searching for Emma . . . finding her. She was alive!

Simultaneously he felt a surge of relief and one of horror. She was alive, but still the Apache Kid's prisoner. He stood behind her, his rifle at her head. Fear had drained the color from her face, making it deathly pale. The Kid's bronzed arm was wrapped around her neck.

They were standing by the ponies, not eight feet from Will, so close he could see that Emma was trembling.

Somehow, the Kid had freed one of the horse's leads and had it secured under his foot.

"I told you to throw up your hands, Kid," Sherman shouted.

Will's eyes flashed to the general. His rifle was aimed at Emma and the Indian.

"You can't shoot!" Will hissed. "You'll hit *her!*"

"You want me to let him go, boy? Let him take her with him? You know what he'd do to her?"

Oh, God! Will looked back at Emma's terrified face. She'd be better off dying quickly than being tortured by Apaches. But he couldn't let her die.

A sense of utter helplessness seized him. He clutched his rifle, immobilized by uncertainty. If they shot, they'd kill Emma. If they didn't . . .

Slowly the Kid bent down for the reins, pulling Emma with him. Slowly he straightened up again, the horse's lead in his hands.

And then Will caught a motion at the front of the engine. An instant later a single shot rang out.

The Apache Kid whirled around, still clutching Emma to him.

Will flung himself through the air, knocking them both to the ground with a flying tackle.

Rifle fire began blasting again. The Kid was no longer holding Emma. Will rolled on top of her and prayed.

Bullets were zinging into the ground around them. Men were yelling. Horses hooves passed so close they sprayed sand into Will's face.

But as fast as the action had begun, it ceased. One final burst and the guns were silent. The only sound was of a horse galloping off, the thunder of its hoofs fading rapidly into nothingness.

"Dammit!" Sherman's voice boomed. "He's gotten away."

"Will?" Emma whispered from beneath him, her voice shaky.

"Oh, Lord, Emma, you're okay," he managed, hugging her against the sand, barely able to believe she was really alive.

"What happened?" she murmured. "What made him let go of me?"

"Someone shot at him from behind," Will said, shifting to his knees, then drawing Emma up without releasing his hold on her. He just might never let her go for the rest of their lives. His arm tightly around her, he turned toward the front of the engine.

"Mr. Dursely!" she cried. "Mr. Dursely, you saved my life."

Buck stood grinning at them, the little Remington still in his hand. "Just followed the general's orders, Emma. He said you might need the element of surprise."

"Oh, Will," she murmured, clinging tightly to him. "You saved my life, too. I didn't think...I thought..."

A trickle of tears escaped down her face, and Will gently brushed them away. "You're all right, Emma. Everything is all right."

She looked at the baggage car, and Will's gaze followed hers.

"John?" she murmured.

Two men were standing in the car. Only two. Sherman and the tall young man.

"John?" Emma repeated, her voice strangled.

"Oh, Lord, Emma," Will said, his gaze once again sweeping the bodies that lay outside the train. Then a third man appeared inside the car, staggering across to Sherman. It was John.

"FIVE, FOUR, THREE, TWO, one...midnight!" Will whispered in the darkness. "July 25, 1887, is officially history. In both our centuries."

Emma hugged John, laughing quietly, not wanting to wake Mr. Dursely in the next sleeping cubicle. Although it wasn't likely anything would wake him. He'd practically been asleep on his feet by the time the Pullman porters had worked their magic, transforming the seats into beds and drawing the heavy curtains—turning the Palace Car into a series of tiny bedchambers.

And surprisingly, sounds didn't carry at all from one compartment to another. The thick fabric of the curtains would muffle any sound softer than a good loud scream, and with the constant clickity-clack of the train, even a scream might not be heard.

"I wish we had champagne to celebrate with," Will said.

"We don't need champagne," she told him. "Nothing could make this any better."

"Oh, I don't know," John said. "I'd feel a mite better without this bullet hole in my arm."

"Don't be a baby," Emma teased. "You were incredibly lucky to have the bullet go straight through without hitting anything."

"It hit *me!*"

"Oh, John, you know what I mean—hitting nothing but flesh. Why, I'll bet you won't even have to wear that sling for long."

"Humph," John muttered. "I just hope that the next time I'm *incredibly lucky,* I don't end up in pain. But at least I got through the day alive. You know, right up until midnight, I was still worrying. Figured I'd survived a hanging judge and the Apache Kid, only to smother to death because you two insisted on crowding in here with me."

Emma smiled, but John was right. The three of them squeezed onto his bed did make things awfully crowded. She glanced at the curtains that defined the sleeping cubicle, wondering if they should try to draw one back.

Not the one on Mr. Dursely's side, of course. But her bed was on the other side. And Will's was next to that.

She was about to suggest they rearrange things when John said he'd like to get some sleep. So she simply kissed him goodnight. Then she and Will slipped out between the curtains—off the end of the bed and into the aisle.

It was almost as dark out there as in John's bed-chamber. The overhead gas lamps had been turned down so far they were emitting only a dim glow.

While she pulled John's curtains tightly together, Will wrapped his arms around her from behind and nuzzled the back of her neck.

His touch sent quivers through her. His body pressing hers made her feel deliciously warm and alive. It was difficult to believe that only this afternoon she'd been certain she was going to be killed, that she'd never be with Will again, that she'd die without knowing how it felt to love him completely.

"I love you so much," he whispered, his words echoing her feelings. "So very, very much, Emma. Even before today, I couldn't imagine what I'd do if you didn't come home with me. And now...oh, Emma, when I thought I was going to lose you, I realized if that happened I wouldn't want to live."

She turned in his arms and he kissed her, transforming her body to liquid. She felt so wonderful when Will held her, so delightfully dizzy when he kissed her, that she wished they could simply stay like this forever. But they couldn't, of course. Not here, like this, in the middle of the train.

Reluctantly she drew away. "I guess it's bedtime," she sighed.

"I guess," he repeated, his arms still around her waist, his gaze telling her he wanted to go on holding her every bit as much as she wanted him to.

Will forced his arms to his sides and forced his feet to move the few steps along to Emma's bedchamber. She opened the curtains, turned back and wished him good-night.

He merely nodded, jamming his hands into his pockets so he wouldn't reach for her again.

He went along to the bathroom, on the far side of his cubicle, lost in thought. "Even before today," he'd told her, "I couldn't imagine what I'd do if you didn't come home with me." But she hadn't responded with the words he'd wanted to hear. She hadn't responded with any words at all. And if she hadn't decided by now that she loved him enough to go with him . . .

He rinsed his hands under the bathroom sink's little pump, then headed back to his own tiny bedchamber and crawled in onto the bed.

His window shade wasn't drawn, and the cubicle was awash with moonlight. It would be so romantic if Emma were here with him, instead of on the other side of that curtain.

He stripped off his clothes, slipped between the sheets and lay listening to the rhythm of the wheels and concentrating on the train's swaying motion, hoping it would lull him to sleep.

A few moments later, he heard a faint rustling of curtains next door, then Emma's quiet footsteps passing his cubicle and the bathroom door closing. He tried to make his mind a blank. It was senseless to lie here and worry. She'd said seeing her parents once more would make it easier for her to go. She'd explain things to them and... and he could just imagine how thrilled they were going to be with the idea of never seeing their baby again. Hell, they'd probably lock her up and throw away the key.

"Will?" her voice whispered from outside.

He sat up quickly and pushed himself to the end of the bed, adjusting the top sheet modestly around his waist before separating the curtains.

Emma was standing in the aisle, wearing a long white nightgown that covered at least as much of her as her dresses always did. It had a row of tiny buttons running all the way from her throat to her waist, and he couldn't take his eyes off them. And he couldn't help thinking how much he'd like to undo them.

"Will," she murmured shyly, "Will, I don't want to be alone tonight. Would it be all right...?"

He swallowed hard. Another night with Emma in his arms, another night of wanting to make love to her and knowing he couldn't, just might be more than he could take. "Afraid you'll have a nightmare?" he managed to ask.

She nodded.

"Well, after fitting the three of us onto John's bed, two will be a breeze." He eased back toward the window and propped the pillow up against the outside wall.

Emma gave him a nervous-looking smile, then climbed onto the bed and closed the curtains. With her hair free, hanging around her shoulders, she looked even more beautiful than usual. More beautiful and more desirable.

She snuggled down beside him, on top of the sheet, and he put his arm around her.

She rested her cheek against his bare chest, almost making him groan. It was going to be a long, long night. He gazed silently down at her, reminding himself for the millionth time that despite her playing at being a modern woman, she wasn't one. She was still Emma McCully, the spinster schoolmarm who'd never even kept company with a man until she'd met him. Still Emma McCully, with 1887 moral standards that said sex before marriage would make her a fallen woman.

He sat with her in his arms, smelling the sweet scent of her hair, acutely aware of her body, wondering if a man could actually die of frustration.

"Will?" she murmured.

"Mmmmm?"

"Will...the other night...when you were telling me about how women act in the future..."

"Mmmmm?"

"When you said that..." She paused, clearing her throat. "You said that if a woman loved a man it was normal for...for...for them to make love. Even if they weren't married."

Oh, Lord! The absolute last thing he wanted to do was talk about sex.

"Even a...a virtuous woman, you said."

"Yes. Yes, I guess I did say all that."

"So...so if we were in your world now...here, like this, I mean...if I was one of your lady rocket scientists..."

"Emma, darling, they aren't *my* rocket scientists. And I'd never want to be here, like this, with anyone but you."

She slid her hand across his chest and began toying with his chest hair.

He inhaled sharply at her touch and captured her hand. "Emma, don't do that, okay?"

She looked at him as if he'd slapped her.

"Emma, it's not that I don't like you touching me. It isn't that at all. It's that you don't understand what it does to me."

"What . . . what does it do?"

He smiled ruefully, imagining how furiously she'd blush if he told her it made him rock-hard, that it made him positively ache with wanting to be inside her. "Emma, it makes me want to make love to you. Right here and now."

"And . . . and if we were in your world, you would, wouldn't you?"

"Emma, things are different in my world. We've talked about that."

"But if we were there," she persisted, "we'd make love now, wouldn't we?"

He closed his eyes, knowing he couldn't look at her for another second without kissing her. And if he kissed her, it wouldn't end there. A man could only take so much.

"Wouldn't we?" she whispered.

"Yes, Emma," he said, praying a definite answer would end this discussion. "Yes, in my world, we would."

She rested silently against him for so long he thought she must have fallen asleep. But she hadn't.

"Will?" she murmured. "I think we should pretend we're in your world."

He swallowed back the words he wanted so much to say. "Emma, I don't think that's a good idea," he said instead.

She gazed up at him, her eyes large and luminous. "Why not?"

"Because... because you're different from women in my world. And because I don't want you to do something you might regret."

She smiled an incredibly anxious little smile. "I don't want to do something I might regret, either, Will. That's precisely why I think we should pretend. Because what terrifies me most about going to your world is that I might grow to regret having done it. Or that you might grow to regret my having done it."

"Oh, Emma, that just wouldn't happen. I'd never regret it if you came home with me."

"Will, you can't know that. I *am* different—just as you said. And I'm frightened I might be so different I'd never be able to adjust to the future. What if I could never learn to be like women there? What if I couldn't learn to think the way they think? What if... Will... I don't know anything about making love. I mean, I know about the biology, but not... oh, Will, what if I don't please you?"

"Emma, you could never, never, not please me."

She slipped her hand up the back of his neck and tangled her fingers in his hair, sending shivers of desire through him.

"Will, I think we'd better make *sure* I'm not too different. Not so different that my going with you would be a terrible mistake."

He exhaled slowly, uncertain if this was right or wrong, but certain he could no longer even try to resist.

CHAPTER FOURTEEN

WILL KISSED EMMA—a passionately delicious kiss. He pulled her toward him and she found herself lying by his side, her cheek nestled in the hollow of his naked shoulder, his arms wrapped around her.

Pale moonlight bathed the little bedchamber, turning her white nightdress silver. And the sheet as well. Her nightdress and the sheet. Those two thin bits of fabric were all that separated their bodies, and Emma's heart was hammering a hundred times faster than the rhythmic clatter of the train wheels. Now that she and Will were actually going to...oh, the prospect was unbelievably scary.

"Will?" she murmured. "Will, I...I'm going to need you to tell me exactly what I should do."

He smiled lovingly at her. "All right, I will. Emma...Emma, you're awfully frightened, aren't you?"

She nodded an admission into his neck. Terrified would be more accurate, but awfully frightened would suffice.

"So am I," he said.

She shifted a little in his arms, so that she could see his face once more. His expression was deadly serious.

"You?" she whispered. "Why would you be frightened?"

"Well, a few minutes ago, you asked me what would happen if you didn't please me. And I guess what I'm afraid of is what will happen if I don't please you."

He gave her another smile and she managed to return it. The thought of Will being frightened, too, made her feel a little less terrified. "Your kissing pleases me, Will," she told him.

"Good. That's a good start. But I want you to like the rest of it, too. I want you to enjoy making love."

He wanted her to enjoy it? But... but this was something a woman had to *endure*. It was a wifely *duty*. "Enjoy it?" she finally murmured.

Will eyed her uncertainly for a moment, then laughed quietly. "I think we've just hit on something else that developed along with equal rights. Women are supposed to enjoy sex every bit as much as men."

He began to stroke her hair, still gazing at her thoughtfully, while his words buzzed about inside her head. Was that really possible?

"Oh, Emma," he finally whispered, kissing her again, teasing her lips with his tongue until she teased him back.

She *did* enjoy kissing him. Incredibly much. And she enjoyed him holding her. It was just that *rest of it* that scared her.

"Emma?" he said softly. "Emma, this would work better if you weren't lying on top of the sheet."

"I ... Will," she mumbled, knowing he had nothing on under that sheet, knowing how furiously she was blushing. "Will, I've never seen a naked man before."

"You don't have to look," he told her, easing the sheet from beneath her. Then, tentatively, he slid his hands down her back and drew her closer... so close that her breasts were crushed against his bare chest. Her nipples hardened at the contact, and she pulled away, dreadfully embarrassed.

"Emma, don't be upset. You're perfectly normal. It's simply your body saying it likes being close to mine." Will propped himself up on one elbow and gazed at her. "Emma, listen to me for a minute. The only real difference between you and women in the future is the way you've been taught to think about some things. So, I'll tell you what. Try not to think. Just go with your instincts and let your body react to what's happening."

She swallowed hard. "I don't think I can manage to stop thinking, Will."

Softly, ever so softly, he kissed her throat. "All right. Then there's something special I want you to think about. Emma, I want you to concentrate, with all your might, on thinking that sex is part of loving. Whatever reactions your body has will only happen because you love me. And because I love you."

"Oh, Will."

He started slowly caressing the side of her neck, and she gradually managed to relax, finally wrapping her arms around him, wanting to kiss him once more.

His lips were firm and hot against hers, and, when he began exploring her mouth with his tongue, she smoothed her hands across his chest and up his back, drawing him closer to her.

He groaned, pulling the length of her body to him so that his hard maleness was pressing against her. It sent her pulse racing frantically.

She began repeating to herself that it wasn't wrong for his body to be touching hers, that it wasn't wrong to be feeling all the strange, exciting sensations she was feeling—the sensations that were growing stronger with each passing minute.

The more possessively he kissed her, the more she wanted him to possess her. The longer he caressed her, the more eagerly her body craved his touch and the less anxious she felt about caressing him in return. She slid her hands up his back once more and tangled her fingers in his hair.

He kissed her even more deeply, his hands slipping down to her waist . . . then stealing back up to her breasts.

Her breath caught in her throat but . . . but what he was doing couldn't be wrong. Not when it felt so good. Not when she loved his touch so much. Not when she loved *him* so much.

His palms grazed her nipples. They were pebble-hard.

He shifted away a little and began toying with the buttons on her nightdress. Then he stopped and gazed into her yes. ''Emma, if you want, we can make love without your taking off your nightgown.''

''I want . . . Will, I want it to be the way it would be in the future. Would . . . would I take it off there?''

He nodded.

She hesitated for a long moment, then slowly undid the top button.

''Let me,'' he whispered.

She barely breathed while his fingers worked their way lower, until the final button at her waist was undone.

Then Will drew her closer again and started kissing her once more, started smoothing tiny circles across the back of her nightdress.

Gradually she began to feel as if she were about to jump out of her skin. Her breasts seemed to be straining against his chest, wanting his touch. And there was an aching throb, low in her body, that was growing ever more insistent.

Her entire being seemed to be melting into a hot liquid. And she was having to concentrate every bit of her willpower on just keeping still.

Will might have told her to let her body react, to go with her instincts, but something must be wrong with her. Surely she wasn't supposed to be wishing he'd stroke her breasts instead of her back. Or feeling that only by moving her body against his could she possibly ease that throbbing ache. Yet she couldn't ask him what she was actually supposed to be feeling and doing without dying of embarrassment.

She managed to remain motionless for a few more seconds, but her body began aching so badly she was almost moaning. Whatever was supposed to happen next had better happen soon—before she had a full blown fit of the jimjams.

Finally, desperately, she murmured Will's name.

"What?" he whispered.

"Will..." Oh, mercy, how could she put this? "Will, you said you'd tell me exactly what to do. But you forgot to tell me exactly when I should be taking off my nightdress."

He shifted back an inch and eyed her closely. "I...I don't want to rush you, Emma. I'm waiting for you to give me a sign."

He was waiting for her to give him a sign? What on earth was that all about? Was he playing some infuriating game with her?

"A sign?" she snapped. "A sign? What kind of sign? Dammit, Will! You said you'd tell me exactly what to do! And you didn't say a word about me having to give you any stupid sign!"

He stared at her with the most taken-aback expression she'd ever seen. And then he began to laugh.

"What?" she demanded angrily.

"Hot damn!" he managed, still laughing. "Oh, Emma, you want me to get on with it, don't you?"

She felt her face begin to burn.

"Oh, Emma," he said again, hugging her to him. "Emma, all we've been through and that's the first time I've heard you swear. There I was about ready to explode and you still felt stiff as a board in my arms, and I thought...well, it doesn't matter what I thought. But if we're really pretending we're in my world, you're going to have to relax. Just go ahead and do whatever your instincts tell you to."

She swallowed hard...then took his hands...then closed her eyes and slipped them inside her nightdress.

"Oh, Lord, Emma," he whispered, cupping her breasts and beginning to fondle them, making her moan as his thumbs caressed her nipples.

His touch brought some of the relief she'd craved, but at the same time made her desperate to have him touch her everywhere.

He brushed the front of her nightdress back, off her shoulders and trailed kisses down her throat to her breasts.

She gasped, startled when his mouth closed on her nipple, the moist warmth of his tongue sending liquid fire blazing through her.

His body was heavy on hers, yet she was moving beneath him without conscious effort, desperately trying to ease the aching inside.

Vaguely she was aware of him pulling her nightgown off, of arching her body to help him, of his hand slipping down over her stomach, beginning to move against the rhythm of her body.

But mainly she was aware of her need to be closer to him, of the excruciating delight of his hands and mouth, of knowing that somehow he could stop the urgent throbbing that was possessing her.

"Emma," he whispered raggedly, "tell me if I hurt you."

But he wasn't hurting her. He was simply stroking her more intimately than she'd ever imagined. And his stroking was making her fight for breath, was making her body move faster and faster until it exploded into a spasm of tiny, jerking motions that she couldn't have controlled if she'd tried.

Will lay for a moment, until she'd almost caught her breath, and then he touched her again, sending another delicious spasm through her, and began moving with her, his body pressing down on her... into her.

She uttered a tiny cry at a sharp stab of pain. Instantly he stopped moving. But the pain was gone in a second, and she wrapped her arms more tightly around him, wanting him to be part of her.

EMMA LAY CUDDLED so closely to Will they were still almost one. His chest hair was tickling her nose, but she felt so warm and secure and loved in his arms that she wanted to stay right there forever.

She was breathing normally again, was able to think once more, and a million different thoughts were scurrying about in her mind. A million different, deliriously happy thoughts.

"Will?" she whispered.

"Mmmmm?"

"Will . . . did I please you?" She bit her lip to keep from smiling. She knew she had, but she wanted to hear him tell her so.

He slipped a finger under her chin and tilted her face up toward his. "Did you please me?" he teased. "Emma, if you'd pleased me even a mite more, I'd have died of pleasure."

She let her smile escape, suspecting it just might remain permanently on her face. "You mean I pleased you as much as a *modern* woman would have?"

"Emma, you pleased me more than any other woman, anywhere, in any time, possibly could have. But what about you?" he murmured. "Did I please you?"

"Oh, Will, you did. Very much."

He grinned down at her. "Shucks, ma'am. T'weren't nothing any red-blooded, twenty-first century man couldn't have done."

"I don't believe that, Will."

"No?"

"No. At least no other man could have done it with me. I wouldn't want to make love with anyone else, Will. Never, ever."

He gently kissed her, then began stroking her hair. "Emma...does that mean...Emma, I love you. Please say you'll come back with me. The uncertainty's driving me crazy."

She gazed at him, aware she no longer had a choice. She'd known Will Lockhart for such a short time—yet felt she'd known him forever. And she was absolutely sure she wanted to spend the rest of her life with him. She took a deep breath and nodded. "I couldn't not go with you, Will. I love you, too. So much."

Slowly, he smiled. The warmest, happiest smile she'd ever seen.

"You won't regret it, Emma. Never, ever. I'm going to love you every bit as much in my world as I do here."

"Not your world," she murmured. "It's going to be our world."

"Our world," he repeated, bending to kiss her.

They lay entwined in the little bed, talking for hours about their future, until the moonlight outside gradually gave way to the first rays of dawn.

"I'll have to wire the school board," Emma murmured. "Tell them I won't be back for the fall term. I'll miss the children."

"We'll have children of our own soon," Will reminded her. "We'll be married and have children of our own."

"Mmmm. You know, Will, I wish there was a way we could get married in San Francisco. It would mean a lot to my parents."

"Maybe we can. We arrive first thing on the twenty-eighth, so we can stay two days and easily get back to Mountainview by the first. If there's no legal waiting

period in California, all we'll have to do is find someone who can marry us. 'Course, we'll have to do it all
over again when we get to 2014.''

"I don't mind that at all," Emma said, nuzzling his
neck. "I'd marry you a thousand times, in a thousand different times, if I had to."

"Only a thousand?" he teased.

"Well...you tell me I tend to understatement." She
reached for her nightdress and started to put it on.

"You're not leaving me?" Will said.

"I don't want to. But I'd better be in my own bed
when John gets up. He's likely to poke his head in to
say good morning, and he isn't anywhere near as
modern-thinking as I am. And I certainly wouldn't
want him to shoot one of us. Especially not now that
we have a happy ending in sight. Oh, Will," she
added, quickly kissing him, "I can hardly wait to tell
John I've decided to go."

ON WEDNESDAY, when they reached Los Angeles,
they had several hours to wait for the overnight train
to San Francisco.

Buck had immediately headed off to visit someone
he knew. Will, Emma and John intended to poke
about the city—what little there was of it, Will
thought, surveying the small adobe buildings in disbelief.

"You know," he said, "aside from Mountainview,
this is the first place I've been—in 1887—that I've also
been to in the future. And you'd never believe it was
the same city. Lord, the population can't be more than
about twenty thousand."

"How big is it in 2014?" John asked, adjusting his arm in its sling.

"Four or five million."

John whistled. "I can't even imagine fitting that many people into one place."

"Well, there are all the high rises. They add a lot to the density. And the city sprawls for miles." Will gestured out across the valley. "That's all built up in the future. As far as you can see there are houses and highways. Of course, you can't see all that far because of the smog."

Both Emma and John glanced at him curiously.

"Smog?" Emma said.

"Ahh... like fog, only manmade."

"Why would people want to make fog?" she asked.

"Well, they didn't really want to. It's an effect of air pollution."

"The air is polluted in the future?" Emma said, frowning uncertainly.

"No, not everywhere," Will said quickly. "But it *is* bad in Los Angeles. There are too many cars, and their exhaust gets trapped in the valley."

"Smog," John repeated. "From car exhaust. Hell, Will, things become so danged different, don't they?"

He nodded, eager to change the subject. He certainly didn't want Emma to start worrying that she'd have trouble breathing in the future.

"Those hills," he said, pointing south, "become a part of Los Angeles that's called Hollywood. Remember I told you about moving pictures?"

"Of course," Emma said. "Movies and videos and television and—"

"Show-off," John teased.

"Well, anyway," Will went on, "Los Angeles turns into the movie-making capital of the world. Most of the film stars live here. And the word Hollywood comes to refer to the American film industry in general. And somewhere along the way, they put gigantic letters on the hills—spelling out Hollywood."

John shook his head. "High rises and moving pictures and cars and highways and computers and everything else you've told me about. Damn, but I envy you going there, Emma. What a lifetime you'll have."

"Maybe you should come with us," Will said.

"You know, Will, if I felt I could, I reckon I just might. I really did want a change from running a business for Buck. I wanted to make an adventure of my life. But now...well, shoot, I sure can't quit on him now. Not after he practically got killed trying to rescue me. And not after he helped save Emma's life. He's a good man, Will. A really good man. But he couldn't run Dursely Oil on his own. Hell, he actually is determined to take on Rockefeller, you know. And that sharpster would hornswoggle old Buck before breakfast, without me to look out for him."

"There's mother and father, too," Emma said quietly. "I mean," she explained to Will, "John and I are the only two of their children they really ever see. And they're going to lose me."

John nodded. "Yeah. I guess it's just as well I'll be living in San Francisco now. But hell, let's not think about losing you, Emmy. Let's just enjoy our afternoon here."

They wandered around the city until it began growing dark, then headed back to the train depot. Buck was already there, waiting for them—slumped on one of the benches, looking incredibly depressed.

"He probably spent the entire afternoon brooding about Dursely Oil," John said.

Will nodded. Last night, he and John had explained stock manipulation to Buck. They'd speculated that someone could be intentionally driving down the prices—simply by selling shares for less than the market would actually have paid for them. And, since hearing that explanation, Buck had grown even more worried about the likelihood of them dropping so low that the bank could seize his company.

He'd accepted the possibility that someone at First Coastal had intentionally inserted that collateral agreement clause as part of a plot to ruin him. But he had no idea who or why. John clearly had his suspicions, though—he'd made a couple of pointed remarks about the bank fellow who'd come to Mountainview.

Buck spotted them and managed a smile. "You three have a good time?" he asked.

Will nodded. "How about you? See your friend?"

"Well, he weren't exactly a friend. He was a lawyer fellow I'd met once. I wanted to get his advice about just how to handle this mess with the bank."

"Good idea," Will said. "What did he have to say?"

"Well, we waited until the stock exchange closed, then wired New York for the closing price."

"And?"

"And it's not good, Will. Dursely Oil shares closed the day at four and a quarter. Could slip as low as four dollars and ten cents tomorrow—easy."

"So what did this fellow suggest doing?" John asked.

"Well, he said I'd be in a much stronger position if I talk to the bank people before the shares get so low they can actually grab them. Said if this really is all a plot, it would likely be harder to get the shares back than to hang on to them in the first place."

"That makes sense," Will said.

"And he advised going straight to the president. I thought I should start by talking to that Mr. Matthews who came to Mountainview. But this fellow said to start at the top—just in case Matthews isn't as honest as I took him to be."

"I think that's a *real* fine idea," John said. "There was something about Matthews that didn't set quite right with me."

Buck nodded. "Well, what I figure is our train gets into San Francisco before eight tomorrow morning. And the bank will be open at nine, but the New York exchange doesn't open until ten. So the best thing we can do is talk to that president first thing—before the price can possibly drop any farther."

Will nodded, thinking Buck was lucky the country hadn't been divided into time zones by 1887.

"Sounds like a good plan," John said. "We'll go directly from the train station."

"You, too, Will," Buck said. "I mean, if you wouldn't mind. The lawyer fellow said that with Butcher Bill stealing my copy of the agreement—well, you're the only one of the three of us who actually read the final version I signed. So I might need you to speak up for me, as well as John."

Will glanced at Emma, knowing she'd want to spend every second she could with her mother and father.

"It's not a problem," she said. "You go along with Buck and John, and I'll go straight to my parents' house. I can visit with them alone for a few hours. And tell them about you…well, maybe not quite all," she corrected herself, smiling. "I think I'll wait until you and John are there to help with the explaining before I tell them *all* about you."

Will grinned at her, then turned back to Buck. "Sure. Whatever I can do to help sort things out."

As THEY GOT OFF THE TRAIN in San Francisco, Emma protested that she enjoyed riding on the cable car, and that she could get directly to her parents' house by taking a car down Clay Street, the way she usually did. Regardless, the men piled her into a horse-drawn carriage.

"We've still got a stack of Wyatt's money to spend before we leave," Will teased, giving her a quick kiss. "Besides, this way John and I don't have to lug our bags along to the bank."

"Right," John said. "You keep ignoring the fact that I have a serious injury."

Emma laughed. "Don't worry. Mother will more than make up for me not fretting over you. When she sees your arm's in a sling she'll be clucking like a hen with an ailing chick."

The driver clicked his reins, starting off, and the three men strolled along to the next carriage in line outside the station.

Buck brushed at his jacket, raising a sizable cloud of dust, then glanced at the station's clock tower. "We've got an hour before the bank opens," he said. "You two mind if we stop by my house so I can clean up? Bankers make me more than a mite nervous, even when I'm looking my best."

Will gazed out at the city as they headed up Washington Street. He'd been to San Francisco before, and some things didn't change with the years. The city was unbelievably hilly. And the hills were incredibly steep. And despite the constant wind blowing in from the bay, morning fog shrouded the city in gray.

"That's the Opera House," Buck said, pointing out the right-hand side of the carriage. "And there's city hall. It used to be the Jenny Lind Theater. And you can see the edge of Chinatown up there," he offered, just before they turned onto Powell.

The horse was laboring by the time they'd climbed the hill to Buck's house. It was precisely as Buck had described it back in Mountainview—a danged mansion on Nob Hill.

Like most San Francisco homes, it had no front yard. But it rose in utter majesty from the street—three stories high and sprawling along the sidewalk of Powell Street with more pillars and arches than Will could believe.

Buck carefully adjusted his battered Stetson, wincing as he pulled it low on his forehead. "That hide the gash all right?"

Will nodded.

"Good. 'Cuz Mary Beth's going to go plumb loco when she sees I been shot. Now, don't you two say nothing to her when we're in there or she'll have me abed and the doctor on his way while the bank's still awaiting. She can be an argumentative hellcat when she gets a bee in her bonnet about something.''

They asked the driver to wait, then started up the stone staircase. Halfway to the front door, it opened and children began spilling out, shouting, ''Pa's here!''

Seconds later, five youngsters—from a toddler to a teenager—had surrounded them and were bombarding Buck and John with greetings.

Another moment and a woman appeared in the doorway.

''Buck!'' she cried, gathering her skirt and hurrying down the stairs.

The children backed off a little, and she threw her arms around Buck, laughing and murmuring to him that he looked a terrible sight.

She was no more than forty, Will guessed. And prettier than he'd expected Buck's wife would be. Blue eyes, pale blond hair, and, despite the five children, she'd kept her figure.

''Will,'' Buck said proudly, ''this here's Mary Beth. And these are our young 'uns. Will's an old friend of John's,'' he explained to his wife.

Mary Beth smiled a greeting at Will, then turned to John. ''I'm so glad to see you, John. Buck thought he'd lost you to ranching forever. But whatever happened to your arm?''

''It's a long story,'' Buck said. ''I'll tell you all about it later, dear. Right now I just got to change and git along to the bank. Maybe you could keep the young 'uns from crawling all over the fellows while they're waiting.''

"Of course," Mary Beth said, giving Buck a final peck on the cheek, then scooting the children back inside, ahead of the men.

"Won't be a minute," Buck said, starting up the sweeping staircase that dominated the foyer. "You two just go on into the parlor."

Will glanced around the elegant marble interior, trying to imagine Buck living in a house that looked as if it should be owned by a Vanderbilt. "Quite the place, isn't it?" he said to John.

"Sure is. I just hope he doesn't lose it."

After a few minutes, Mary Beth reappeared. She chattered away to them, telling them all about life in San Francisco, until Buck came back downstairs. He'd changed into a clean suit and decent hat—again pulled low on his head.

"Oh, before you go, dear," Mary Beth told him, "a wire came for you yesterday." She fetched an envelope from the mantel, then fussed with his tie for a moment before letting him escape.

Buck waited until they were back in the carriage, then opened the telegram and read it with painful slowness, underlining each word with his finger. Gradually a smile crept onto his face.

"So help me Moses!" he finally exclaimed, grinning across the carriage at Will and John. "That danged Sheriff Slaughter did it! Will, your map led him right to that hideout and he's got Butcher Knife Bill in his jail."

Buck peered back down at the page for another minute. "And he says the posse killed three other yellow skunks who tried to fight their way out. Well, I'm deuced glad he got that polecat. And he got my case, too. Says there was still a bunch of money in it. Says it's evidence right now, but that I'll be getting it back after the Butcher's trial. And let's see... there's a bit more...."

Will resisted the temptation to grab the wire from Buck's hands. Instead, he waited, impatiently watching Buck silently mouth more words. A frown slowly replaced his grin.

"What is it?" John asked. "What else does it say?"

"Well, John, Slaughter says he thought he should tell me about something Butcher Bill had on him. It was a telegram addressed to Bill Christian, in Marble Canyon, Arizona."

"Bill Christian," Will repeated. "Reverend Bill. That was the name the Butcher was using when he was playing preacher."

Buck nodded. "And he got on the train at Marble Canyon. That's where I first met up with him."

"But what did the telegram he had on him say?" John pressed.

Buck stared down at his wire again. "It said...

CONFIRM DURSELY DEAD TO MR. B. STOP. CARE OF WELLS FARGO. STOP. MONTGOMERY STREET, SAN FRANCISCO. STOP. PAYMENT WILL FOLLOW.

"So... whoever paid to have you killed was in San Francisco," Will concluded slowly.

"Mr. B.," Buck murmured.

"Do you know anyone whose name begins with a *B*?" John asked.

"That's probably too obvious," Will said. "It's more likely a code."

"But someone in this city paid to have me killed," Buck said quietly, peering out of the carriage. He cleared his throat and straightened his shoulders. "Here we are at the First Coastal. I'll have to worry about who Mr. B. is later."

They made their way to the other side of California Street and into the bank. A skinny male receptionist, seated at a large mahogany desk, guarded the entrance to a corridor of offices.

"I want to talk to the president," Buck told him.

The man's gaze swept them. "You have an appointment with Mr. Whipple, *sir?*"

"No. But I want to talk to him."

"I'm sorry, *sir*, but the president of a bank has a very busy schedule. It's necessary to make an appointment to—"

"This man," Will snapped, nodding toward Buck, "is the president of an oil company. And an important customer of this bank. And he has a very busy schedule, too. So I suggest you tell your Mr. Whipple that Mr. Buckingham Dursely and his associates are here to see him. Right now."

The receptionist blinked rapidly. "I...I'm afraid Mr. Whipple really *is* very busy just at the moment, sir. He has Mr. Rockefeller in his office. And, of course, Mr. Rockefeller is the chairman of The First Coastal's board of directors."

Will glanced at John and saw his own surprise reflected in the other man's eyes.

"Mr. John D. Rockefeller?" Buck said.

"Of course, sir."

"The Mr. John D. Rockefeller who's the president of Standard Oil."

"The same, sir."

"But he lives in New York. So how can he be the head of this bank?" Buck demanded.

"He's not really the head, Buck," Will whispered. "The board of directors only meets now and then. And it simply advises the bank management."

"But... but he must have a lot of say about the bank's business," Buck murmured, looking from Will to John, silently asking them a question: since Rockefeller controlled a vast segment of the oil industry, how much interest would he have in seeing a new competitor destroyed?

"What a coincidence that John D. is here today," Will said to the receptionist, thinking furiously as he spoke. "I have to talk to him—as well as to your Mr. Whipple. I intended to call on John D. the minute I got back to New York. But you can save us all some time by interrupting that meeting and saying we'd like a moment with them."

The receptionist blinked rapidly again, looking extremely uneasy.

"It's perfectly all right, my good man," Will insisted firmly. "John D.'s wife, Cettie, is my cousin. And he'd have your hide if he found out he missed me. Simply tell the gentlemen that Mr. Dursely, Mr. Lockhart and Mr. McCully need to speak with them immediately. On a most urgent matter."

The receptionist slowly pushed back his chair, mumbling the three names to himself, then nodded to them. "Just a minute please, gentlemen."

"Cettie?" John demanded as the skinny man started down the corridor. "How the hell did you know that?"

Will shrugged. "Back when I took a lot of business courses, I read a couple of biographies about John D. Guess the name just stuck in my mind."

"Then you don't really know him?" Buck hissed, turning purple. "Or his wife, neither?"

"Ah . . . no."

"Then what in damnable blazes are you doing?"

"Buck, what I'm doing is trying to find out what the hell's going on. Just as fast as I can."

CHAPTER FIFTEEN

MR. WHIPPLE and Mr. Rockefeller sat listening, without interrupting, to Buck's story about the altered loan agreement.

Will couldn't take his eyes off John D. Rockefeller. Not that the man's physical appearance was particularly prepossessing. He was about fifty, with thinning brown hair, noticeably large ears and an extremely bushy mustache. And seated, at least, he looked to be only average height. But he had an undeniable presence.

"And both Will and John here," Buck concluded, "are convinced someone's been pushing down the share prices."

When Buck finished speaking, Rockefeller ordered Whipple to fetch Matthews. "And don't tell him what this is about," John D. added.

The bank president practically fell over himself getting out of his office.

Rockefeller's gaze focused on Will, making him instantly uncomfortable. John D. had eyes that seemed to see right through a man. "You aren't my wife's cousin," he snapped.

Will shook his head. "No, sir. But we had to get in here to speak to you."

"Humph! Well, I wish Cettie *did* have a cousin with your gumption, Mr. Lockhart."

"Thank you, sir."

Whipple scurried back in, followed by another middle-aged man who glanced around the office. When he saw Buck and John, the color drained from his face.

"Mr. Dursely has a problem with his loan agreement, Matthews," Rockefeller said. "What do you know about it?"

Matthews swallowed hard. "Know, sir?"

"Yes, dammit! *Know.* These gentlemen tell me there was a clause added to the agreement between the draft and the final version. Is that true?"

Will's glance followed Matthews's to Whipple. The bank president was staring at the floor.

"Ahhh . . . well," Matthews stammered, looking at Rockefeller again, "well, sir, yes. It is true. After I'd had a chance to review the draft, I realized the bank should have more protection."

"Protection." Rockefeller repeated. "Protection from what?"

"Ahhh . . . protection of our investment, sir."

Rockefeller simply glared at the man. "Don't you horse with me, Matthews. 'Cuz the president of the New York Stock Exchange is a good friend of mine. And I can wire him faster that you can say stock manipulation. So you just better tell me what he'd find if he ordered an investigation into recent Dursely Oil trading."

Matthews's face grew even paler.

"Well?" Rockefeller demanded.

"I . . . I did it for you, sir. I saw the opportunity to eliminate competition in the oil industry and I took it. I . . . I assumed you'd be grateful, sir."

"Grateful?" Rockefeller shouted. "You assumed I'd be grateful to find I'm the chairman of the board of directors of a bank that has a dishonest vice president? A man who would take it upon himself to destroy one of our valued customers? And what was in it for you, Matthews?"

"Nothing, sir! Absolutely nothing. I did it all for you."

"Bull!" Rockefeller roared. "You've got your own private little pile of Dursely Oil shares tucked away, haven't you? Shares that you've been buying at a depressed price. A depressed price that will go up again as soon as you stop playing your game. Well? How many shares would my friend find registered in your name if he checked?"

"A . . . only a few thousand, sir."

"Only a few thousand! Well, this is not the way a banker I have any association with operates, Matthews!"

Banker. The word began echoing in Will's mind. There was something about it that . . .

"I'm an honest man!" Rockefeller raged on. "And I expect those I deal with to be honest, as well. I want you out of here. Immediately."

Matthews hesitated a second, then turned toward the door.

"Mr. B.?" Will called.

Matthews wheeled around. His gaze froze on Will.

"Mr. B...Mr. Banker," Will said quietly. "There's one more thing. I expect the police will want to talk to you about plotting to have Mr. Dursely murdered."

"What?" Matthews whispered.

"Buck and John were the only two people who could have testified that you'd amended the loan agreement. Did you intend, right from the start, to kill Buck?"

Matthews exhaled slowly, then shook his head. "No. I'm no murderer. I was just keeping track of his activities on the off chance...just to be certain he didn't realize...I honestly didn't think he would."

"Keeping track of his activities?" Will said.

"I have...I have contacts at Wells Fargo. And when I learned that Dursely was going after McCully...well, I figured there could only be one reason. I had no choice, then."

HOURS LATER, THE POLICE left, taking Matthews with them.

"I just can't believe it," Whipple murmured as they shut his office door. "All those years Charles has worked for me. I just can't believe it."

"Greed does strange things to men," Rockefeller said, turning to Buck. "Mr. Dursely, on behalf of the First Coastal Bank of California, I apologize to you. That clause, of course, will be stricken from the loan agreement. And on behalf of Standard Oil, I look forward to the challenge of your participation in the oil industry. I welcome competition with open arms. It's competition that makes the game of business exciting. It's competition that makes this country of ours great."

Will managed not to smile. But he knew Mr. Rockefeller wasn't a man who'd welcome competition in the slightest, let alone with open arms. Hell, he'd maintained a virtual stranglehold on the oil industry for most of his lifetime. According to one of those biographies, the government had spent over four years prosecuting an anti-monopoly case against Standard Oil.

Of course, now that John McCully hadn't died, now that he would be running Dursely Oil...well, with any luck John and Buck could manage to present John D. with a damned good challenge. That would be a mighty interesting thing to see.

"Well, thank you, Mr. Rockefeller, sir," Buck was saying. "It's been a pleasure meeting you. And it's a pleasure," he added, grinning at Will, "to know that both Butcher Knife and Matthews will spending a long time in jail."

"Mr. Lockhart," Rockefeller said, "you've got a fine head on your shoulders—to have figured out how deeply Matthews was involved, I mean. Anytime you're in the market for a good job, let me know."

"'Fraid I've already spoken up about that, sir," Buck said. "If Mr. Lockhart wants a good job, he knows he's always got one with me."

They shook hands all around, then Buck, John and Will left. Outside, afternoon sunlight was streaming down onto California Street.

"Lord," Will muttered, "we were in there for hours. Emma must be wondering where on earth we are, John."

"It won't take long to get to the house," he said, hailing a carriage. "Buck, you won't mind if I don't start work until next week, will you? With Emma and Will leaving for... for Boston, I'd like to spend whatever time I can with them."

"Of course, of course," Buck said. "And I know you'll be needing time off to arrange about your things back in Mountainview. Well," he added, shaking Will's hand, "I'm real pleased you and Emma are getting married. And I'm real grateful for all the help you've given me. Like Mr. Rockefeller said, you've got a fine head on your shoulders. And if you ever decide to leave Boston... well you just keep that job offer in mind."

"I will, Buck. And it's been great to see you again after all these years."

"Give my regards to your pa, you hear. And to that purty woman he married."

Will nodded, climbing into the carriage after John, thinking how incredible his father and Erica were going to find this whole story. Hell, they were undoubtedly worried sick because he'd been gone longer than the single day he'd said the trip would take—probably figured he was lost someplace in time and space.

He looked out onto California Street as the horse clip-clopped along. Like Los Angeles, San Francisco was far different now than in the future, but in a different way. In a hundred and twenty-seven years, Los Angeles had gone from primitive adobe to modern glass and chrome. But even in 1887, San Francisco was a sophisticated city. Almost none of the buildings standing now, though, were... "John?" he said.

"Yes?"

"John, if you and Buck are still in California in 1906, if your parents are still here—"

"Yes?"

"Well, you don't want to be in San Francisco then. There's a major earthquake. And a fire, afterward, that burns for days. Most of the city is destroyed."

John first looked skeptical, then slowly shook his head. "You're serious, aren't you?"

"'Fraid so."

"Nineteen-oh-six," John repeated. "I'll keep it in mind. Any other disasters I should know about?"

"Let's see . . . don't ever ride in a dirigible called the *Hindenburg*."

"Will, I don't even know what a dirigible is."

"It's a kind of hot-air balloon. Anyway, don't ride in the *Hindenburg*. It burns up. And don't take an ocean liner called the *Titanic*. It sinks. And don't be touring Europe in 1914. A world war breaks out."

John grinned across the carriage. "You're just full of cheery knowledge, aren't you?

"That's the house, right up there," he said a minute later, pointing along the street to a modest two-story, perched halfway up the hill. "Looks as if they've got company," he added, nodding toward the small black rig sitting directly outside.

They paid the driver and strode across the street to the McCully house. John opened the front door and shouted a greeting. A moment later, Emma appeared at the top of the stairs, her finger to her lips, silencing them.

One look at her and Will realized something was terribly wrong. She started quickly down the stairs, and the closer she drew the more terrible he knew the problem was. Her face was pale, but there were brightly flushed patches on each cheek. And she'd been crying. Her eyes were red and looked as if they were about to overflow with more tears any second.

She reached them and threw her arms around Will. He hugged her to him, afraid to ask what was wrong, strangely certain it was going to be worse than he could even imagine.

Without speaking, she drew away from him and put her hand on John's good arm.

"What?" John murmured. "What's happened?"

"It's father," she whispered.

John started for the stairs.

"Wait," Emma said. "Don't go up now. The doctor just arrived. He's been coming twice a day since..." She swallowed hard, unable to go on.

John wrapped his arm around her shoulders and led her to the parlor.

She sat on the settee, Will beside her, clutching her hands firmly in his, her brother slumped in the chair across from them.

"Emmy, tell me exactly what happened," John said.

Emma shut her eyes. The morning was etched in her memory. Slowly, she related what had happened.

As John had just done, she'd opened the front door and called a greeting, not even bothering to bring the bags in from the steps first. "Mother? Father? Surprise!"

Silence. The house was silent... and where was the welcoming aroma of breakfast she'd expected?

And then Sarah McCully had appeared at the top of the stairs, looking more like a ghost than a woman. But a ghost dressed in black. And she never wore black except to funerals.

Emma simply gazed up the staircase, not quite making sense of what she was seeing. Her mother seemed a hundred years old—deep wrinkles where there'd been tiny laugh lines. And her blue eyes, always sparkling, looked dead.

"Mama?"

"Oh, Emma! Emma, my baby."

Tears began streaming down Sarah's face. "Oh, Emma, when I sent the wire to Mountainview I didn't know if you'd be able to get here before your father... before he..."

Emma began racing up the stairs, heart pounding, throat tight, feeling tears filling her own eyes. Before he what? Before he died? Before he was buried? No! That couldn't be!

She wrapped her arms around her mother. "Tell me, Mama. I didn't get your wire. Tell me what's happened."

"It's his heart," Sarah managed. "Three days ago, Emma. Since then, he's been barely..."

"Mama, is he...will he...is he going to be all right, Mama?" She waited in agony for the answer.

"The doctor says," Sarah said in a choking little voice, "that he might die."

Emma closed her eyes, but that didn't stop her tears from escaping. She loved her father so much. "Can...can I see him, Mama?"

Wordlessly Sarah led her down the hall to the front bedroom. Emma paused at the doorway, furiously wiped her face, then took a deep breath and stepped into the room.

Her father was lying in the bed, his face pale and drawn, blue veins clearly visible beneath his skin. And his breathing... oh, his breathing sounded horribly labored. Her own lungs began to hurt with each tortured breath he took.

She blinked hard and moved closer to the bed. Close enough to take his hand in hers.

His eyes flickered open, and a glimmer of recognition appeared in them. "Emmy," he whispered, as if simply speaking her name took all the effort he could muster.

He squeezed her hand—so weakly she barely felt the pressure—and it was all she could do to keep from sobbing out loud. This man who'd once carried her on his shoulders, who'd tossed her into the air and easily caught her in childhood games, was suddenly an old, old man... who the doctor said might die.

"Papa," she murmured past the gigantic lump in her throat. "Papa, I'm here. And John is, too. He'll be along in just a little while."

Her father's lips moved slightly. An attempt at a smile. Then he closed his eyes again.

Emma fought for control of her emotions, then glanced back to where her mother was hovering in the doorway. She clearly hadn't slept in days. "Mama, put on a nightdress. I'll make you some tea and then I'll sit with Papa. You can rest in the other bedroom."

Sarah nodded obediently, as if she were the child and Emma the mother. "Emma," she murmured, taking a nightdress from the bureau, then crossing the room to embrace her daughter once more. "Darling, I'm so very, very glad you came. I've been so frantic. And so afraid. And so alone. Oh, Emma, I don't know what I'd have done if I'd had to bear this by myself for even another day."

The sound of a man clearing his throat jolted Emma back to the moment. It was the doctor, standing in the parlor doorway, his medical bag in his hand.

"Dr. Hoskins, this is my brother, John," she murmured. "And our friend, Will Lockhart."

"May I see my father now?" John asked.

The doctor nodded, and John headed up to his father's room, his footsteps telling Emma he was taking the stairs two at a time.

Hoskins cleared his throat again. Emma eyed him silently, praying.

"Your father is improving," he said, smiling at her.

Will squeezed her hands reassuringly.

"But he looks so...so very ill...so weak," she said, afraid to read too much into the doctor's smile.

"He is. But since he's made it through the first three days without a setback, we have every reason for optimism. He'll need a good deal of rest and care, of course. But now that you're here...and your brother, as well, naturally. Although a son is never the same as a daughter in situations like this.

"At any rate, I must say your arrival was most timely. I was growing extremely worried about your mother. I've seen *her* health starting to deteriorate over the past few days. She isn't strong enough to carry on the way she's been doing—certainly she can't keep it up. But she won't hear of a nurse. Each time I suggested it, she insisted your father needed family caring for him. But now that you're here...well, I'm very hopeful they'll both pull through this just fine, Miss McCully. And after a few months, you'll be able to get on with your own life."

Will's hand tightened on hers again, but this time she knew it wasn't a reassuring squeeze. She looked at him and saw fear in his eyes. The same fear she felt. Fear that they were going to lose each other, after all.

THEY SIMPLY STOOD in the train station as the locomotive began hissing to life. Emma, Will and John. Three utterly despondent figures, saying goodbye.

"I could handle it, Emmy," John told her again. "Father's going to be all right. Even in the past couple of days he's started looking better. If you went, I could explain to them about time travel. I could explain where you've gone. I could hire a nurse. I could—"

Emma shook her head, cutting him off. "It wouldn't work, John. We've been through this. You'd be away all day. And mother doesn't want a nurse. If I wasn't here, she'd try to do everything herself. And neither of them is in any shape to deal with me disappearing—or with you giving them an explanation for it that they'd think was insane. John . . . John I appreciate the offer. And so does Will. But we know I have to stay."

John jammed his hands into the pockets of his suit jacket and took a step back. "I'll give you two a few minutes alone, then," he said, turning away.

Emma bit her lip, trying not to cry. But she couldn't help looking at that train. And every time she did, she imagined it was already pulling out of the station, carrying Will to Mountainview, carrying him away from her.

She forced her eyes from the train and stood gazing at Will, trying to memorize everything about him. He was wearing the suit he'd worn when he'd first appeared on her front porch. Their time together had flown by so quickly, that might have been yesterday.

"Emma..." he murmured.

"Don't," she whispered. "I can't talk about it anymore, Will. We've been talking about it for two solid days and...and we both know this is the only solution. And the three years—until the next time hole opens—isn't forever."

He wrapped his arms around her, and she pressed her cheek to his chest. This was the last time he'd hold her for three years. She couldn't leave her parents when they needed her so. And Will couldn't disappear from his life in the future without a word. He had all those responsibilities. His job. His parents.

Before they'd decided to come to San Francisco, when she'd believed that, if she went with Will, her parents would never know what had become of her, she hadn't been at all sure she could do it. So she understood why Will had to go back. He couldn't leave his father and Erica thinking he was dead.

But once he *had* gone back...would he really come for her again in three years?

"I love you, Emma," he whispered. "So very much."

"I love you, too. So very, very much." But three years was so very, very long. And their time together had been so very, very short.

What if it had been so short that he'd gradually forget her? What if he fell in love with someone else? A modern woman who wouldn't have any adjusting to do to fit into his life? What if he decided he'd been crazy to even suggest Emma McCully go to the future? What if...?

Of course, Will was always telling her not to worry about *what if.* But how was she going to live without him for three years? Or, possibly, for the rest of her life?

"If only we hadn't had to cut this so close," Will said. "If only I had time to go home, get hold of Dad and make it back here again. I would if I could, Emma. I'd spend the next three years here with you. But by the time the train gets to Mountainview, and I get from town out to Broken Hill and back to 2014...well, I'd just make it to a phone and be calling Dad in Boston, when that time hole in the mine closed."

"I know," she whispered. They'd been through all of this a hundred times. And his staying was no more a possibility than her going.

The train whistle blasted—a long, mournful wail that made her feel impossibly worse. And made her cling to Will impossibly tighter.

"I'll think about you every day, Emma. Every single day."

"Me, too," she whispered.

The whistle wailed a second time, and the engine began to hiss more loudly. John appeared back beside them. "They'll be calling all aboard any minute," he said quietly.

Will nodded, then bent to kiss Emma.

Her lips were trembling when they met his. This kiss would be her last for three years.

She wanted to kiss him forever. His mouth was so warm and wonderful on hers. But too soon...far too soon ... the conductor's voice rang out and Will drew back.

She clung to him for another second, ordering herself not to cry. She didn't want him remembering her in tears and tried to smile. If she had to look at him for one more second, though, she knew she'd be done. "I don't want to get on the train to say goodbye, Will. I ... I'll just say it here."

"Oh, Emma," he murmured, his voice breaking. He hugged her tightly once more, then picked up his bag. "I ... hell, why am I taking this?" he said, setting it down again. "I won't be needing these things for three years. And the computer's in there, John. It's yours now. Emma ... Emma, I love you. And I'll be back. Wait for me, love."

"I will. You know I will," she managed. She wanted to tell him she'd wait for him through all eternity if she had to, but speaking had become impossible.

"I'll see you onto the train," John mumbled, starting off with Will.

She watched them stride toward the coaches, no longer able to hold back her tears. They streamed down her face, and Will and John became blurred figures walking ever farther away from her.

And then the whistle cried out a final time, and the train jerked into motion. The station filled with the chugging throb of the locomotive, the rhythmic rumble of a hundred steel wheels grinding against the rails. They seemed to be speaking to her—repeating the same words, over and over again. "Three years ... three years ... three years."

The sound hurt her ears. And threatened to break her heart. Gradually the train picked up speed. She waved unseeingly at the passing coaches, knowing Will was on one of them, waving back. In no time, the last of them had passed, and the caboose trundled by. In another minute the train was gone. The station felt empty. And Emma felt empty.

Forlornly she glanced along the track, looking for John. But the man standing there, looking back at her, wasn't her brother.

"Will?" she murmured, unable to believe her eyes. "Will!" she said again, starting across the station toward him, racing into his outstretched arms.

"Oh, Emma," he said, gathering her to him. "Oh, Emma."

She simply held him, certain he had to be an illusion. But how could an illusion feel so solid and real and loving in her arms?

"John went instead," Will finally whispered into her hair.

She drew back, taking Will's hands and gazing up at him.

"He's going to the future, Emma. He's going to see my father and tell him what's happened. And he's going to have that adventure he wanted so badly."

Emma shook her head, uncertain which of a thousand questions to ask first.

"We can tell your parents he had to go back to Mountainview to sell the house and whatever," Will went on. "Then, when your father's stronger, we can explain the truth."

"Is John going to come back? In three years?"

Will shrugged. "I told him how and when he could. I guess he'll decide between now and then. But he'll be fine. I gave him a couple of my credit cards. And once he gets to Boston, Dad and Erica will give him any help he might need."

"Oh, Will," Emma murmured, hugging him tightly again, almost unable to believe he was really still with her. "And what about you? What are you going to do for the next three years?"

"Well, Buck's offered me a job about eighteen times. And with John gone, he's going to need someone to help run Dursely Oil. I know a fair bit about business. And I've still got the computer to help us out. And hell, what could possibly be as challenging as going up against John D. Rockefeller?

"And what could possibly be as enjoyable," he added quietly, "as coming home, every day, to you?"

EPILOGUE

"HAPPY NEW YEAR," Will murmured. He gave Emma a long, loving kiss, then clinked his champagne glass to hers. The crystal danced with reflections of light from their crackling fire.

"Happy 1890," she replied, taking a tiny sip. 1890. This coming August, the three years would be up and they'd be going to the future. Time had flown so fast. And thinking about trying to adjust there still made her anxious. She loved their life here. And they were so very happy. What if...?

She sternly told herself to stop what-ifing and glanced across the parlor—to where Will, Jr., was sleeping in his cradle. "He'll be walking before August," she said, snuggling closer to Will on the settee.

"Just wait until Dad and Erica see him," Will told her. "Their first grandchild. They'll be so darned proud of him."

"As proud as you are?" Emma teased.

"Close," Will told her, taking her hand. "Close. Emma... about August... about our leaving..."

"Yes, Will?"

"Emma...how would you feel about living in New York?"

"New York? I... Will, I thought you said it became a bad place to live in the future. That there was a lot of crime. And that—"

"No, Emma, I'm not talking about the future. I mean, what if, instead of living in the future, we lived in New York? Today's New York. The New York of the 1890s."

She gazed at him, confused. What was he suggesting?

"Your heart's set on going to the future, isn't it?" he said quietly.

"No! No, Will, it really isn't. I just... well, I've always known how much you want to go back and... and, well, I want us to live wherever you'll be happiest. But why New York?"

"Because Buck and I have decided Dursely Oil's head offices should move there. And because... oh, hell, Emma, because I like life in this century. Living in San Francisco has been great. And I enjoy my job—especially getting to drive John D. Rockefeller crazy. And the future... well, there's a lot that's good about it, but a lot that's bad, too. I'm not sure I want our children growing up with all the stress and pressure of the twenty-first century."

"But, Will, I don't understand. You were just talking about seeing your father and Erica and—"

"I was thinking of just visiting them, Emma. The time hole in August will be open for a few weeks. And I was thinking we could visit the future and then come back and move to New York. In its heyday, it was really supposed to be a great city. And we could get one of those big stone houses in Manhattan. With lots of room for more children. And a separate apartment for your parents."

"My parents could come with us?"

"Of course. They're both so darned healthy again that I bet they'll still be around in 1906. We can hardly leave them here with an earthquake coming. So...so, what do you think, Emma?"

"I think...oh, Will, I think I love you more than any woman has ever loved any man."

"You only think you do?"

"Oh, blast it, Will. I'm sorry. I just can't seem to stop making those darned understatements."

HISTORICAL

CHRISTMAS

STORIES·1991

Bring back heartwarming memories of Christmas past
with HISTORICAL CHRISTMAS STORIES 1991,
a collection of romantic stories
by three popular authors.
The perfect Christmas gift!

Don't miss these heartwarming stories,
available in November
wherever Harlequin books are sold:

CHRISTMAS YET TO COME
by Lynda Trent
A SEASON OF JOY
by Caryn Cameron
FORTUNE'S GIFT
by DeLoras Scott

**Best Wishes and Season's Greetings
from Harlequin!**

XM-91R

Harlequin Superromance®

COMING NEXT MONTH

#478 TROUBLE IN EDEN • Elise Title

Gillian Haverford had worked hard to establish her resort inn at Big Sur, California. Now a saboteur was threatening her livelihood—and her life. Police chief Joe Devlin felt out of place among the rich and famous, yet he found himself drawn to Gillian. He soon realized she meant much more to him than just another case....

#479 OVER THE HORIZON • Kaye Walton

Gail Montgomery never knew she had a twin sister. Yet, now she was being asked to impersonate her. As if that weren't enough, she had to juggle two men—her twin's fiancé and Alex, the man Gail herself was falling in love with....

#480 THREE WAIFS AND A DADDY • Margot Dalton

If they hadn't found the three orphaned children, Sarah Burnard was sure she could have gotten away with it. But now that she was helping Jim Fleming take care of the three waifs, how could she keep her secret? Jim was bound to not only learn her name, but to find out she was pregnant—with his child.

#481 SEVENTH HEAVEN • Pamela Bauer

Even though her three daughters were all grown-up, Kate Osborne felt she had to watch out for them. But it seemed that she wasn't the only one watching! Her oldest daughter's mysterious neighbor appeared to have a telescope trained on her bedroom window! Protest would finally lead to passion as Kate discovered Police Commissioner Donovan Cade's true interests.

HARLEQUIN
Romance®

A Christmas tradition...

Imagine spending Christmas in New
Orleans with a blind stranger and his aged
guide dog—when you're supposed to be
there on your honeymoon!
#3163 Every Kind of Heaven
by Bethany Campbell

Imagine spending Christmas with a man
you once "married"—in a mock ceremony
at the age of eight!
#3166 The Forgetful Bride
by Debbie Macomber

*Available in December 1991, wherever
Harlequin books are sold.*